I0780086

RETURN OF THE FAE

THE FAE BOOK THREE

By Alex McGilvery

Return of the Fae
By Alex McGilvery

Copyright Alex McGilvery 2024

ISBN: 978-1-989092-97-2

Celticfrog Publishing
Clearwater BC

CHAPTER 1

Robin slowed at the edge of a field showing the beginning sprouts of a crop, but Robin couldn't identify what it was. No matter, she'd walk around the edge of the field and avoid disturbing it. A small village occupied the far side.

She ended up circling halfway around the village before a track led her between fields to the village. A few houses clustered around a well. She didn't see any evidence of businesses unless they were run out of the inhabitants' homes. With no clear choice of door to knock on Robin used the well to refill her waterskin, then washed her face.

An old woman crept out of a house and over to Robin.

"Are you a deserter or a spy?"

Robin laughed, then scanned the houses. Curtains twitched as people peering past them at her jumped back.

"My apologies for my rudeness." Robin bowed slightly to the old woman. "I am neither, but it struck me as odd to ask so directly. Surely neither a deserter nor a spy would admit it so easily."

"You are here, in armour with a sword where the young and fit have been called away."

"I'm just passing through." Robin leaned against the stone lip of the well trying to look less threatening.

"To where?" The old woman set her chin.

"That way." Robin pointed in the direction she was being called to. "I can't say more than that, I don't know why."

If anything, that made the old woman more nervous. She glanced at the houses, then sighed. "You might as well come in for tea."

Robin followed her to the smallest of the houses. The door opened straight into a single room. A hearth held a fire to her right. An old man slumped in an upholstered chair near the fire with a colourful quilt wrapped around him. Robin sat in the stool next to him instead of the other chair.

"Good morning."

"He don't talk no more." The old woman lifted the kettle from the hook over the fire and placed it on a rickety table while she sprinkled a few leaves into the teapot. "Sorry, miss, the tea will be weak. I don't have much leaf left."

Robin dug into her pack and retrieved her bag of tea leaves.

"Use some of mine." The old woman sniffed at them then added a generous pinch to the pot. She reluctantly passed the bag back to Robin.

While replacing the tea, Robin brushed up against her food supply. She'd given Adam some cheese, but still had a decent amount left. If the woman had that little tea, would it be fair to expect her to serve any of her food store?

The old woman's eyes widened when Robin placed her bread and cheese on the table.

"I couldn't..."

"Don't refuse gifts from the fae," the old man mumbled. His hands tightened on the arms of his chair, then he slumped. "Can't greet you properly, Lady Fae. Don't hold it against m'wife."

Robin throttled the urge to flee the cabin. It would only make it certain in their minds they'd offended the fae.

"No offense." She patted his arm, then looked at the woman who might have fallen over but for the support of the table. "There aren't many who speak of the fae these days."

"He says he met a fae woman in the forest when he was young, he could spin the most fantastic tales, have the whole village laughing and crying."

"That does sound like a fae gift." Robin used her belt knife to slice the bread and cheese. She handed the first slice to the old man, the second to the woman. There wasn't much left, but she cut a slice for herself as well. What remained wasn't worth packing up, so she left it on the table.

"What do the fae want with such as me?" The woman attempted a curtsy.

"I'm passing through from here to there." Robin said, "but a cup of tea and a meal shared is always welcome. Sit down and tell me about yourself."

The old woman sat in the other chair after pouring the tea and handing it out.

"M'name's Marta. I grew up in the next town along. Roderick here captivated me with his stories on market days, so against my father's wishes I married him and moved here. All my children left for other places leaving just Rod and me. But I don't regret a thing. The others in the village are kind to an old lady and her storytelling husband. They're great nephews and nieces from Rod's side, but until the emperor called up all the young and healthy, there was more people than work to be done."

"He called for them during the winter, or after the seeding?"

"After the seeding, Lady. They only left for the next town a week or two back. It's been lonely without them young folk."

"I imagine." Robin sipped the tea and sighed. It would taste so much better without the ever-present urge to run north and east. She chatted with the old woman about the seeding and the half a dozen young people who'd left to serve the emperor. If Robin had any choice in the matter, they'd all return home with nothing more than tales of training to tell.

"I've enjoyed our visit. I'll leave the crust for you and Rod to share." She put her hand on the old woman's hand. "You have my gratitude for your hospitality."

After bowing again. Robin left the house and jogged along the track out of the village, by the time she'd reached the trees, the urge made her run as if to punish her for an hour visiting Marta and Rod.

***

Marta waited in her chair until Eva from next door knocked and entered the cabin.

"You okay?" Eva stopped to stare at the crusts of bread and cheese on the table.

"Fine, Eva." Marta grinned. "T'was like one of Rod's stories." She related what had happened and poured out a cup of tea for her friend. At Marta's urging Eva cut thin slices from the cheese and bread. Soon others came until the tiny room was filled and overflowed onto the dirt road outside. Everyone tasted the tea and had a sliver of the cheese and bread. Yet somehow when they'd all retreated to their own homes, there was still tea in the pot and a crust of bread and cheese on the table.

***

Robin bypassed the next village, only slightly larger than Marta's. She didn't want to be stopping everywhere to deal with questions. Her sword went into her pack and the cloak covered the chain mail well enough. The pull to her destination had been so strong she'd never considered how her armour and weapons would look to the casual eye. Perhaps she needed something less conspicuous to travel in.

That night she built a tiny fire off the road, still little more than a track and chewed at her smoked meat and crusty bread. Her bag held enough that she had no need to forage except for a few greens to go with her meal.

Just before she'd rolled up in her cloak, two men stepped out of the gloom. One held an axe, the other a broken sword. They smirked at her.

"Give us whatever you have, and we might let you live." The one with the axe waved the axe in what Robin guessed was supposed to be a threatening manner.

"Might." The holder of the sword licked his lips.

Robin sighed; she'd been looking forward to a quiet rest.

"Well, if you're going to rob me, you might as well have at it." She looked up at them and rolled her eyes. "Now would be good. You're interrupting my rest."

Axe wielder frowned and stepped back, but the one with the sword charged in sword raised like a club. Robin rolled to the side and stood as the bandit's swing lodged the sword in a tree. Robin struck his temple and crushed the bone. He fell boneless to the ground. The axe man dropped his weapon, screamed and bolted, unfortunately straight into another tree. Robin winced as he too dropped to the forest floor.

When she checked, they were both dead. She didn't feel sorry for them, but it did mean she'd have to find another place to spend the night. Fire out, she loped along the moonlight road and past another town before retreating into the forest to curl up in her cloak and rest.

In the morning, she headed through the forest since the road travelled in the wrong direction. The interlude with Marta was pleasant, with the bandits less so, but the pull on her didn't allow for more such times.

Two days later, she hit a road going in the direction her call pulled her. As she loped along the road the sound of chopping echoed through the woods. Maybe it she could put her disguise to the test and get some more suitable clothes. Robin stashed her bag in the hollow under a tree and crept closer to the sounds.

Two men, not much less rough looking than the bandit hacked at a tree, it finally groaned and fell with a great deal of crashing and snapping of branches. A woman appeared with a waterskin and a cloth bag.

"Time for a break." She passed the waterskin to one man and handed a chunk of bread from the bag to the other.

"Thanks, Leila." The man with the waterskin moved away from the fallen tree. "We'll dress this one and have enough to get the haulers to drag the trees to the mill."

The other man came and sat beside the first, leaning against a tree. "Maybe we'll have earned enough to buy you a new dress."

"What would I do with a new dress out in these woods?" Leila crossed her arms. "The goal is to earn enough to build a house in town for you and your wives, once you find some."

"No new houses until the emperor sends everyone home." The man with the waterskin handed it to the other and took a piece of bread from Leila. "All this is for weapons for the army, not building homes. If we weren't foresters, you'd be alone with Pa."

Leila shuddered. "Fae forbid. He wants to marry me to that fool of a mayor's son."

"It is the mayor or the son who is the fool?"

"Both." Leila scowled. "They act like the emperor himself gave them rule over the town. No maid or purse is safe. 'Tis why we're better here where neither is brave enough to come."

"Not with you telling your stories of the fae." The men laughed.

"Never thought grandma's tales would be of such use." Leila sighed and turned away. "I'd better get back. The wash on the line's probably dry. Need to get it in before it blows away."

"You're always finding excuses not to hang out with your brothers." One clambered to his feet and pulled Leila down to sit with them. "Relax for a minute. Pa's not watching."

Robin snuck back to her bag, then circled around the three. She followed the narrow track Leila had used to where the laundry hung. The brothers were right. Leila did need a new dress, the one on the line was more rag than dress. Robin plucked it off the line, then fished in her purse for a coin or two to leave behind.

A twig cracked not too far away, so Robin flung a couple of coins onto a stump near the laundry line and dashed away.

The scream that rang through the woods made Robin feel guilty, but in a moment, Leila would find the coins, and everything would be, if not all right, at least better.

***

Robin gazed longingly at the firelit windows of the town. She'd changed into the dress and tried to remember the last time she'd worn a dress, aside from the brief period she'd played at being fae to scare imperial soldiers. It kept wrapping around her in odd ways, inconvenient at best, deadly if she got into a fight.

Her bag, except for a bit of food in a sack and one or two copper coins, lay hidden in another hollow tree. The biggest concern would be if squirrels made a nest in it. She squared her shoulders and ran through her story once more before knocking on a door, praying it didn't belong to Leila's father.

A woman opened it and stared down at Robin.

"Do ye have any work I c'n do in exchange for a meal?" Robin slipped into the street talk years of training had eliminated.

"What?' No." The woman started close the door, then stopped. "Where did you get that dress?" She frowned at Robin. "It's far too big on you."

"Stole it from a rag bin, ma'am." Robin looked down and scratched a line in the dirt path.

"Hmmph." The woman sounded as disgusted as Robin would have expected. The door creaked but didn't close. "Ah well, you might as well come in." She stepped well back to avoid any contact with Robin.

The spotless entryway barely held Robin, the woman and the open door. The woman backed into what Robin guessed was the kitchen. Robin pushed the door closed and waited.

"Fanny!" the woman called and backed farther away. A young girl, no taller than Robin appeared. "She --" the woman pointed at Robin. "—needs a wash, a dress, and she can help you clean. Make sure she doesn't steal anything."

"Yes ma'am." Fanny bobbed in a brief curtsy then peered at Robin. "You, this way." She led the way to the back of the house and out a door to what Robin's nose told her was a stable. A water trough collected water from the roof and held it for whatever animals resided in the stable. Robin peeled out of the dress and used it as a washcloth. From Fanny's face, the cleaning job didn't accomplish much, so Robin's disguise was probably safe.

Fanny disappeared briefly once Robin started washing and appeared with a bundle of cloth and a towel. "No good putting a new dress on wet." She shoved the towel into Robin's hands. Though clean, it was only a step above a rag. Robin patted herself dry and put on the dress. It fit much better than Leila's.

Fanny used a stick to lift Leila's dress and toss it into a corner. "Ain't fit for rags," the girl pronounced. She dragged Robin back into the house. "Your small clothes aren't as horrible as that dress." She handed Robin a broom. "You done run away, didn't ye?"

Robin started sweeping the hallway. "My pa drives wagon. Delivers cargo to towns. He brung me along cause he ain't got a son. Wasn't...nice." Robin scrubbed at the real tears flowing down her cheeks. How long was it since she'd seen her father? Suddenly she desperately needed one of his hugs that lifted her up and spun her around.

Fanny's arms wrapped around Robin and held her close. "Mistress is strict, but kind. Showed the master a knife and told him what she'd cut off if he touched me. You're safe here."

Robin couldn't get her voice to work, worse the tears flowed stronger until she bawled into Fanny's shoulder.

The door to the back hall opened and the mistress stood arms crossed glaring at the girls.

"Can she work here, mistress?" Fanny didn't let go of Robin. "You can pay her from my wages."

"Nonsense." The mistress frowned. "If she works, she'll make her own wages. Now stop that noise, the master will be home soon and doesn't want to listen to that."

Robin took a deep breath and shoved the grief and loneliness deep inside her.

"Thank you, ma'am." Thankfully her voice had recovered.

"Didn't say you'd work here." The woman's frown softened. "I need to talk to the master. Fanny, I need your help in the kitchen."

Robin swept the hallway, then behind one door she found a room full of split wood. She tidied the wood pile, swept the wood chips up and used a piece of bark to lift them into a box of kindling. The other door was locked, so continued sweeping out in the back, tidying up an outside wood pile. She was debating starting on the stable when Fanny came and fetched her.

"We don't work outside after dark." The girl stared at Robin wide eyed. "The fae will get you if the loggers don't."

"The fae?" Robin asked.

"Long 'fore humans were here, the fae lived in the forest. They play tricks on people, get them into trouble."

"They're still here?"

"Who knows? But no sensible person wants to find out."

After a meal of mostly potatoes with a tiny bit of gravy, Fanny led Robin up a steep set of stairs to a tiny room in the attic. They had a window for light.

"Mistress says you can't stay here," Fanny whispered, "but the baker is looking for someone to work in the shop, maybe you can get a position there."

"Maybe." Robin lay on her back and examined the roof within easy arm's reach from the thin pad on the floor. She expected the call to travel north and west to yank at her, but it had gone quiet, as if her destination was this small town on the edge of the forest.

***

The baker was indeed looking for a worker. He was the biggest person Robin had ever met, yet he moved in the tiny kitchen without the slightest problem.

"You won't be baking," he informed Robin. "My son will take over the business. You will keep the front clean and help the customers."

"Thank you, sir." Robin curtsied. The baker gave her an odd look, but turned back into the kitchen and left her alone with the baked goods.

"Good grief." A woman as slender as the baker was big came in. "Hal is great in the kitchen, but he hasn't a thought in his head outside it. I'm Millie, his wife." She walked Robin through the cases, naming the different types of loaf and sweet, and the price for each.

"If you don't mind me askin', why aren't you doin' this?"

"I need to watch the children." Millie sighed. "Three daughters who would die to bake in the kitchen and a son who thinks of nothing but being a soldier."

"And master wants his son to take over the business." Robin rolled her eyes while Millie giggled.

She met the daughters during the day. The oldest had be about Robin's true age. She pretended to be a customer, but looked so much like Millie, Robin had no doubt who she was. Once Robin got all the prices right and showed she could sweep without getting dust on the baking, Chella warmed up.

"You'll never guess what happened." She whispered to Robin. "The woodsman's daughter found a gold coin on a stump where she'd been doing the wash. Says it must be payment for her singing while she worked."

Gold? Oops. Robin shook her head. She'd been sure she'd left copper, but maybe in the rush? At least Leila wasn't going on about a stolen dress. Last thing Robin needed was mistress putting two and two together and getting five.

The middle daughter looked like the baker. She laughed and giggled the whole time she visited the shop, even while Robin helped an old woman choose a single bun for her supper.

"Papa would get so mad at me for putting an extra bun in the bag for the old dear," Paula winked at Robin.

The youngest daughter stalked into the bakery and circled around Robin, she had to be a year or two younger than Robin was pretending to be. "I never liked that dress, but you look all right." Heddi sniffed and left again.

Robin quick grew used to the girls dropping in. In their own way, each was fascinated by the bakery, though none did more than glance at the door leading to the kitchen.

A week after she started in the bakery, a boy burst through the door cussing like a soldier and holding a hand up to his bleeding nose.

"Don't be getting blood on the bread." Robin ordered him.

He spat on the floor then ground it in with his foot.

"And what if I do?" He glared at her, then moved toward a shelf of bread.

"No, you don't." Robin took his elbow and dragged him outside.

"That's my bakery, I'll do as I please," the boy tried to pull his arm from Robin's grip.

"It is your father's bakery." Robin sat him on a bench set outside the door. Heddi came down the street, took one look at her brother, then turned and left.

The baker stormed out the door and glared at his son.

"Fighting again? Wes, when is it going to stop?"

"It's training, not fighting. I'm going to be a soldier, not some fat, weakling baker." Wes wrenched himself loose and ran off.

"What am I going to do with him?" The baker plunked down on the bench, making it creak dangerously.

"You can't make him something he doesn't want to be." Robin crossed her arms. "Trying will only make you both miserable."

"You sound like Millie." The baker's face crumpled. "All I want is my son to take over the bakery."

"And your daughters?" Robin leaned against the door frame. "They come in every day, just to breath the scent of baking bread. They're kind, careful, and thoughtful."

"I know." He put his head in his hands. "But they wouldn't be able to lift the flour sacks or knead the dough."

"Chella said the town is having a strong man competition as part of a festival next week."

"They have it every year." The baker snorted. "Waste of time, the woodsmen use it as an excuse to come into town and get drunk."

"Enter the contest." Robin said. "I'll bet you're stronger than any of them."

"What if I am?" the baker asked, peeking through his fingers. "What if I'm not?"

"Enter and find out."

"You don't sound like a young girl." The baker dropped his hands on his knees. "I'll do it." He stood up and stomped away toward the guardhouse.

***

The day of the contest arrived, and the baker stood in line for his turn.

"You can do this, Osarl. Just pretend it's flour." Millie kissed him on the cheek, then each of his daughters gave him a hug. Wes preened in front of a huge soldier who laughed and slapped the boy's back sending him tumbling to the ground. Wes laughed, but his face was red. He glanced over at his father, then turned his back.

Osarl wished Robin was here, but she insisted on watching the bakery.

"I don't need to watch to know what will happen," she'd shooed him out onto the street.

A huge round of wood sat in the centre of the square. Osarl had watched two loggers lift it down from the cart, cheered on by a woman in a brand-new dress. That was the woodsman's family. Strong and beautiful. Word was the mayor's son wanted to marry the girl. The woodsman sat with the mayor and his sun under an awning.

Osarl watched the first few people in line struggle to move the round. The two who had delivered it each lifted it a few inches from the cobbles, earning a round of applause. The big soldier strutted over, though Osarl was next in line. He wrapped his arms around the piece of tree trunk and hoisted it easily, then dropped it on the cobbles with a crack. Parading around with his arms raised, the man ignored the half-split log behind him.

Osarl walked up to the round and, then around it.

"You're going to lift that?" the big soldier sneered. "Go back to your bakery." He slapped Osarl on the back. It might have been a fly landing on him.

"I'll lift it with you sitting on it." Osarl pointed to the round. "Be careful you don't get anything important caught in the crack."

The crowd roared with laughter, whether at his jibe or the idea of him lifting the piece of tree and the soldier. The soldier reddened and sat on the round and crossed his arms.

It's just flour. I've lifted flour sacks this big. Osarl rubbed his hands together, then placed them on either side of the wood with the crack in the middle. He glanced over at Wes who stood rigid with his fists clenched.

Osarl breathed in deep and filled his mind with the memory of his kitchen. He had bread to make. Before he realized it, he'd hoisted the wood off the cobbles. Where the soldier had dropped it to parade about, Osarl marched around the square holding the soldier, clutching desperately at his unstable seat. Finally he put the round and its passenger back in the centre of the square.

The crowd cheered so loudly Osarl thought he might go deaf, but he heard the soldier mutter.

"I won't forget this, baker."

Osarl put his hand on the man's shoulder and squeezed a little, like kneading bread. "Wes admires you. I won't have you pushing him around, bloodying his nose in what you call training." He squeezed a little harder. "I might have to have a word with your commander if it happens again."

The soldier winced and growled, "If I had my sword."

"If you had your sword, you'd be in the guardhouse awaiting the rope." A man much smaller than the soldier stood casually with his hands behind his back. The soldier wilted and hung his head.

"I'm impressed sir baker." The man nodded at Osarl, then chased the soldier out of the square.

"Wow, I didn't know you could do that!" Wes stared at Osarl with eyes wide.

"I lift a lot of flour." Osarl smiled at Wes. He hoisted his son to his shoulder and walked over to where Millie and his girls waved at him.

"You have to collect your prize." Wes jumped down and tugged at Osarl's arm.

By the time he'd talked to the mayor and half the town, the sun was dropping behind the trees. When he arrived home, Robin was sweeping the step, in front of the bakery.

"Sold out. People couldn't wait to try the bread made by the strongest man in town."

CHAPTER 2

Allin looked forward to arriving in Dordnom. The coach was easier than walking, but not very comfortable. General Mihone had made sure there were no more incidents, but it meant having guards dog their every footstep. Henry appeared as relaxed as ever with Magpie at his side, but Allin wondered how he'd do facing the man who had claimed the title of emperor in his place.

They approached the walls, traffic clearing away to allow the coach to pass. As they passed through the gate, city guards stood at attention saluting stiffly.

The cobbles of the city streets made the ride even rougher, and Allin told himself it was only for a bit longer. Magpie and Rebecca peered out the window and pointed out landmarks to each other. They soon passed through the area they knew and rolled past grander buildings until they arrived at the palace.

Allin had been expecting something luxurious and expansive, but the ancient keep they stopped in front of spoke only of utility.

"This is the oldest building in the city." General Mihone said. "The emperor doesn't feel the need for luxury and the show of wealth."

"I envy him." Henry stretched. "The palace in Acanopolis was a nightmare. After all the additions and changes there were servants who did nothing but guide people from place to place. Even those who'd grown up there got lost on occasion. There are stories of undersecretaries who still wander after years of trying to find their way."

"How interesting." General Mihone glanced at Allin and shrugged. Henry had given up pretending he wasn't the emperor in Acanopolis, but the stories he told weren't of grandeur and power. Allin suppressed a grin. General Mihone clearly didn't know what to do with this down to earth emperor.

"I hope we are given time to bathe and refresh ourselves before meeting Emperor Ordamy." Rebecca tugged at her travel creased dress.

"He will meet with you tomorrow at noon." General Mihone opened the door of the coach and climbed out. He gave his hand to help the women down the steps. Henry and Allin were left to navigate the rickety steps on their own.

"Lady Wren will show you to your suite. If you have any questions she can't answer, she will send for me."

A solidly built women in a dress perfectly tailored to fit her body curtsied.

"If you would follow me." She spoke in a musical alto tone, almost as if she sang her words. Allin and the others trailed after her. "You will be staying in the new wing. It was built a century or two after the main keep."

"The main keep was built almost a thousand years ago," Rebecca whispered to Allin, "So don't expect all the modern conveniences."

"Correct." Lady Wren didn't turn around. "But there have been continuous upgrades over the years, and some things that have been lost in other places are maintained here. I'm sure you will enjoy the heated floors in the bath. There is only the one bath in the wing, so you will need to take turns or bathe together."

"We'vc been on the road for ages." Rebecca said. "We are comfortable in each other's presence. There was an incident which would make us women uncomfortable bathing alone."

"As you will." Lady Wren bobbed her head. "I will let the women know what to expect."

"Thank you." Allin said. "It will be wonderful to wash away the crust of travel."

Lady Wren stopped by double doors. "This is your suite. You may arrange things to suit yourselves. The servants will aid you as you need. I will go inform them to get the bath ready and send someone to fetch you. There are robes and slippers in the suite for you to wear to the bath." She pushed open the doors and waved them in, closing them behind her before they could thank her.

Allin walked around the suite. The walls were stone, so secret passageways would be difficult, but not impossible. Tapestries hung on the walls and rugs covered the floor. The servants, two girls and two young men were already showing the others the rooms to the side.

"Henry and I will take one room." Magpie took Henry's hand.

"I can sleep in the main room if that makes you more comfortable." Allin came over to join them.

"I don't know if I could sleep in a room by myself." Rebecca sighed. "It has been so long, there is a couch, if you aren't comfortable on the bed with me."

"We will work it out when the time comes." Allin smiled at her. "Make sure there are extra pillows and blankets on the couch." The servants nodded and one opened a cupboard to reveal a vast array of bedding and pillows.

"Is there anything else you need?"

"We will need our clothes washed, and perhaps fresh clothes. What we have with us is no longer suitable to meet an emperor."

"We will take your clothes when you change into your robes for your bath." One of the girls turned pink. "Perhaps the men will undress in the other room?"

***

The baths were as marvellous as Allin had hoped. The huge room held a range of pools from barely knee deep to deep enough to swim in. They washed by the entrance with the help of women in simple black dresses. All of them were older than Allin and didn't show the slightest reaction to scrubbing the backs of the men.

Once they were clean enough for the bath attendants, the four of them lounged in the shallow pool, also the warmest and let the heat undo the knots in their muscles. One of the attendants massaged ointment into Allin's hand and offered to give him some to take to his room. The scar didn't feel as tight, so Allin thanked her and accepted.

Henry and Magpie tried out the other pools. Some had salts in the water, others a strong current, though Allin couldn't figure out how that was done. They ended up in the deep pool swimming like otters and laughing anytime their faces were above water.

"What is going to happen to us?" Rebecca sat not quite close enough to touch to Allin. "I can't see how the emperor is going to be able to let us just wander about. We arc all too important. It will have to be imprisonment or death." She shuddered. "To be honest, I'd prefer death. After being so free for this time, I can't go back to being confined in a room, no matter how luxurious."

"Wait and see." Allin crossed his arms. "I don't think Emperor Ordamy is going to be much like the emperors in Ancanopolis. From what General Mihone has said about him, he is more interested in creating order than the title. Maybe there's a way we can help him."

"I don't know. I'm afraid." Rebecca pulled her knees up to her chest and wrapped her arms around them. "What I really want is to return to my people, but that isn't going to happen.

***

At a knock on the door the next morning, Allin let in the servants who brought them their clothes, washed and repaired.

"There isn't time to make new outfits," the oldest girl said. "The emperor has said these will suit. He is more interested in the people than the clothes." She bustled the men into the other room to get dressed.

"She seems more in charge this morning." Allin commented as he dressed. One of the young men rolled his eyes. "Lady Wren spoke with her. That means she is responsible to carry out the Lady's instructions.

"Lady Wren is a hard mistress?"

"You have no idea." The young man looked around the room and lowered his voice. "She's scarier than the emperor."

"You've met the emperor?" Henry looked over.

"Everyone working in the palace meets the emperor. We have to talk to him before he decides if we can stay."

"What kind of questions does he ask?" Allin tugged on the hem of his coat. He'd lost weight and it wouldn't sit right.

"He doesn't. We talk to him for a few minutes, then either we're in or not." The young man glanced around again. "You'll see."

Once they'd finished dressing a servant opened the door to Lady Wren, who stood like she'd known exactly when the door would open.

"Please come with me." She walked away down the hall without looking to see if they followed. They passed into a part of the building with much larger stones making up the walls.

Probably we're in the old part of the palace. Allin ran his fingers along the wall. It reminded him of the one section of the palace in Fhayde remaining of what the fae had built. There was more to it than just stone. Some force of will held it together. He wouldn't want to be the general trying to capture this keep. The stones themselves would fight against him.

They arrived at a set of double doors. The only thing marking them as special was the guards standing outside them. They opened the door for Lady Wren.

"Introduce yourselves to the emperor. Each of you speak for yourselves." Lady Wren waved them in. "Your guests have arrived."

Allin led the way into the chamber. It wasn't large, not like the one in the emperor's palace in Ancanopolis and only a few people were gathered there aside from the man on the throne.

The throne looked to be made of oak older than the walls. There was no cushion, no upholstery. Emperor Ordamy sat on it like he was part of the throne, or maybe the other way around.

Allin bowed. "I am Duke Allin of Fhayde. I bring greetings and a hope that we can build on the peace we made after the battle on the border of our lands."

"Did you offer this peace to others?" The emperor's voice was soft, like old stones grinding together.

"To those who would listen." Allin met the emperor's gaze. "Those in the palace weren't interested in peace, so we were forced to flee."

"Yet you fled north."

"We did. There was war to the south."

Emperor Ordamy nodded. Allin stepped back, suddenly tired, wishing he had a chair to sit in.

"I am Henry, once emperor in Ancanopolis. There was a plot against my life, my companions aided me in escaping with my life. I have left that life behind along with all the names and titles given to me. If you took me back to Ancanopolis and offered me the throne, I would refuse. If you tried to force me into it. I would fight to the death to avoid returning to that prison."

"You had a ruby which connected your will to that of the land." Emperor Ordamy leaned forward slightly. "What became of it?"

"I tossed it down a well in the first village we passed outside the city." Henry shrugged. "I expect it is still there."

"That ruby held immense power."

"I gave up the throne, so I gave up that power." Henry shrugged again. "I could not be free of one and keep the other."

"Could you show me this village on a map?"

"If you require it, I can." Henry looked at the emperor and set his shoulders back. "Allow me to offer a warning. The stone wields the emperor as much as the emperor wields the stone."

"I will keep that in mind." Emperor Ordamy leaned back.

"I am Rebecca Ormsdottir, once Third Wife of the emperor. Now just Rebecca. I seek to return to my home and perhaps help fashion a peace for my people."

"I remember Orm." Emperor Ordamy tilted his head. "He was a stubborn man. Someone I could respect. I was saddened to hear of his passing in a skirmish with the clans."

Allin jumped to catch Rebecca as she slumped to the floor.

The emperor clapped his hands. "Chairs for my guests." The people in the room jumped into action and chairs appeared like magic for Allin and his companions. The emperor stood and came to Rebecca.

"My apologies, Rebecca Ormsdottir. I should have known you wouldn't have heard of his passing. I didn't mean to wound you with my words."

"The old fool always had to personally attend every battle." She gasped and buried her face in her hands. "What of the north?"

"The clans were sent packing. I sent a legion north to secure the border for now."

"For now, you mean until you march south."

"I do not wish to claim Ancanopolis, but the person who calls himself emperor there may give me no choice."

"I see." Rebecca slumped further into herself.

"We will speak more on this." The emperor returned to his throne.

"I am Magpie." She took Henry's hand.

"I am told you gave yourself to the emperor in place of your mistress, the Voice of the Emperor."

"I did." Magpie tightened her grip on Henry's hand. "Only I would say I gave myself to Henry the man, not the emperor. He needed someone to see the man, as my mistress saw me, not a slave."

"May I be so fortunate." The emperor nodded to her, and a murmur rippled through the room. "You may return to your rooms. We will speak more in the coming days."

***

Alekar waited until the four had been escorted out of the throne room before approaching the throne.

"Are you going to give them to me, as we discussed?"

"No." The emperor glared at Alekar, and he almost backed away.

"I gave you their location. In return you were to give them to me. I can't allow them to live unpunished. Already the streets are more dangerous for my people."

"Your people are your concern not mine." Ordamy leaned forward. "They are too important to cast away to your petty revenge. Our agreement was that I would meet them and decide what happened to them from there. If I didn't need them, they were yours."

"You need me and my people to keep the city calm." Alekar stepped closer to the throne. "You're only on that throne because we helped you."

"If you believe that, I suggest you stop helping me and see where it gets you." Ordamy stood and moved until he stood nose to nose with Alekar. "You are a convenience, not a necessity. Go think on that."

Alekar backed up. His fury made it difficult to breathe, but even this angry he wasn't stupid enough to take on this man directly. As he stomped away through the halls, plans already swirled in his mind. If he needed to remove Ordamy to get his vengeance, he would.

If he removed Ordamy, he'd take that throne for himself. Emperor Alekar sounded good to him. He'd pull all his people in, and while they gathered, he'd make plans. He wouldn't be the first king under the streets to take a city for his own.

Chapter 3

In the week following the strongman competition, the bakery became a madhouse. Osarl had to bring Chella and Wes into the kitchen to help, while Paula and Heddi helped in the front. Robin spent her time sweeping the step and talking to people who had lined up to buy bread. Osarl had let slip that she was the one who assured him he'd win, and a surprising number of people wanted her advice on a bewildering breadth of subjects.

Apparently, it wasn't just the draw of Osarl's display of strength, but the baking itself was extraordinary. Even the mayor's servants lined up, much to the disgust of the mayor's cook who had prided herself on being the best baker in the town. The mayor's son stopped by once, but when Robin wouldn't let him in ahead of everyone else, he left and never returned, much to Robin's relief.

He'd spent the entire time bragging about how he could have won the contest if his father had let him enter. The boy was soft as new cheese and didn't look like he'd done a day's work in his life.

"My daughter doesn't want to get married." A woman in fine clothes didn't quite look at Robin. "She insists she found a gold coin in the forest and is now obsessed with going out there every day to help her brothers."

"Didn't she do that already?" Robin asked.

"You know her?" The woman almost faced Robin.

"I've heard the stories." Robin shrugged. "She wouldn't have found the coin if she hadn't already been in the woods."

"But now she thinks she's too good for the mayor's son."

"She is." Robin snorted. "I've met him. No woman deserves him."

"Don't let the mayor hear you say that. He dotes on the boy."

"It shows." Robin shrugged and waved the next person into the shop. "But why would the mayor care what a servant girl thinks?"

"There are a lot of people who care what you think." The woman sniffed. "You need to think more carefully about what you say."

"You're right." Robin sighed. "I'll keep that in mind."

"It may be too late." Leila's mother swept into the shop.

A smallish man took her place. "Sword training, bow too." He lifted her hand and peered at it. "When you showed up at Mistress Henry's house, you talked like an urchin, now you speak like a knight born and bred, though with an odd accent. I'd wager you didn't grow up in Anca."

Robin's heart sank as the man released her hand.

"Don't look so down. Join me for supper at the guardhouse. Our bread isn't as good as the baker's here, but it is palatable enough." He met her eyes and Robin got the impression that if she didn't show up for supper, guards would find her and escort her there.

"I would be delighted." She choked out. He gave her a half salute and wandered away.

***

As the sun set, Robin knocked on the door of the guardhouse. A giant of a soldier answered and glared at her.

"What do you want?"

"Let her in, Seth. She's a guest." Robin's visitor from earlier in the day strolled up behind the giant. She was sure he'd emphasized 'guest'. Seth stood aside, scowling.

"You're the reason I lost that contest." Seth said.

"Osarl was always stronger than you." Robin replied tilting her head to meet his gaze. "That is true, contest or not. Blaming me isn't going to make you stronger."

The smaller man laughed and pointed to the back. The giant hung his head and slunk out of the room.

"Come now. Sit. Seth will be out to serve our meal in a few minutes. I'm Commander Willem, but please call me Willem."

"I'm Robin." She followed him to a table set as immaculately as the king's table in days when she'd been a trainee.

"Tea?" Willem poured her a cup without waiting for her to respond. "I'd offer wine, but sadly, I'm no longer allowed to drink it."

"Tea is fine." Robin added honey and milk to her cup and sipped at it, barely holding back the sigh of enjoyment. Willem smiled and nodded as if she'd just proven something to him.

"There are a few interesting stories we've heard in the last week." Willem sipped at his clear tea. "For instance, a young woman visited a tiny village on the edge of the forest a weeks' journey to the east. She visited with an old couple, then revealed she was a fae, testing their hospitality, and left a crust of bread and a bit of cheese behind for them to share. According to the story, that bread and cheese still hasn't run out despite everyone in the village tasting it. Someone sent to investigate insisted that it was the finest of bread and cheese and claimed it for themselves. It vanished from their pack on the way back to report to their lord. One hopes it is back in that village."

Robin put her teacup down and tried to process the story. She hadn't announced anything of the sort, but Rod had been sure she was fae. The rest had to be exaggeration.

"Somewhere between that little village and here a man came on the bodies of two men known as murderous bandits. Being a good citizen, he reported the bodies. The guards who buried the bandits said they couldn't see any wounds on them. As if they'd fallen over dead. They reportedly suggested the men had attacked a fae and died from a curse."

Robin snorted. "Don't believe in curses."

"Neither do I." Willem smiled and waved Seth over. He placed plates of roast and vegetables in front of them, then retreated.

"Do eat while the food is hot." Willem picked up his knife and fork and started at his own plate.

The food was delicious, better than what she'd eaten while on the march with the Thousand. Robin almost said as much, then bit her cheek. This man didn't miss anything. There was a reason he was telling these outrageous stories.

Maybe he suspected she was a spy. She'd already been too careless.

"Closer to home, Mistress Henry's girl Fanny says that the girl they let in at night swept the back hall, tidied the wood room, and swept the courtyard outside in the few minutes that she and her mistress were talking about what to do about the girl. Fanny claims the back hall and wood room no longer need much in the way of cleaning. The mattress she loaned to the girl now feels like a feather bed.

"Mistress Henry doesn't claim to know about the mattress or the hall, but it seems Master Henry's wandering eye has settled, and he no longer stays late every night at the tavern. She'd hesitate to say it is the work of the fae, but she'd all but given up on the man."

"They were kind to me," Robin said, "but I have no power to give such blessings."

"Then there is our baker." Willem sat back and tilted his head. "A man who barely left his kitchen, even to go home, suddenly decided to enter a contest. He said you told him to enter and all but promised that he'd win."

"I thought if Wes saw how strong his father was, he'd consider working with him." Robin poured herself more tea. "He picked the biggest, strongest soldier to attach to, one who didn't have any real interest in training the boy. Showing that his father was stronger would shift his attention. He's still too young to really know what he wants to do with his life."

"Interesting." Willem leaned forward and eyed Robin critically. "I'm guessing you're older than you present. Not a knight yet, but well trained. Probably better than my boys. I'd love to see you in action. I had some of the local boys out looking in hidey holes. One of them got scratched to pieces by a pair of squirrels, but they found a bag."

Seth walked into the room and dumped Robin's pack on the floor. She winced as her sword clattered against the short bow she'd been carrying. Coins rolled on the floor.

"Touch them and you'll regret it." Robin snapped at Seth. He jumped back. "Don't you have the slightest respect for another's belongings?" She picked up her herb satchel and checked it over. "You're lucky you didn't break any of the vials, some of them could have unpleasant effects."

Seth recovered and sneered at her. "What you going to do girlie?" He reached for her. Robin's annoyance blossomed into a fire in her gut. Everything Rick taught her flowed into her muscles as she twisted Seth's arm and slammed him into the floor, then held him there by pressure on his wrist.

Willem slapped his knee and roared with laughter. "Let him go, Robin. He'll behave, or I'll tell the squad how a twig of a girl bested him at his own game."

Seth growled as Robin released him and stepped back. She held his eye until he wilted. "Everyone I trained with was bigger than me. Size doesn't scare me, and if you have any notions of getting your own back, know I could have killed you easier than subduing you."

He muttered something under his breath and slunk from the room.

"My apologies for the violence in your dining room, Willem."

"I enjoy my semi-retirement here in Shadetown. As you might have noticed I have a hobby of collecting stories. Some of them include the news of a thousand Fhayden soldiers led by a girl who defeated the emperor's army at the border. Curiously they marched under a white flag until quite recently."

"I had considerable help at the border." Robin's hands twitched toward her gear still splayed on the floor. We were betrayed by treachery at Westburg. Haffmon corrupted two of the commanders."

"Haffmon is now calling himself Emperor Haffmon, and his story is very different." Willem picked up her sword and weighed it in his hand. "He doesn't have the palace bureaucracy in his pocket yet, but he does mostly control the city. Emperor Ordamy is watching him. I expect he will be interested in hearing your opinions."

"So, are you arresting me?" Robin retook her chair and sipped at her tea.

"I don't have any orders to do so." Willem put her sword down. "I will send a message to General, rather

Emperor, Ordamy. I would be happy to accept your word that you will not try to escape or cause harm to the people I watch."

"But?"

"But the mayor has heard your opinion of his son. He is displeased and would like to see you locked in a cell. It would be troublesome to get on his bad side."

"I see." Robin shrugged. "Where I sleep is of little importance, but I don't want my friends hurt because of me."

"The mayor thinks you to be a fae. In the tales they are often outspoken. I have suggested that disturbing the people you call friend would be a bad idea."

"I appreciate that." Robin sighed and caressed her satchel before pushing it over to Willem. "Guard this carefully. It is dangerous in the wrong hands, and it means more to me than my sword."

"You have my word." Willem stood. "Now, Lady Robin, I will guide you to your chamber."

The chamber turned out to be a stone walled cell with a solid oak door and a tiny window. The cot had a mattress and a blanket. A pot nestled beneath the cot.

"It will do." Robin said and sat on the cot. "Thank you for supper. It was delicious."

"I will let Seth know."

"He is a much better cook than soldier."

"He would say no one respects a cook."

"Tell him to cook for more people." Robin lay down. "Good night, Willem."

The door closed followed by a thump as a heavy bar dropped into place.

What are you playing at? Robin asked the land, but all she heard in response was laughter.

***

Allin followed Lady Wren to a small room with only two chairs and a fire. Glasses and a bottle sat on a small table opposite the fire.

"Come in, Allin." The emperor stood and waved him to a seat. Lady Wren poured wine in glasses from the bottle and offered them to the emperor and Allin.

Allin accepted one and sipped at it. He sighed and lowered himself into a chair. "A vintage from my homeland. One of our better years."

"Lady Wren reminded me we had the bottle, and suggested I share it with you." The emperor sat in the other chair. "In this room I am Gurdin, and you are Allin. We are two men sharing some fine wine."

"As you wish, Gurdin." Allin glanced around, but Lady Wren had already left. "To what do I owe this pleasure?"

"First a warning. The head of the thieves' guild offered to keep order in the streets while I consolidated my hold on the northern province. I accepted as much to keep them out of my hair as anything else. Now he is threatening me because he wants me to turn you over to him."

"That does sound like the man who has been harassing us." Allin shook his head. "Some of his less capable thieves tried to rob us. It went badly for them. Several times. He isn't much of a strategist."

"So I've gathered. My soldiers have put down a few petty riots. None of the rioters could explain what was going on. Only that they'd been ordered to cause a disturbance."

"Maybe he's trying you out. If there were riots all over the city, would putting them down leave you vulnerable here?"

Gurdin laughed. "If he thinks I'm tough, let him try Lady Wren. She ran this place before I took it as my seat of government. Our agreement is that while I run the country, she runs the keep."

"She is a most formidable woman." Allin took another sip, conscious there only was one bottle on the table.

"You and your companions are far too valuable to hand over. I will caution you, if you go out in the city, do not go without guards."

"I will keep that in mind." Allin shifted slightly in the chair. "We are comfortable enough here for the moment, but if you need us as bait, let me know."

"I will." Gurdin got up and poured more wine into Allin's glass, then topped up his own. "I wanted to ask what you know of the fae."

"Just what our histories tell us." Allin swirled the glass and took in the perfume of the wine. "They held our country before we arrived. Taught us how to work in partnership with the land when farming or harvesting from the forest. A long time ago they left for Caldera and never returned. We eventually settled Caldera."

"I keep getting reports about a slip of a girl who leads a thousand soldiers under a white banner. She defeated a giant in one city. Built a fort in Ancanopolis that the soldiers there couldn't open. Some claim she committed treachery by Westburg, but others suggest she fought free of treachery by the Ancans and repelled the attack on the city. Such a person is dangerous to have wandering through the countryside. There have been no new reports since the battle at Westburg, but I'd like to know where she is."

"All that happened after I left on my peace mission to Ancanopolis." Allin drank more of his wine. *Maybe Gurdin has a different bottle stashed away.* "I would dearly like to meet her. She sounds like a very interesting person."

"I have my people listening for more information. I expect we'll know more when Ancanopolis tries to take Westburg again. They've created a situation where backing down and writing a trade agreement is impossible."

"What would you do?"

"Nordfin is our centre of trade with the eastern plains, but it isn't set on the plains as Westburg is. We have people from the plains trading in the city. They keep a low profile, unlike the nobles, but they are there. If they can hold Westburg, it gives them a legitimate trading centre. I would recognize the plains as their own land and craft a trading agreement that would fail on any military venture into my territory." Gurdin stood and stretched. "I appreciate your company. Unfortunately, with the present situation it is unwise for me to drink more than a couple glasses of wine. I can arrange a bottle to be sent to your quarters if you'd like."

"If I may, I'll finish my wine here and find my way back to our suite." Allin smiled and swirled his glass. "It is much too fine a vintage to drink quickly."

"Take the glass with you." Gurdin set his own glass on the table. "I can't allow you to stay here without my presence."

"I understand." Allin pushed himself erect and followed the emperor out of the room. A guard walked him to their suite and saw him inside. Allin sat in a chair to finish his wine. The suite was silent, the others had to be asleep. For the moment, as comfortable as it was, the suite was still a prison.

CHAPTER 4

Lencely woke in his cell. Rud still snored on the other side of the tiny room. He hadn't been able to breathe properly since a guard broke his nose for asking after Sarge one too many times. Lencely's dreams had him in his armour with sword in hand facing down that guard. Awake, he was no hero, and no matter what he had, that guard would beat him. He'd taken pleasure in humiliating any of the captive Fhaydens he could.

Commander Paychen had complained to the commandant of the prison, but the scuttlebutt was he'd been laughed at and threatened with whipping if he spoke up again.

The third occupant of their cell turned away from the bars.

"So you're finally awake. Wish I'd been in the army and could sleep in every morning." Daggins looked to be about Lencely's age but acted twice that.

"What else is there to do?" Lencely stood and started his exercises. "Sarge told us to never let a chance to sleep or eat pass us by."

"Sounds like a sharp fellow. Explains why he's working for Haffmon now."

"I'm sure he has his reasons." Lencely squashed the resentment rising like bile in his throat and concentrated on his movements.

"You going to ask him?"

"When I get a chance." Lencely sped up until sweat poured from his skin.

The conversation woke Rud who sat on his mat and waited his turn to exercise.

"So you keep saying." Daggins didn't sneer at Lencely, but his expression was one of a person with much greater life experience pitying a fool. "Once Rud is done with his nonsense, we'll continue our lessons?"

Daggins refused to join in the morning exercise, but he was fascinated by the 'lordly' manner of fighting, also he enjoyed demonstrating his superiority in the enclosed space of the cell.

He crouched against the wall and waved for Lencely and Rud to attack.

Today Lencely charged in and tried to keep Daggins occupied while Rud circled around to wait for an opportunity. When Daggins swivelled to push Lencely toward Rud, Lencely grabbed Daggins' arms and lifted his feet from the floor. His weight pulled them both to the floor. Rud jumped on Daggins and tried to get an arm around their friend's neck. Somehow Daggins squirmed free and rolled away, his own arm around Rud's throat.

Lencely laughed and picked himself up from the floor and brushed the dust from his new scrapes.

"You win again."

Rud nodded and Daggins released him.

The boys then spent the remaining morning attempting to teach the basics of sword play with neither swords nor the space to move.

"Enough of that." A guard banged on the bars, then looked around. "You want to earn some extra comforts?" He leaned close to the bars.

"You're new, ain't ya?" Daggins slipped back into the street slang he'd been working on changing.

"What of it?" The guard put a finger to his lips. "Happens some of us are bored. Some lad's fighting might be just the thing for entertainment."

"Betting you mean." Lencely leaned against the wall arms crossed. "What's in it for us?"

"I can arrange better food, maybe blankets. If you're good, maybe a woman."

"Ye c'n keep your women." Daggins spat on the floor. "But more food would be nice. Real meat, not the half rotten slop you serve us."

"It can be arranged."

"What about the commandant?" Rud rubbed his nose.

"What about him? Can't complain about what he don't know."

"Fine, but we want a proper meal before, need to know you're serious." Daggins stopped just short of poking the guard through the bars.

"Tonight, after lights out." The guard winked at them. "Enjoy your supper."

"Don't trust him." Lencely walked over to the bars and peered through them. "Did you notice the cells across the way and beside ours are empty? When did that happen?"

"You're right." Daggins kicked the wall. "What do you think he's after?"

"Blood." Rud sat on his mat. "He smells like the one who likes to beat on the prisoners. "We may get a good meal, but it will probably be our last."

"Not that we have a choice." Daggins frowned. "We need to have a plan if we're going to survive."

***

"Word with the Commander, urgent." Lencely bumped into one of the other Fhaydens. The woman nodded, then pushed him away. They had a few minutes in the courtyard each day, watched by guards looking for chances for violence.

Another Fhayden, one Lencely didn't know well bumped into him, then cursed and shoved him up against the wall. Leather scraped on stone as the guards above shifted position.

"You need to watch where you're going kid." He slammed Lencely against the stones again.

"Back off soldier." Commander Paychen didn't raise his voice, but the soldier stomped off. "You okay, Lencely?"

Lencely filled the commander in on the events of the morning as quickly as he could while the commander examined his back and arms for injury.

"We've been expecting something like this. Go in with your eyes open, stay alive." The commander slapped his shoulder and walked away.

In the cell waiting for the evening meal, Lencely repeated what the commander had told him.

"Don't help us much." Daggins smacked the wall with his open hand.

"Our first job is to stay alive." Lencely leaned against the wall where he could see down the hallway of strangely empty cells. "The guards behind this don't want it getting out. How much trouble was it to empty this section just to isolate us? We're young, so in their mind, we aren't dangerous. From what the Commander said, they have guards helping us. Unless they have another large space with a gallery to watch from, the fight will be in the courtyard."

"Great, so if there's trouble, they shoot us with crossbows." Rud clenched his fists.

"That may be a problem, but they chose us because they think they can control us. Crossbows would imply that they're scared of us. Even if they have weapons, I think they will limit them to a few who are running the fight. Don't want the audience murdering each other over a lost bet."

"Right, then what?" Daggins stomped over to Lencely.

"We stay alive until it is no longer an issue." Lencely met Daggins's eyes. "Keep in mind they think we're harmless kids. Probably the biggest concern is whether we'll fight. I expect them to offer the winner their freedom. Pretend to believe it. Hey, what do you think they'll feed us?" Lencely spoke normally and tapped his head.

"Hope it's roast beef and potatoes." Rud laughed. "I'd even eat vegetables."

"Here you go." The guard passed the tray under the door. "It's better than what I ate." He turned and marched away before they could respond.

"It ain't roast beef, but it ain't porridge either." Daggins pulled a leg from the chicken and took a huge bite. Lencely and Rud weren't far behind. They'd eaten the bird down to the bones and all but licked the tray clean before Rud sat bolt upright.

"What if it's drugged?"

"Why would they drug us if they want us to fight?" Lencely asked.

"Not all drugs make you sleepy." Daggins warned them. "They may have dosed us with something to make us fight harder."

"Drugs cost money." Lencely said after a moments' thought. "We're their first try at this. Pay attention to what goes on in your mind, but I think we're safe. They aren't picking us up until lights out. But be careful of any water or drink they give us."

"Aye, commander." Daggins saluted Lencely with a twisted grin. "When I was a little sprat, I wanted to be a soldier. This looks to be as close as I get to it."

"Good to have you in my squad." Lencely reached out a hand. Daggins took it, and Rud covered their hands with his.

Lights out came after a long silent wait. Instead of putting the torch outside their cell out, the guard opened the door for them. He carried a short sword and made them walk ahead of him. As Lencely suspected, their destination was the courtyard. A full moon filled it with light and shadow. The spectators on the guardwalk were edged with white.

When they entered the courtyard torches lit up in braziers around the courtyard. Guards stood beside each brazier forming a square around a rope circle on the ground. Lencely counted four guards at braziers, all with short swords, plus the one behind them. He couldn't see much in the 'gallery' but there had to be a few dozen at least to make the betting worthwhile.

"Go stand in the circle." The guard behind them gave Lencely a shove. "Friends. A warmup exercise if you will. The last one standing in the circle will get a drink. Betting will open at the conclusion of the first fight. Start!"

Lencely lunged at Daggins. "Make it last."

Daggins laughed and threw Lencely almost to the edge of the circle. Rud swept Daggins' legs from under him, and they wrestled on the sand. Lencely tried to drag them to the rope.

When the laughter died down. Lencely rolled too far and landed outside the rope. It didn't take long for Daggins to push Rud out of the circle, and he lifted his arms in victory.

One of the guards at the braziers handed Daggins a waterskin. He made a show of drinking but spilled most on himself.

Lencely lounged on the sand with Rud and Daggins while the crowd argued odds and placed bets with guards.

After the chaos slowed. The guards pushed Lencely and the others into the ring and tossed three knives into the sand.

"This time they will fight until only one remains standing. The winner gets to walk out of here tonight."

Lencely picked up the knives. They were old and rusty. He ran a thumb down one's edge. Butter knives were sharper. He spun and threw them against the stone wall. Two of them broke.

"You want us to fight for our freedom and you give us toys?" He spun on his heel. "I thought you wanted a fight, not comedy. Are you afraid of blood?"

"Yeah, give us something to put up a proper fight." Rud yelled.

"I want a cut of the pot when I win." Daggins pointed at the guard who stared open mouthed at them. "Freedom ain't any good without some coin to enjoy it."

The audience roared with approval.

"Give them swords." Someone shouted and the crowd took up the call.

"Fine then." The guard running the fight shouted. He pointed at three of the guards by the braziers. "Give them your swords."

"No way," one said and stepped back.

"They're just kids." Another unsheathed his sword and dropped it to the sand. "I want double my take if the kid with my sword wins."

"Fine, fine." The guard threw his hands in the air. "Just let's get this going before the moon goes down."

Lencely picked up a sword and tested its edge. It was marginally better than the knife. Rud didn't look any happier. Daggins wiggled the blade uncertainly.

"Rud, let's give them a demonstration. Form five." He leapt into the series of moves, making the sword whistle through the air. They finished and stood back to back with Daggins.

"You don't have gold enough in this place to make us harm each other. We're a squad, and we live together, or die together."

"Fine, then die." The guard who'd brought them drew his sword. "You may be flashy, but you're still just kids."

As he stalked toward Lencely, the three swordless guards drew batons and the last one his sword. He pointed it at Rud.

Lencely found his centre. He'd trained with Lady Robin, and she'd said he was good. He'd find out what that was worth tonight.

The guard grinned and made a feint so obvious, Lencely didn't bother reacting to it.

"You've got too much weight on your front foot, and your stance is narrow. I'm guessing you're used to fighting in a line." He slid to the right, then drove in for a cut. The guard batted it away and scurried back. Lencely chased him around the courtyard keeping up his commentary on his opponent's weaknesses. One of the baton wielding guards tried to come at him from behind, but Lencely read the danger in his opponent's eyes and spun to club the guard down with the flat of his sword, continuing the spin to bring his sword down hard on the guard's sword arm. The crack of bone preceded the man's scream. Lencely clubbed him silent. Rud's opponent lay bleeding on the sand. Another of the baton wielders lay motionless. Daggins had the last guard in a choke hold on the sand.

"No one move!" Doors opened into the gallery and soldiers held swords and crossbows on the people in the crowd.

"Back to back." Lencely yelled and met Rud and Daggins in the circle. The wave of people over the wall stopped and those on the sand backed into the wall, hands in the air.

Soldiers went through the crowd sending some away and pushing others to jump onto the sand, where other soldiers forced them to kneel.

One soldier sheathed his sword and walked over to Lencely.

"Should have had the commander tell you not to kill anyone."

"Don't think anyone is dead, quite." Lencely withheld the urge to salute. "It is good to see you, Commander Themson."

"I'm Guardsman First Class Bodan here. Follow me."

Lencely waved Rud and Daggins to stay with him as Commander Themson led him down a corridor he hadn't seen before. They stopped in what had to be a storeroom.

"Find uniforms to fit. Make sure they don't have any bars or the like on them. You're going to be guards. In our report to the commandant, you'll have been thrown into solitary. He will be discouraged from any investigations of his own. He's not one of Haffmon's flunkies but got assigned to the prison because he was sloppy and lazy. We will allow him to continue in his ways. By some coincidence the division our uniforms come from is a pro-Haffmon division. He won't want Haffmon knowing the man was running a gambling ring without giving the emperor his cut.

"Even me?" Daggins stood with his back to the wall.

"He's part of my squad." Lencely stepped back and put a hand on Daggins' shoulder. "I expect his knowledge of the city will be useful."

"I will leave him in your care. Now get into uniforms and I'll show you to the barracks."

"Yes, sir." Lencely peeled off the ragged remains of his squire's clothes and found a uniform to fit. He was one step closer to getting back to Sarge.

***

"We're supposed to train some young fighters for Haffmon's arena games." Lencely sat with Rud and Daggins in the corner of the barracks. "He liked the idea, just not being cut out of the money."

"I thought he was already rich?" Rud shook his head.

"Bribes are expensive." Daggins grinned. "He'll be paying off the thieves' guild to not cause trouble for any of his people. Then there are the commanders of the city guard. He has the top dog in his pocket, but that doesn't guarantee that others won't decide to put a nose in where Haffmon doesn't want it. All that is copper to gold when it comes to keeping the bureaucrats off his back."

"Where do we find people who are going to be willing to fight for a sliver of that pie?" Rud asked.

"If we start with the street gangs, they're fighting each other all the time anyway, so getting paid for it would bring them in for sure." Lencely nodded at Daggins.

"Happens I know a few we could talk to." Daggins grinned. "We don't want to go in uniform, or the discussion might be more hands on than we want."

"It might not be a bad idea to demonstrate that we have something to teach." Lencely pointed at the baton on his belt hung on the end of his bed. "It would help to establish a neutral space for training. We don't want to waste time stopping fights."

"I know the perfect place." Daggins jumped up. "Might as well wear the uniforms since we'll be knocking a few heads anyway."

They put on their belts and grabbed rain cloaks as they went out the door. The drizzle was heavy enough to keep the dust down, but not to turn the streets they walked on to mud. The buildings shifted from stone, to solidly built wood to ramshackle. People in the street eyed them balefully, some spitting on the road behind them.

Around one corner a man was beating a woman. Daggins strolled up to the man and knocked him to the ground.

"What are you doing?" the man shouted and climbed to his feet. "Do you know who I am?"

Daggins knocked him down again. "I know you. You're a coward who only beats women."

Two other men appeared from alleys, they were bigger and looked meaner than the man Daggins faced.

"I'll take the one with the knife." Lencely spoke loudly as he nudged Rud. "You take the one with the club. Let's try not to kill them this time."

"Fine." Rud rolled his eyes and hoisted his baton. "But it's easier to kill them."

"More paperwork, and I'm the one has to do the paperwork."

The men slowed as Lencely lifted his baton.

"You talk big for little people," the one with the knife said.

"Then why are you trembling?" Lencely smacked his hand with the baton. "Or maybe you're late taking your drug? That's going to slow you down. Sure you want to deal with the pain over that guy?" He pointed his baton at the man grovelling in the dirt as Daggins recited the impossible family tree of the man.

The knife man charged Lencely who side stepped and tripped the man. The man slammed into the ground and oofed before rolling on his back. The knife had stuck in his shoulder.

"Didn't you learn not to run with a knife in your hand?" Lencely knelt beside the man. "Do you want me to fix that, or would you rather keep it there as a warning to others?"

The man snarled and wrenched the knife out and slashed at Lencely who slapped the knife away with his baton then tapped the man's head, rendering him unconscious.

"Can't be that bad." He poked at the wound, then bound it up after dusting it with the herb Robin had given them to prevent infection. "Probably a waste of time, you'll just ignore it and get it infected anyway."

Rud's opponent lay on the road. "He's breathing." Rud wiped his baton on the man's shirt. "For now, anyway."

Daggins crouched beside his man. Whatever he was saying had the man shaking on the road. He stood and looked around. "Blast, the woman is gone. I wanted to talk to her."

"Don't blame her for bunking it." Rud nudged his man. "She probably didn't expect this outcome."

"Most of the guards in this area are bribed to stay out of such things." Daggins shrugged and looked around. "This is going to cause us trouble, but I was hoping to get a message to my sister."

"Maybe next time we talk to the woman before we take out the muscle." Lencely dusted his pants off and put the baton back on his belt. "Shall we continue?"

They walked along the street. The housing grew even worse. He'd never imagined people living in such terrible conditions. The buildings were more ruins than complete structures, they leaned against their neighbours. Naked children ran through the rain while adults slumped in whatever cover they could find.

"Home, sweet home." Daggins muttered frowning. "Never thought I'd be back. Should have died in prison." He led them into a opening where it looked like someone had tried to clear the ruins, but gave up.

"What is this place?" Rud looked around.

"Daggins is here. Anyone want to talk to me, better show your face." Daggins shouted. "Now we wait. Shouldn't be too long."

"What do you want?" A woman sauntered into the clearing, stopping a dozen paces from Daggins. "You figuring on trying to take over from the guild again?"

"Not today, Kat." Daggins shuffled his feet. "We come to train people to fight in the arena."

"We're going to shed our blood for our emperor?" Kat spat in the dirt. "Prison changed you; time was you'd die rather than wear that uniform."

"In a way, I did die." Daggins stood straighter. "I'm here knowing there's no easy change to our lives."

"So you've given up." Kat's shoulders slumped.

"I said no easy change. Change will be hard, but I have help and an offer."

"An offer? To put on the emperor's colours and bow to his cronies?"

"We shed each other's blood to hold onto tiny bits of useless territory. The rich still own us. What if we take our fights to the arena and get paid as we solve our arguments. The fights aren't to the death, even the losers will get a few coins."

"And the bully boys will come and take those coins from us." Kat sneered.

"We pay them off, same as the emperor does. The bully boys are about business, easier to take bribes than fight for control."

"Maybe. I'll take the message to them, but you beating Mac and his boys already sent a message."

"True." Daggins stepped toward Kat. "We pay them, we aren't their slaves. Mac and those like him need to learn that beating their workers costs them money. The choice is easy money or war. The Guard's changing, they won't allow anything that gets in the way of the emperor collecting his gold."

Kat laughed and waved a hand at him as she walked away.

Men and boys walked out of the ruins carrying knives and clubs.

"Big words, Daggins," a man shouted. "But ye're going to leave your blood on the dirt here."

"Back to back." Lencely ordered. "No mortal wounds if you can avoid it."

Rud and Daggins moved into position.

"No speeches?" the man called.

"Come and fight, Os," Daggins sneered. "Or are you going to hang back and let others shed their blood for you like usual. No wonder you're the bully boys' best girl."

Os swore and pointed at the three. "Get them."

No one moved, some of the younger boys stepped back.

"I'll have anyone who doesn't move beaten within an inch of their lives."

"You'll have them beaten?" Lencely stepped forward. "Not beat them yourself? Not much of a threat if you aren't around to make the order." He walked forward slowly. A man rushed him, and he swatted him aside casually.

Os ducked behind a group of boys. "Stop him you cowards."

Lencely pulled his purse out and dangled it in the air. "I will leave this for anyone who can land a blow on me, one on one." He dropped it on the dirt. "Just don't let the coward run away."

"How do we know there's any money in it?" Os pushed the boys aside.

"Come and find out." Lencely spread his arms. "I don't have all day."

Os wrenched a club from one of the boys and stalked toward Lencely.

"I'm going to kill you and take that purse."

"Then what?" Lencely grinned at him. "You think the bully boys are going to let you spend it? You talk big, but you're nothing but a snitch, kissing ass to get a copper coin. The bully boys are watching. Now's the chance to show what you're made of."

"How do you know they're watching?" Os gulped and stepped back.

"If I ran the bully boys, I'd be watching." Lencely put his hands behind his back. "I tire of waiting."

Os threw the club at him and bolted for the edge of the clearing.

Lencely caught the club and inspected it.

"Not much use." He snapped it over his leg. "Don't bring rotten wood to a fight."

"What do you want?" the boy who'd owned the club ran up to Lencely.

"We are going to train you to fight in the arena." Lencely picked up his purse. "Any who want to learn. We'll be here each day. The first thing is to work on your strength and stamina. Ten laps around the clearing, fast as you can run.

The boy took off, followed by others, after the first lap some of the men joined in, others walked away.

CHAPTER 5

Lencely worked their trainees mercilessly. When some girls and women wanted to join, he just waved them into line. A big man punched a woman who got too close to him.

"Rud if you would explain to him the proper treatment of his fellow trainees."

Rud jogged over to the man and stood between him and the woman. "Punch me."

"You'll just hit me back," the man crossed his arms.

"But she won't?" Rud pointed to the woman crouched on the ground holding her face.

"Nah, she's just a woman. Only one thing she's good for." The man leered.

"What's your name?" Rud raised a brow.

"Cabel." Cabel puffed up, until Rud stepped forward and punched him in the gut. Cabel folded and collapsed on the ground.

"Until your fellow trainees have the skills to hit back. I will stand in for them. Woman, boy, man, I don't care. Your first concern is the safety of your partners. If you can't work with them, I can't work with you." Rud turned and helped the woman to stand. "What's your name?"

"Edit, sir."

"Call me Rud." He checked her face. "Bruises, but no broken bones. Back in line when you're ready, Edit."

She nodded and stepped back into line beside where Cabel gasped for air.

"Save the fights for when you know how to fight." Lencely told his trainees. "If you really want to fight, challenge one of us. But we won't be gentle. If you don't follow our orders, you're out. We don't have time to waste on fools."

Cabel struggled to his feet. "Sorry, Edit."

"Don't do it again." Edit said and turned her attention back to Lencely.

"Now, we will start on your stance." Lencely waved Daggins and Rud to him. "Split into three groups. Each of us will work with a group."

After they split up, Lencely worked his group on how to stand and how to walk until they gasped for air.

"You need conditioning." He dropped to the ground and demonstrated the push ups Sarge had taught them, then sit ups and other exercises they could do on their own. "Train every morning and evening. If you can run safely, run for a candle each day. No fighting outside this arena. There will be no second chances. If someone threatens you, report it to us and we will deal with it. Dismissed. We will be back tomorrow."

The twenty trainees turned and left. A man walked out to Lencely.

"Ballsy, to expect them to obey when you aren't around to enforce your rules."

"Obeying the rules is part of the training. I don't have time to babysit them."

"So what if other people start fights with them? How you going to deal with that?"

"The guards have been bribed to stay out of your business." Lencely stretched out a cramp in his shoulder. "How much would it cost your boss if they stopped being bribed?"

"We've taught guards their place before." The man put his hand on the knife on his belt.

"And how much did that cost your boss?" Lencely pointed to where other men hid. "You have four men with you, armed with knives, maybe poisoned. You think I don't know the stink of assassins? Here's a message for your boss. You start something with our trainees, the guard grows a spine. Anyone who attacks us has a coin's toss of a chance of living. If you do somehow kill us, the guard will decide they need training in city fighting. Full armour, bows, swords, the works. See, you think you're threatening three kids, but you're threatening the emperor's business. If you think you can take on the emperor, go ahead. What are your lives worth measured against the gold the emperor plans on making?"

The man slipped his blade out, almost faster than Lencely could follow. A knife buried itself in the man's throat. Daggins strolled over, kicked the blade from the man's hand, then pulled his knife free.

"Anyone else? A message has already been sent to the old man. Here's a second."

"An arrow in the back will kill you as easy as a knife." Another man stepped out of the shadow holding a small bow.

"Sure it will, and when we don't show up for evening roll call, our commander will send the guard in. Why do you think he sent us here? We're a test. You're failing. I doubt your boss will be happy." Daggins grinned at him.

"You're lying." The man lifted his bow, but a knife came around his throat.

"He's not lying," Rud said. "Drop the bow or die."

"How?" the man dropped the bow and reached for his belt.

Rud ran his knife lightly along the man's throat, then hit him with the hilt. "You are a fortunate fool, but someone needs to carry the message. Your scar will talk for us."

Lencely waved him over. "The others?"

"Sleeping." Rud nodded. "As ordered."

"Good." Lencely slapped Rud on the back. "Let's get home before they wake up."

"I didn't think it would work." Daggins joined them.

"Distraction is a useful tool. Keep in mind they will look to use it against us."

"Right, they know we stopped to help a woman, so they'll send a woman against us next?" Daggins asked.

"Perhaps, or they'll use a woman as a shield. We need scouts." Lencely rubbed his chin. "I'd rather not be the cause of a war."

"I know who to talk to." Daggins sighed. "I swore I'd never go back, but they are exactly the kind of people we need. This way." He turned sharply to the right and wove through alleys until they arrived at an abandoned tavern.

"You have nerve coming back here." A man stepped out of the doorway. Other jumped through windows until they faced a dozen men. "You'll have to fight me to return."

"I'm not returning, Kraog. You were right enough to name me a fool." Daggins put his hands out from his side.

"I haven't changed. We are renegotiating terms with the bully boys."

Kraog roared with laughter. "And you want us to protect you?"

"Not exactly." Lencely stepped forward, also with his hands out. "We are looking for people to scout out trouble while we walk to and from the place where we're training people for the arena. We've sent a message to the boss that we'll pay to be left alone. A few of the bully boys were thinking they didn't need to wait for the boss to make up their mind."

"You thought the three of you could take on the bully boys?" Kraog sneered, "you're stupider than you look."

"Our captain expects we'll be sent to Westburg soon enough. He wouldn't mind some training in fighting in a city. The guild would be a reasonably good target. There's space at the top, and he has a mind to fill it. We offered peace in return for being left alone. We will of course pay for the privilege. The emperor is paying us generously to train people for the arena. Can't have games to bet on if no one plays." Lencely bared his teeth. "I expect the boys we left have woken up and either they're coming after us or running to the boss. It's getting late and I'd rather not have to fight my way out."

"You knocked them out and left them alive?" Kraog shook his head. "They'll be out for blood."

"Maybe." Rud said. "I left them with something to think about. They may not want to try their luck a second time."

"You took them out?" Kraog's eyes widened. "Alone?"

"They were distracted." Rud shrugged. "It wasn't that hard. The problem with hiding in the shadows is your friends can't see you either."

"I'm almost impressed, but you could be lying."

"Get us out tonight." Lencely tossed Kraog his purse. "Then you can check on our story for tomorrow."

"And if we decide to make a present of you to the bully boys?"

"You could try." Lencely crossed his arms. "But you might want to count the cost before you try. Three boys without armour and swords are an easy enough target, but tackling the guards would be a different matter."

"The guards aren't here now." Kraog raised a hand. "We could take your heads to the boss."

"Tradkin." Lencely lifted his hand. "A demonstration please." Three bolts thudded into the dirt in front of Kraog. "The captain wanted to know where to start the war if we didn't return. We've had people watching our backs the entire day."

"Now what?" Kraog snarled.

"You decide. Are you going to scout for us or not?"

"You expect us to help you out now?" Kraog yelled. "The guards know where we hang out."

"We already knew." A voice floated down from the roof. "You aren't as clever as you think. If we wanted you dead, you'd be bleeding already. Just happens I like these boys, they're going to train up to be decent soldiers, but we don't have time to babysit them until the guild decides what they're going to do."

"The money is real." Lencely pointed at the purse. "Why don't you have a look?"

Kraog sidled forward to pick up the purse and dump it into his hand. "You've been walking around with this on your belt all day?"

"The one on my belt is filled with pebbles." Lencely laughed. "Are you in or out?"

"We're in." Kraog put the money in his own purse. "We'll meet you where you laid a beating on Mac."

"Good, until then." Lencely nodded to Daggins and Rud.

"One more thing." Kraog called. "If I want to fight in this arena, who do I talk to?"

"You can be in the first fight." Lencely said. "It will be in a week. I'll let you know tomorrow for sure."

***

Lencely, Rud and Daggins finished their meal and sat back.

"You did well." Commander Themson took a long pull from his tankard. "The right amount of violence to be convincing and a lot of bravado. Tradkin will be keeping an eye on you for a while, but don't get careless. There will be more than one fool trying to make a name from taking you down."

"It did help having his guys take down the other bully boys." Rud looked down. "I don't like playing the thug."

"Good." Commander Themson put his drink down with a thud. "As long as you know you're playing the part, you won't get carried away. We're walking a tightrope until we hear from the guild. They'll be checking with the emperor's people, but we've fed them the same story. Westburg is going to be a thorn in Haffmon's side, anything that looks to make it easier to take will play well with him."

"Will he attack it soon?" Lencely sipped at his water.

"If he was smart, he would have a delegation negotiating peace. He doesn't want a war in the east while he's trying to claim the throne. This is Haffmon, so you can count on an attack soon, probably within a month. He needs to secure the city before he sends more guards out to fight." Commander Bodan sighed. "We'll need to figure out how to rescue our people before then."

"We can't do anything now?" Rud asked.

"We have about a hundred soldiers. There's about a thousand Ancans in that camp. With luck we could get in, but we'd not get back out again. There's better minds than mine working on it."

"What about Sarge?" Lencely asked. "Is there something we can do for him?"

"We know he's safe for now. Haffmon brags about him, but we haven't been able to get anyone close. Haffmon is keeping his circle small. Probably on advice from Sarge. Hard to sneak a mole into a group who all know each other."

"Right." Lencely slumped his shoulders. "It also keeps Sarge isolated and only feeds him the information Haffmon wants."

"We have people walking by, but the inn is part of a more upscale neighbourhood. We did get a few messages asking for information, vaguely threatening Sarge, but those have stopped as if Sarge has become more important than whatever information we might have."

"Anything on who owns the inn?" Daggins leaned forward. "They'd have family. Even if Haffmon has taken over the place, they'd still need to buy supplies and such."

"All the businesses in the area are old family run places. Again, hard to place someone there. I will let you know if anything changes." Commander Themson caught Lencely's eyes. "You are not to do anything or try to find Sarge. It could put him at more risk. If he stops being useful to Haffmon. He becomes just one more disposable hostage.

***

Sarge sipped at the soup. In other company, he'd have taken time to enjoy it. Haffmon made all food tasteless. It didn't help that most of Sarge's strength hadn't returned. It had been a miracle he'd woken and been able to move, but the miracle didn't extend to giving him even the little strength he'd had before the coma.

"The games will start in a week." Haffmon grinned and munched on chicken leg. "I'll have the money to pay the army and we'll take Westburg and control the flow of food from the east."

"It is important to keep the populace fed." Sarge whispered.

"Yes, yes, you've told me." Haffmon waved a hand. "They will get their bread. I still think we could have some prisoners fight to the death. Give the crowds a proper show."

"Hostages have no value when they're dead. If you start killing them, you lose leverage."

"What do I need their leverage for? That commander person says most of the Fhayden army went home. Cowards, I could have used them."

"Mercenaries are expensive, and dangerous." Sarge took a long drink of water.

"Tell me something new." Haffmon frowned. "You keep saying the same things."

"Saying something different won't change reality."

"Give me a new weapon we can use against that rabble in Westburg."

"I've explained the use of pikes and shield walls." Sarge coughed and drank more water. "They are most effective against untrained troops."

"I know that." Haffmon banged his hand on the table, spilling his wine. "I want something new and devastating."

"Your technology isn't ready to build such a thing. Maybe..." Sarge trailed off into a fit of coughing.

"What?" Haffmon shook Sarge. "Maybe what?"

"Siege engines." Sarge gasped, then slumped in Haffmon's hands. *Let the idiot think he's killed me.*

"Serena!" Haffmon screamed.

The innkeeper's daughter came and mostly carried Sarge back to his bed.

"Poor old man." Serena covered him up and rubbed his back. Sarge liked Serena. She was doing her best. It wasn't her fault her pig of a father and Haffmon had embroiled her in this mess.

"I saw Tom walk past today." Serena said. "Every time I see him, I'm afraid he will have a new girl with him. Not that he was ever the type to have a new girl every month, but it's been so long. He looked so handsome in his uniform. Tom said we'd get married when he became a guard, but I haven't been able to do more than wave at him through the window." She rattled on as Sarge dove into sleep, hoping it would take him to memories of Robin.

***

The sun woke Sarge. He didn't remember any dreams, but he'd decided what he'd give Haffmon. Something complicated enough to take a month to build and test, something to buy him a bit more time. The only reason he knew Robin was alive was through Haffmon's cursing her treachery. She was in that city he wanted to take. So close it was only a week's march from Acanopolis, so far away it might as well have been on his old world.

"I have a secret." Serena whispered. "Promise you won't tell."

"Promise." Sarge croaked.

Serena fetched him a cup of tea, then helped him drink it.

"I snuck out last night and saw Tom. He said there was trouble at the prison and a bunch of guards lost their jobs."

"Yes?" The incident had sparked Haffmon's obsession with fights to the death.

"He's been appointed to work at the prison. No more walking the dangerous streets."

"Tom likes it there?" Sarge's voice worked better after the tea.

"Sure does. All he needs to do is watch the prisoners, and none of them are causing any trouble." She leaned close until her lips brushed his ear. "He says a lot of them are your friends. They talk funny."

"Is that so?" Sarge smiled. It had been so long, it felt strange on his face. "Does he still want to marry you?"

"Oh yes." She clutched her heart. "He's been walking past just to see me in the window. I want to run away, but he says it's too dangerous with *him* in control."

"I fear that he's right." Sarge struggled to hide the elation in his voice. There had to be some way to use this thin thread to contact the Fhaydens.

***

"No problem, Tom." Lencely handed the boots back to the newest guard. "It is our job as the juniors to help out our seniors."

"Good to hear you know your place." Tom pulled the boots on and obviously looked around for something reflective to admire himself.

"You look good." Lencely fought his face to dead pan.

"I still wish I had a sword."

"You heard about the riot?" Lencely lowered his voice. "Some of the prisoners took swords from the guards and almost broke out."

"No mere prisoner would take anything from me." Tom puffed up.

"Of course not, but then everyone would want one." Lencely shrugged. "And not everyone is at your level of skill."

Partially mollified, Tom marched out of the barracks, not forgetting anything this time, so Lencely could give into a fit of silent laughter. He shook it off and finished his own dressing before jogging down to the mess to collect Rud and Daggins.

"We have to report to Commander Themson before we go out." Rud told him past the piece of bread he was stuffing in his mouth.

"Better eat in a hurry." Lencely slapped together what Sarge had called a sandwich and gulped it down.

They collected full waterskins at the mess counter then went to the commander's office.

"I was exploring the contraband room and found a few interesting things." He pointed at a pile on table to the side. "The standard uniform doesn't allow for any armour for rank-and-file guard. Some took it on themselves to improvise. See if anything there fits you. It isn't as good a proper stuff, but it will probably turn a knife blade."

Lencely found a leather vest with thin plates sewn onto it. It wouldn't stop a thrust unless the point hit a plate exactly right, but it would protect him from slashes. Most of the moves Daggins used in their training sessions had been slashes. Daggins and Rud both found something as well.

"Don't use these except in the direst emergency." Commander Themson pushed three batons over to them.

"A bit heavier than normal." Daggins weighed his in his palm.

Commander Themson took one and gave the long part of the baton a sharp twist. It slid off revealing a wicked looking blade. Shorter than a sword, but deadly in close combat.

"Punishment for owning one of these ranges from immediate dismissal to hanging. Some guards wanted more than batons to control the prisoners. They ended up killing a few people. Normally not a big problem, but one was a hostage to a group outside the prison. The death caused a lot of political problems and almost lost the Commandant his job."

"The Commandant isn't exactly brilliant, is he?"

"Don't complain about your enemy's shortcomings." The Commander re-assembled the baton. "I'll trust you to know when to use these wisely. There will be rumours about you three spreading through the city. We've been careful to make you sound useful to the right people. There will be other stories about, so the confusion will work in your favour. We don't want anyone trying to take you out to prove themselves. One of the reasons we revealed your escort last night was to take you down a peg."

"Thanks, sir." Lencely saluted. "We will endeavour to continue to show the proper level of ability."

"Get out of here." Commander Themson tossed Lencely the baton, but he grinned at the same time.

They reached the clearing without any issue. The only sign they had of Kraog's people was the occasional whistle. Twice the number of trainees greeted them. Some were already running while others stood and chatted until Lencely called them to order.

"Good morning," he said. "Ten laps around the arena. Full speed." He ran them through the complete warm up Lady Robin had taught them. Many of the trainees were groaning by the end of it, but none quit. Again, they worked on stance and footwork, but by the end of the morning, Lencely added basic punches and blocks.

"When do we get proper weapons?" One man who had gone through all the warmup without breathing hard asked.

"When we can be sure you can use them without hurting yourselves." Rud responded. "For some of you that will be sooner than others."

The week passed quickly. Lencely sparred with a few of the trainees and declared that four of them were ready to fight in the arena the next day.

"The goal is to be better than your opponent, not to kill them. It is a harder task than fighting to kill. These aren't death matches, so you will need to demonstrate your prowess by ending the fight. Either your opponent gives up, or they can't continue. That also means if you are outmatched it is better to resign before you're injured. Remember you get paid even if you lose. Your real job is to entertain the crowds. So where a soldier is told not to be flashy, I'm saying create a style to catch the crowd's attention."

"Are you going to be fighting?" the man who'd asked about weapons tilted his head.

"What's your name?" Daggins asked.

"Ulfred." The man squared his shoulders as if he expected them to know the name.

"Ulfred, we are trainers. We won't be fighting. But I see you want to try us out." Daggins dropped his belt and stripped to the waist. "Let's spar and give the trainees a bit of a show."

Ulfred took off his shirt and squared up against Daggins.

"You start when I tell you and stop when I say. No blows after the end of the fight will be tolerated." Lencely held his hand between them. "Fight."

Ulfred almost brushed against Lencely as he lunged forward. His fist flashed toward Daggins' gut. Daggins scooted backward and the blow hardly touched him. Ulfred tried a variety of attacks, most of which they hadn't taught him. The man was probably a bare fisted fighter. He stayed in close where his arms would reach. Someone used to weapons would likely be less comfortable at such close quarters.

Daggins grinned as he wove and dodged. Lencely recognized the expression from their training in the cell. His friend was having fun.

Ulfred dropped and swung a leg, trying to sweep Daggins feet from under him. The smile broadened.

"Anytime now, Daggins." Lencely looked up at the sun.

Daggins drove forward into Ulfred while the other man was stretching to hit him. Their feet tangled and they crashed to the dirt. Daggins pinned Ulfred's right arm with a foot and drove a fist down stopping a hair's breadth from Ulfred.

"Fight to Daggins." Lencely said.

Daggins jumped up and offered Ulfred a hand.

"You could have finished me at any time." Ulfred furrowed his brow.

"What's the fun in that?" Daggins laughed. "If I was allowed, I'd bet on you tomorrow."

CHAPTER 6

Adam's stomach growled. Though the fae lady had told him not to eat only the white roots, he hadn't been able to find anything else.

The fox who had eaten the last of Adam's cheese still followed him.

"Why are you still here?" Adam pointed at the fox.

"You're amusing," the fox answered.

Since he'd met the fae lady, Adam hadn't been surprised that the fox talked, but it sounded too much like his older sister. He'd named the fox Zella after his sister, but most of the time called it fox. It was too hard to think while he was hungry.

"There's a village up ahead." Fox sat and curled her tail around her. "I will watch you from here. I don't want to draw too much attention."

"I guess." Adam walked far enough to peer through the branches at the quiet village with a well in the centre square. "I do need more water. The Lady Fae told me to fill my waterskin whenever I could."

"She also told you she wasn't a fae."

"They don't." Adam waved off Fox's statement. "It's part of the test."

Fox rolled her eyes.

"I didn't know foxes could roll their eyes." Adam checked his empty backpack, but there was nothing there.

"I learned it from you." Fox rolled her eyes again to demonstrate.

"Do I roll my eyes that much?" Adam tried, but wasn't sure if he had it right.

"Go, before my eyes fall out and run away from me." Fox swished her tail, a sure sign she was losing patience.

Adam pushed his way through the branches and walked slowly toward the village. He tried to think of a story to tell, but thinking wasn't one of his strong points. No one came out as he arrived at the well. He lowered the bucket until he heard it splash, then hoisted it back up, he could taste the cold clean water already.

Then the bucket stuck just below him. He tried jiggling the rope, but it didn't loosen the bucket. If he reached over the edge, he could almost reach it. Maybe if he stretched farther, he could free it. The problem was he needed to hold the rope to keep the bucket close. He wrapped the rope around one hand and put it on the rim of the well, then braced the other hand on the opposite side of the rim.

He was missing a hand.

Adam lifted his hand from the rim to reach down to the bucket and fell into the well. A strong hand gripped his leg before he could fall completely. He lifted the bucket free of the wall and squirmed back out of the well with the hand pulling his leg. As his waist passed over the rim, his knife fell into the well. It flashed once, then landed with hardly a splash far below.

"Blast." Adam finished his journey out of the well and fell to the ground. A girl stood peering down at him with one blue eye. Her brown eye looked out at the horizon somewhere.

"Were you trying to fall into the well?" she asked.

"No." Adam dusted himself off and looked over the rim. "My knife fell."

"That's too bad." The girl put her hands on her hips. "You have to lift the rope up the centre of the well or the bucket drags and drops moss into the water."

"That's bad?" Adam stood up to face her. He had to look up to see her face.

"Do you like drinking mossy water?" Her brown eye fixed him to the spot.

"I don't think so." Adam said. "I drank a lot of water in the forest. Some of it was mossy."

"You see?" She switched to her blue eye.

"I need to go get it." Adam looked for a way to tie the rope.

"Not happening." The girl shook her head. "Moss is nothing to a corpse, and you'd be a corpse if you went down there."

Adam lifted the rope. "You could hold this."

"This is rope for buckets not for fools." She frowned at him.

"Do you have any rope for fools?" Adam asked. "The lady who gave me the knife told me not to lose it."

"You met a lady?" The girl's frown deepened.

"In the forest," Adam explained. "Not someone to ignore their commands. She also gave me cheese, but I ate that."

"Stop, you're making my head hurt." The girl rubbed her temples. "I'll ask my father if he has any rope for fools." She stomped away to one of the houses.

Adam filled his waterskin and fastened it to his belt next to his empty sheath.

"Becca says you want to go down into the well to fetch a knife you dropped." The man's height made Adam tilt his head so far back he almost lost balance.

"Yes." Adam said.

The man shook his head and dropped a coil of heavy rope on the ground, then tied a loop in one end. "I'll help you, but you must give me whatever else you find at the bottom of the well."

"Okay." Adam nodded his head to be sure the man knew he had a deal.

"You're going to wash before you go down there." Becca had her hands on her hips again. "I don't want to drink water tasting of some muddy fool."

She made him take his clothes off while she poured water over him. It reminded him of home. Neither of her eyes was looking at him, so he didn't mind much.

Naked as the day he was born, Adam climbed onto the rim of the well, put his foot in the loop and hung on as he was lowered into the well. The water made him gasp with its chill. Winter snow wasn't as cold as this well. His feet sank into damp sand when the water made it up to his chest. The wall of the well closed in so he could only bend his knees and feel around on the bottom. While he was searching for his knife, the bucket came down beside him.

"Put whatever you find in the bucket," the man shouted down to him.

Adam couldn't talk for the chattering of his teeth, so he concentrated on his search. He found his knife when he stuck his finger on the point. The knife went into the bucket and his finger into his mouth so he wouldn't get blood in the water, also stopping his teeth hitting each other. His other hand scrabbled on the bottom and came on a purse. He put the purse in the bucket.

"Up," he shouted then put his finger back in his mouth The bucket vanished above him, then he was hauled up. On the way up he spotted something hanging on a rock. One hand held the rope, so he used the hand from his mouth to snatch up the thing. It flashed briefly, warming him from his hand down to his toes.

***

When the boy reached the top, Becca's father stopped hauling him up.

"Hand me that necklace."

The boy looked at the thing in his hand. It had a big red stone on a yellow chain.

"I found it on the wall on the way up. Not at the bottom." He slipped the chain over his head.

"You give it to me, or I'll drop you back into the well." The man let the rope slip a bit.

"You'd spoil our well over some bauble?" Becca stomped her foot. "You're a bigger fool than he is. You made a deal, keep it, or I'll tell everyone in the village how you spoiled our well."

"I'll have that gem," Becca's father let the rope slip a little farther.

Becca reached into the bucket and lifted out the purse. It broke in her hand and spilled gold on the ground. Her father let go of the rope and grabbed for the gold. Becca took hold of the rope. It burned her hands, but she pulled it up until the boy could climb over the rim.

She wrapped her shawl around the boy.

"A deal is a deal."

"You're a princess," the boy clutched the stone in a hand which dripped blood from one finger. She took the hand to wrap the finger in her kerchief.

Warmth filled her. She was a princess, it didn't matter that she'd been born to a man who grubbed in the dirt for gold and a woman who lay in the dirt beneath a gravestone.

"If I'm a princess, are you a prince?" Becca asked.

"I'm just the youngest son of a famer," the boy met her blue eye. "But maybe I can become a prince."

"I'm Becca." She finally let go of his hand.

"I'm Adam." The boy tried a bow, but the shawl slipped, and he tried to catch it and ended up at her feet. "Sorry, I'm a bit clumsy."

"So I've seen." Becca lifted Adam's knife from the bucket and replaced it in the sheath before handing Adam his clothes. "Come in and I'll get you something to eat."

Adam ate like the simple bread and cheese was the best he'd ever eaten. He listened to her like she was clever and wise.

"Does the world look different when you look at it through your blue eye or your brown?"

Becca froze. Her eyes had been a source of misery all her life, she'd never paid attention to the world she saw through them. Covering her brown eye, she scanned the room. Roughly constructed but sturdy; it did what it needed without any extra. The bread and cheese was the food she'd always had along with vegetables from the garden. Adam was a boy, a bit strange and a bit clumsy.

When she covered her blue eye, she saw a house no better than it needed to be. Food that filled the stomach but the making of it fed her soul. Adam looked her and saw her. Not her wandering eyes. Not the body better suited to working the garden than drawing the eyes of men. Somehow, he saw the princess.

"Yes." Becca dropped her hand. "The blue eye sees what is. The brown what it means."

"I wondered." Adam smiled and took another bite of bread and cheese.

"I never did, until you asked." Becca scanned the room again, then grabbed Adam's pack and put spare clothes in it, some bread and cheese, some tired carrots from the winter. "I see that now my father has his gold, he doesn't need me. Finish your meal and we'll head to the city. Between us we should be able to make a living." The last thing she took was a pot, which she tied to the outside of the pack.

They walked past her father, still sifting the dust, afraid he'd missed a coin. He didn't even glance in her direction.

"We aren't that far from the city, but I've never been." Becca carried the pack easily. "Don't mention my eyes, or that gem you found. There are people who would use us until we're worn thin."

"As you say." Adam patted his knife at his belt, then his waterskin. "I have what the lady gave me, and you at my side. We'll be fine."

As the sun lowered behind them, a fox sauntered out of the forest to join them.

"Hello, Fox." Adam waved at the animal. "Right, this is Becca. She's joining me to travel to the city to make our fortune."

The fox barked at Adam, and he frowned. "That's rude. Better apologize." The fox bobbed its head and whined what Becca assumed was an apology.

"Sorry, Fox asked if you were as foolish as I am." Adam looked up at Becca. "Though he doesn't count himself as foolish for following me."

More barking and Adam laughed. "Such loyalty for a piece of cheese."

The fox barked more, making Adam laugh harder. "He says it is for the possibility of more cheese."

The conversation between Fox and Adam continued until it started getting harder to see Fox.

"He suggests we find a farm and offer to work in return for shelter."

"Smart fox." Becca pointed to lights in the window of a house beside the road. "We could start there."

"Fox says they have no dog, so he agrees. He promises not to eat their chickens but would like us to save some of what we eat for him."

Adam knocked on the door. "Greetings, we are looking for work in exchange for a bite to eat and a place to rest our heads."

"I've no interest in sheltering vagrants." The woman frowned and shut the door.

After trying a few more houses, they found an old farmer who set them to splitting and stacking wood. Becca did the splitting because watching Adam with an axe was terrifying. There was a nanny goat who Fox said wanted to be milked, so Becca did that too. The farmer made no mention of the pail of fresh milk. He sat them at the table with old bread and moldy cheese. Becca would have complained but he sat down to the same meal.

"Excuse me a moment." Adam jumped up and left the house. Becca had choked down one slice of the bread when he arrived back with his shirt filled with greenery.

"Do you mind?" He went to the counter without waiting for the old man's response and sorted out the greens. He used the knife at his belt to cut them up and took the pot from their pack to dump them in. He splashed them with water then put the pot over the fire. Other greens he used to wrap pieces of cheese he trimmed most of the mold from and put them on a plate on the hearth. At a scratch at the door, Adam went over and bent down to pick up something. Becca expected a chicken, but it was a squirrel. After some struggle and a couple of cuts on his fingers, Adam had it skinned and cleaned. He tossed it into the pot with the greens.

Becca watched him work. He was no less clumsy, dropping things and fumbling the knife, but he looked like he knew what he was about.

"You live alone?" She reached over to touch the farmer's hand who stared at Adam in a daze.

"Oh, yes." He nodded and went back to watching Adam.

"Have you been alone long?"

"Most of my life." The farmer glanced at her briefly. "My beloved was turned into a bear by a fae. She'd been gathering nuts in the forest."

"A bear?" Becca shook her head, then peered at him through her blue eye. He was old and tired, no reason to stay but the lack of a place to go. Through her brown eye she saw his hope that somehow his love would return from the forest, even now after all the years.

He only nodded, eyes on the food Adam prepared.

"You didn't tell me you could cook." Becca pushed away from the table.

"Gran taught me." Adam hung his head. "It's the only thing I'm even a little good at."

"You're a good person." Becca lifted his chin. "It isn't just what you can do, but what's in your heart."

***

Adam insisted that Becca sleep in the loft on the only mattress. The farmer slept in the rocking chair, same as he always had.

He lay on the floor by the fire and stared into the banked coals. What was in his heart? He always meant well, but life didn't cooperate. Then there was Fox. Maybe he imagined what his friend said, but that would mean imagining things he couldn't imagine. It made his head hurt, so he stopped thinking about it and went to sleep.

He and Becca spent the next day helping the old farmer but set off at sunrise the following morning. They walked until the farms grew closer together and richer. No one at these places would give them work.

"This is as far as I go." Fox sat down on the road. "Cities are dangerous places for foxes. I should get back to my territory anyway."

"I'll miss you." Adam knelt and hugged Fox close. The first and last time he'd do so.

"You have Becca now. Listen to her the same as you listened to me, and you'll be fine." Fox shook himself loose and trotted away up the road until she vanished into a fence line.

"You okay?" Becca asked.

Adam stood and breathed in deep. "I'll be fine. We need to find somewhere to hide the gem. It will get harder to hide in the city. I don't see any wells."

Becca laughed and scanned the area they were in. "How about under this thorn bush?" She pointed to one beside a fancy gate.

Adam crawled under the bush and discovered a family of rabbits. "I'm going to leave this with you." He put the gem in a hollow beneath the trunk and covered it with a rock. "Don't let anyone take it." The rabbits stared at him, then one lay on top of the rock he'd just put down. "Be safe, gem."

He crawled back out, stood, and put his shoulders back. "We need to find a part of the city that isn't quite so rich."

They headed into the city. Becca looked at it with both her eyes and guided them along roads until the houses got smaller, then rickety, then vanished altogether.

In the middle of the clearing people were fighting while three young men walked about correcting the fighters. One of them noticed them and waved them over.

"You come to learn to fight?"

Becca shook her head, but Adam's heart leapt.

"Yes."

The young man pointed over to where a half wall formed a seat for a few people. "You can wait over there, miss. I'll see what I can do with your young man."

"Her name is Becca." Adam handed her the pack and his belt with his knife and waterskin.

She smiled at him and walked over to the wall.

"Now," the young man tapped Adam on the shoulder. "We'll start with you running around the clearing. Ten times."

Adam ran, tripping only a couple of times on the dirt until he was exhausted and had lost count.

"That's enough." The young man waved him over. "I should introduce myself. I'm Lencely, my friends are Rud and Daggins. Our squad's job is to train people who want to fight in the arena."

"Why would people want to fight in an arena?" Adam wasn't sure what an arena was, but it sounded like an odd place to fight.

"Some people like to fight." Lencely lay on the ground. Hands at shoulder width. "Lie down like this."

Adam did as he was told.

"Now push yourself up, keeping your back straight."

It wasn't as hard as Adam thought, though Lencely was up and down twice before Adam made it up once. Lencely jumped to his feet.

"Keep it up until you can't push yourself up anymore." He circled Adam and made him move his hands and straighten his back. "Some people fight because they get paid. Work is hard to come by here."

Adam tried to push himself up one last time, but his arms refused. He rolled onto his back and gasped.

"Good start." Lencely crouched beside him. "Now put your hands on your shoulders like so." He demonstrated. "And put your feet flat on the ground so your knees are up. Next try to touch your elbows to your knees without lifting your feet. Just use your stomach muscles."

Adam got most of the way to his knees. He tried again, and again, until his stomach ached.

"Do you need a break?" Lencely leaned over him.

"No." Adam stood up and Lencely steadied him.

"Be careful standing up too quickly, it can make some people dizzy. When you're ready I'll teach you how to stand."

"I'm standing now." Adam looked at Lencely. Lencely pushed Adam's shoulder gently and he staggered back.

"We're going to learn how to stand so it isn't so easy to push you over."

Lencely moved Adam's feet, made his shift his toes, bend his knees differently and more. Adam had never spent so much time thinking about how he stood.

"We're done for the day." Lencely said. "Good work. You can stay and watch the sparring or head on home."

"We don't have a home yet. I'll watch." Adam walked carefully over to Becca. Now that he'd started thinking about his feet, it was hard to stop. They watched men and woman box or wrestle in circles scratched in the dirt.

"They aren't using swords." Adam observed.

"They say they'll bring swords tomorrow, or maybe the next day." A boy beside Adam said. "You're lucky. You had time with Lencely all to yourself."

"Lencely is special?" Adam wondered if he should pay attention to how he sat, the same as when he stood.

"Wait until the end." The boy chuckled. "You'll see."

The fights in the centre of the clearing ran out, but no one left.

"I can guess what you're waiting for." Lencely picked up a stick from a pile on the ground. One of the other teachers also did. "We will bring training swords tomorrow. It's harder to hurt yourself with a wood sword, but still possible."

The crowd laughed.

"Ready when you are." The other young man hoisted his stick.

"That's Rud, the other one is Daggins."

Lencely and Rud faced each other in a circle, raised the sticks and pointed them at each other, then they started fighting with the sticks, moving faster than Adam could follow. Still Lencely kept up a running commentary on what they were doing and why.

Adam watched Lencely's feet and saw that what he'd learned made him a kitten to Lencely's bear. "So that's why."

"Why what?"

"All that about how to stand and stuff. He knows where his feet are all the time."

"I guess." The boy shrugged.

Lencely called a stop to the demonstration, then he, Rud and Daggins picked up their gear and marched out of the clearing.

"See you tomorrow." Lencely called as they passed the edge.

"Do you know where we can sleep tonight?" Becca asked the boy.

"What's in it for me?" The boy crossed his arms.

Adam picked a plant from beside his foot. "I can cook you some greens for supper."

"You can eat that?" The boy made a face.

Adam dusted the leaves off and munched on it.

"It's nicer steamed." Becca laughed. "All we need is bit of ground to stretch out on and some water."

"I'm Dofson." The boy jumped of the wall. "Water is a bit of a walk. We'll do that first."

Adam examined the houses as they walked to the well. He stopped here and there to pick greens, but then had to run to catch up. Becca was paying careful attention to everything Dofson said. They filled the pot and Adam's waterskin with water. That done Dofson led them along more broken-down streets until they arrived at a dirt lot. A ruined house leaned in one corner.

"You can stay there. I live across the street."

"That's good." Adam wandered through the lot picking plants until he had an armful. "I may have picked too much. Would your family like some?"

Dofson gave a shrill whistle. A girl younger than him and two boys younger yet appeared from the house. "This fellow says we can eat green stuff with him."

The children came over and squatted in front of Adam. He built a fire and lit it with Becca's help, washed the greens with a splash of water from the pot, then stuffed them in and set it on the fire.

"Here's a bit of cheese while we wait for the water to boil." Becca broke off pieces and set them in the children's hands. Their eyes widened like they'd never seen cheese before. Adam laughed as they nibbled it, then stuffed it in in their mouths.

Their squeals of delight brought other urchins and Becca crumbled pieces of cheese for them. Adam made her eat the last crumb. He hadn't considered how they were going to eat the greens, but the children fetched a variety of boards and he put piles of green on each board. They didn't giggle and squeal over the greens, but they vanished as quickly as the cheese.

They all sat around the fire until it grew dark.

"Where are your parents?" Becca asked.

"Who knows?" Dofson shrugged his shoulders. "We must have parents somewhere, but they aren't here."

They all slept in a heap as the fire died down to coals.

CHAPTER 7

Robin woke in her room; it was too nice to be called a cell. She stretched and did what exercises she could before Seth knocked on her door to invite her to breakfast.

"Breakfast, Lady Robin." Seth had become excessively polite since the mayor's son had transferred his interest from Leila to Robin.

"Coming." Robin checked that her dress fell properly. The exercises did strange things to it. She'd prefer her uniform, but she was out voted by everyone around her.

Lyle, the mayor's son sat at the table. Robin spun on her heels and returned to her cell.

"Seth, remind the intruder that I will not be disturbed at breakfast. He may join us for supper, but before that, I will remain in my cell rather than speak to him."

Unfortunately, the builder of the cells had seen no reason to put a lock on the inside of the door. Robin sat in the chair facing the window and stared out at the forest. It called her, in a different way than the call to the north had, but she felt it especially at times like this. Or perhaps it was her discontent with her situation.

Lyle knocked on her door, and Robin ignored it. Finally, he opened it and came into the room.

"It displeases me that you ignore me."

Robin clenched her teeth and continued to look out the window.

"I have a lot of power in this town. Unfortunate things could happen to other people if you continue to reject me."

At least he'd learned not to make specific threats, his father had some hand in that after Robin threatened to break out, beat the entire guard and disappear back into the forest. Willem had assured the mayor with a straight face that she was perfectly capable of doing that.

Lyle had to have been drinking late, she could still detect the stale liquor from where she sat. Sadly, he was still drunk enough to grab her shoulder and slam her against the wall.

"I will have you." He tried to kiss her, but Robin slammed her knee up between his legs, then dragged him by his collar to the front door of the guard house.

"Seth, open the door." She snarled at the big man.

"Lady Robin, you can't." Seth stood between her and the door.

"He's going out the door whether it is open or closed."

"But..." Seth sighed and stepped out of her way. "I tried to stop him." He opened the door as Robin threw the still puking man out into the street.

"I'm sorry, but my room needs cleaning. Better yet, give me a different room. One with a key that only Willem holds." She stomped over to the breakfast table and poured a cup of tea, adding cream and honey though she didn't deserve it.

The mayor arrived while she sipped her second cup. The rage had reduced to a simmer, but not so far that she regretted the outburst.

"You should stand and greet your mayor properly." He stood with arms crossed.

"I am Lady Fastheart Shieldmaiden of Fhayde and Caldera, friend of the King and Commander of a Thousand." Robin put every bit of ice she could into her introduction. "Your son assaulted me in my chamber. If a man under my command did such to any maiden, I'd hang them."

The mayor wilted and sat across from her. "I'm sorry, I don't know what to do with him."

"Start by giving him consequences when he's an ass. He will learn nothing when his father covers up all his crimes. I doubt I am the first he has assaulted."

"He's my son, he's all I have left."

"What happens when he takes over as Mayor?" Robin poured tea for the man and pushed the cup over to him. "Is that the legacy you want to leave your town?"

"What do you suggest?" He sipped at his tea, cheeks wet with tears. The last of Robin's anger faded and she sighed.

"Send him away to join the emperor's army. He'll learn that bluster will get him nothing. Maybe he'll grow up." She refrained from adding that it was probably too late.

"I will tell him he must join the army in Stronghaven."

"Very well." Robin spread butter on a slice of toast and ate it while she let the silence stretch on. The mayor stood, bowed to Robin, and walked out looking like he'd aged years over the course of their conversation.

Robin walked down into the basement of the guard house. The cells here were cold and damp with dirt floors. She sat in the centre of one and closed her eyes.

Talk to me. She sent out to the land. Again, the only response was laughter.

If you won't tell me what is going on, I'm going home. The tug to travel north hit her like a blow, but the desire to return south, see her family and the people she cared about was stronger.

An old woman sat across from Robin. She looked like Robin might if she lived as long as Sarge.

The land needs the fae. No one is listening. The emperors will fight each other and the land will burn. Only the fae can set things right.

I'm not fae. Robin clenched her hand in the dirt.

You hear the land, and the land hears you. You are fae.

No. She stood up and broke the connection with the land. Her chest hurt from the effort. All her life people had told her how she looked like the fae. Then she'd become a shieldmaiden, something other than her dreams. The land pulled her this way and that, and now it wanted her to give up herself to become something out of legend.

She ran out of the cell and up the stairs, she was outside the door of the guardhouse before she stopped. Running away would change who she was more surely than the land's machinations. Robin slumped to the ground and pounded the dirt.

"What's wrong?" Willem came over to her.

"I can't win." Robin gasped and hit the dirt again.

"If you're going to hit things, you might as well train with us." Willem pulled her up and dragged her to the training yard.

She took a wooden sword and ran through her forms. The dress made it extremely weird, but not impossible.

Seth appeared in front of her with a leather breastplate and a buckler.

Robin strapped the breastplate on and hefted the buckler. "You'll want a proper suit of training armour."

He looked at her doubtfully but put on grieves and bracers.

"I doubt I'll find a helmet to fit, so no blows to the head." Robin pushed her hair back. It had grown longer and was in her way. She was about to ask for a knife to cut it off when another guard came with a bit of leather thong and tied it for her.

Robin saluted Seth and waved for him to come at her. He attacked slowly.

"You'll need to do better than that." She held her sword ready. Again, he moved in slow motion. Robin growled and leapt to the offensive, chasing Seth around the training ground landing blows on his armour until he tripped and she put the point of her sword at his throat.

"This time you're going to attack properly."

Seth's sword work became faster, but he still pulled his blows.

"Pretend I'm the baker." Robin shouted at him. "If I don't feel some energy behind your blows, I'll hoist you up and carry you around the grounds like a sack of flour."

This time Seth gave her a proper fight and she laughed like a maniac. When was the last time she'd had a proper bout to cleanse her soul?

When Seth stood heaving for breath, Willem stepped up and took the sword from the huge man.

"My turn." He saluted Robin and attacked. He was on a new level from anyone she'd faced before. She might have been a raw recruit facing a full knight, and Robin loved it. As they circled the training yard, she was barely aware of a crowd gathering to watch. Not just guards either.

Townspeople interrupted their day to stand as if struck to stone.

Robin's arms ached, and bruises littered her body, but somehow she kept going. Her sword flashed like it never had before. Then the sword broke, so she took the blow on her shield and it broke too. The point of his sword stopped a hair's breadth from her throat.

"Do you know why I collect stories of the fae?" Willem wasn't even out of breath. "I met one in the forest once. It must have been in a good mood. It asked me what I wanted. I said 'to be the best swordsman in the world' it laughed at me and vanished."

Robin pushed his sword aside and hugged him. "You poor man." He dropped the sword and clutched her close. He might have been laughing or crying, maybe both. "What did you trade for your skill?"

"Everything." Willem gasped. "My life. I'm too dangerous to be near my General, no one wants to be near me unless they want to learn to kill."

"I've learned what I needed from you." Robin released him and stepped back. "Let's go have some tea."

"You don't want me to train you?" Willem stared at her, like she'd slapped him.

"No." Robin dropped the pieces of her sword and shield, then her breastplate. "I would like some tea."

She left Willem and the crowd to go inside. Seth was still outside, so she put the kettle over the fire and sliced some bread and cheese while she waited for it to boil. A bit of dried sausage hung in the corner, she sliced that too and added it to the plate. The kettle boiled and she warmed up the teapot and added the leaves, then poured in the boiling water. While the tea steeped, she carried the tray with the plates and cups out to the table. By the time she returned for the teapot, cream and sugar, her heart had stopped feeling like it had been broken.

At the table she sat and poured tea. She'd forgotten the cream and honey but didn't feel like getting up to fetch it, so she drank it clear.

You aren't making me that cruel. Robin told the land. *Play your tricks or don't. I will not become fae.*

So you say now. Everything you've done could be undone.

True, and the people would continue. They don't need you. You need them. Hurting them won't make them believe.

Cursing is a form of belief.

It doesn't last. Robin helped herself to bread, cheese, and sausage. *Hate will only lead to burned forests and ravaged land. Will you curse yourself to change my mind?*

Willem came in and sat across from her. He poured tea and sipped it.

"The tea tastes better."

"The fae gifts always had two edges." Robin said. "I studied them extensively in Fhayden. The stories were all very clear on that. But I don't think it means we are powerless. We can make choices."

"Like drinking tea?" Willem took another sip.

"Like drinking tea." Robin put cheese and sausage on bread and put the plate beside Willem's cup. "I don't need to be the best swordswoman in the world. I don't need to be all powerful, or perfect. I want to be me, warts and all."

"Yet you have strewn blessings in your wake like flower petals."

"The land wants me to be fae. An emperor is no longer good enough. I refused."

"That seems like a dangerous thing to do." Willem frowned and bit into the bread. His eyes widened.

"It is." Robin nodded. "The land is fractured where once the emperor held it together. Already the east has turned its back on the empire. I suspect the lands close to the southern border will make their own peace with Fhayden. Haffmon has declared himself emperor in Acanopolis. General Ordamy has made himself emperor in Dordnom, the forest between them is probably the last bit of true wilderness south of the northern forests. It wants to be a power again. I'm its tool."

"Right. What happens when Emperor Ordamy calls for you?"

"Who knows?" Robin made up another slice of bread. "This would be nice toasted."

"Maybe Seth could bring a brazier out here?" Willem finished his and sighed. "My message should arrive in Dordnom in the next few days. I don't think the emperor will be slow in responding."

"Maybe a week or so?" Robin shrugged. "If you could keep Lyle away from me for that time, I will be forever grateful."

***

Lyle used the chair to smash the last bit of glass in his window. His father had not only told him he couldn't have that Robin woman, he'd ordered Lyle to go to Stronghaven and join the army. In Stronghaven he'd be a nobody. The fat son of a small-town mayor. He couldn't deal with that. Running away wouldn't help. He had to stay here, and he had to have Robin. Her refusal was making him a laughingstock at the tavern.

Lyle stared out the window at the forest. That's where she came from. Willem insisted she was an emissary from Fhayden, but he knew better. Maybe there was someone else like her in the forest. Someone who could make him stronger.

He jumped out the window and climbed down like he used to as a kid. He never scratched himself as a kid, and dropping the last few feet left him with a twisted ankle. Limping and cursing, Lyle headed for the forest.

The branches opened up for him like they were welcoming him a path led him to a cave.

The woman in the cave didn't look up from her fire.

"Welcome. Sit."

"I want—"

The woman raised her hand and his voice cut off. "I know what you want. First, sit."

Lyle's legs gave out and he collapsed to the floor of the cave. She served him a bowl of stew.

"You can't waltz up to the emperor and tell him you're the strongest in the world. He'll believe you, and try to put you in chains, or not believe you, and laugh."

Lyle opened his mouth to argue, but nothing came out. He ate the stew to cover his fear.

"You'll head west through the forest. It will train you and make you stronger. When you get to the edge of the forest, there will be a giant destroying a village. The emperor's soldiers may be there trying to stop it. You'll fight it. If you win, that will be your first step toward what you really want."

He shook his head and tried to talk again, then tossed the bowl to the floor in anger.

"Think of it as your first test." The woman pointed to the cave entry. "Better get on your way."

Lyle stood up and walked outside. He turned to go back and argue with the woman, but the cave was gone. At least his ankle didn't hurt, and the stew warmed his belly. He picked up a stick and beat on a tree. When that stick broke, he picked up another one, and another until his hands were raw and his muscles like jelly.

He didn't know which direction was west, so he walked where the forest let him move.

***

"Lyle's missing." Willem told Robin in the morning. "The mayor thinks he went into the forest."

"Why would he do that?" Robin tried to speak to the land, but got nothing. "I think he may be right. I can help search."

"You'd go back into the forest?"

"I'd be a fool to say it is just a forest, but it is a forest. I may be the best equipped to deal with it."

"It doesn't matter." Seth staggered in the door. He was covered in scratches and bruises. "No one is being let into the forest, not even the wood cutters."

"Are the roads open?" Willem asked.

"For now." Seth looked ready to fall over so Robin gave him her chair.

"I'll go get my medicine kit. I should be able to patch you up before they get here."

"Who gets here?" Seth slumped in the chair.

"Whoever the forest calls to take me away." Robin ran to her cell in the basement and snatched up the kit, the only thing Willem had let her keep of her gear. She was still putting ointment on Seth's wounds when the door banged open.

"We're here to arrest the one called Robin Fastheart for spying on the emperor." The two soldiers had their hands on their swords.

"Be right with you." Robin glanced over at them and went back to work on Seth.

One of the soldiers grabbed her arm painfully. She broke the grip, then slammed him on the floor, standing up in time to kick the other soldier's sword from his hand before sweeping his legs from under him.

"I said I would be right with you. Even if you're arresting me, there is no need to be rude. It reflects badly on your commanding officer." She finished helping Seth as the soldier moaned on the floor. "Okay done, let's go." She hauled the soldiers to their feet. "I'm not impressed with your training if a little bump like that puts you so out of sorts."

"You going to be all right?" Willem handed her the medical kit.

"The forest thinks it's found a way to get what it wants. What it hasn't realized yet is that what it wants could destroy it. I did warn it. Give my farewells to any who need it. The forest can withdraw a blessing, but it can't take away what is already innate in us. You will need to hold onto that."

She dragged the soldiers out to the closed in carriage with barred windows and shoved them toward the front while she climbed in the back and closed the door after her.

The soldiers refused to talk to her. She took care of her needs by ignoring them. She'd been longer without meals than it should take for the carriage to make to Stronghaven even at the crawl they'd set.

Farms made a wide swath between Stronghaven and the forest. The carriage stopped briefly at a guardpost where the guards reported, still surly, before driving to a small keep complete with a wall taller than two men. They pulled up in front of the office and left. Robin waited in the carriage until the sun had sunk most of the way to the horizon. She laughed; they must have told stories about her.

She pushed open the back door, picked up her medical kit and strolled into the office.

"Aren't I supposed to be under arrest?" She plunked the kit down on the counter. "Don't touch anything in this. A lot of it is poisonous in the wrong hands. Keep it safe, I will be most annoyed if something happened to it. I'd have to mention it to the emperor. Now who is guiding me to my cell?" She scanned the faces. One young man near the back standing under a portrait was stifling laughter. "You, in the back. Please show me to my room."

He straightened and came over to her. "This way my lady." He led her along the hall to the last cell. "We haven't used this one in a while, so it may be musty, but it is clean." He locked the cell door after her, checked it was locked and gave her a wave.

Robin settled in. The straw mattress was musty, but nothing worse. A thin blanket lay on top of it. She sat on the mattress, wrapped the blanket around her and reached for the land. It gave her the mental image of an old woman sticking her tongue out at her. Robin tried to reach past the forest, but either the emperor's land was distracted, or the forest was blocking her.

Either way she had time to think, maybe too much time. From what Willem said there were two emperors, plus the one she'd thought she was looking for. What was she supposed to do? It didn't look like anyone would be telling her. She'd have to figure it out for herself.

***

The commander of the Stronghaven guards came in so full of self-importance she was surprised he fit through the door. He wore an expensive tunic and had a finely decorated sword at his waist. She recognized him from the portrait.

"Why are you here?" he demanded.

"You arrested me." Robin sat with her back against the wall and fixed her gaze on his knees.

"You know what I mean." He loomed over her. "Why are you spying on us?"

"I'm not spying." Robin shrugged. "You don't have any information I need."

"If you don't cooperate, I can make things less comfortable for you."

"Please move back, you're crowding me. I don't like it."

He moved forward and leered at her.

"I take it you didn't pay any attention to the report of the guards who brought me here." Robin stood and put a finger on his chest and pushed until he had to back up out of the cell.

"Good. Close the door and lock it. If you come in again without permission, I will throw you out."

"Who do you think you are?' The commander tried to push back into the cell.

"I am Lady Robin Fastheart, Shieldmaiden of Caldera and Fhyade, Commander of a Thousand, though most of them I've sent home. I wouldn't mind sitting down to talk with your emperor, but I will not be bullied by the commander of a small outpost on the edge of the empire."

The Commander reddened and stepped back. "Teach her a lesson."

He pointed at a man, who while not the size of Seth, still would have to bend down to enter the cell. The big man stalked into the cell.

"What's your name?" Robin leaned against the back wall of the cell.

"Huh?"

"Your name. I don't like fighting people I don't know their names."

"You think you'll be fighting me? I'm going to—"

Robin didn't wait to hear the recital. She launched herself at him kicking with both feet on his chest and kicked him back out the door to crash into the door across the hall. She landed and returned to her spot against the wall.

"I don't tolerate rudeness well. Are you going to give me your name?"

"I'm not going back in there." The man muttered to the commander.

"I'll have you locked up for disobeying orders." The commander put his finger between the man's eyes.

"Okay." The big man opened the cell door behind him and walked in, pulling the door closed after him.

"I suggest you send a letter to the emperor letting him know what you've done, before the rest of your guard have locked themselves down here."

The commander stepped toward the door, hand on his sword.

"Don't." Robin crossed her arms. "I'm done being gentle, and I don't want to go through this again with your second in command. You'll want to be sure your affairs are in order before you step in here with a drawn sword."

He hesitated in the doorway.

"You heard a few rumours and decided you'd steal a march on Willem. You have no idea what kind of mess you've created for yourself. Don't make it worse."

The commander drew his sword and charged at her. Robin slid aside at the last second. The thrust meant to pierce her heart ground against the stone, twisting the sword in his hand. She snatched the sword from him then beat him with the flat of the blade chasing him out of the cell, along the hallway, and up into the office.

"Stop her. Kill her." He ran behind two of the guards.

"Just because you've arrested me, doesn't mean you can be rude." Robin stabbed the sword into the back of the desk. "If you want to talk. Introduce yourself and don't make stupid threats." She scanned the room and the guards scuttled back, then stalked back down to her cell and pulled the door closed.

"My name's Sam," the guard in the cell across from her said. "I'm really sorry."

"Pleased to meet you Sam." Robin sat on her mat. "Tell me a little about yourself."

CHAPTER 8

Allin walked with Rebecca on his arm as they viewed the market. Henry and Magpie had stayed in the suite. Lady Wren explained very politely that they were hostages to Allin's cooperation in the day's operation.

In the week since they were brought to Dordnom the manufactured discontent had increased. Allin couldn't see how Alekar thought he could beat Emperor Ordamy and his legions, but he had never acted other than in predictable and foolish ways. As Rebecca pointed out as they dressed for this outing, he was cunning, but not very bright.

The single guard who followed them, and carried Rebecca's purchases, hadn't spoken a word since leaving the keep. A servant walked with them and pointed out interesting stores and told histories of the city landmarks. The tour led them gradually, but inexorably toward the quarter Allin and the others had wintered over in.

Allin guessed the servant was Alekar's agent, he hadn't seen the young man before this first trip into the city. Without a doubt, the emperor had plenty of people in the crowd around them. The closer they got to Alekar's domain, the harder it would be to hide those agents from the guild.

A roar started up behind them.

"What a nuisance." The servant looked around. "We'll have to take another way back to the keep."

Allin almost laughed. The servant should have at least pretended to be a bit nervous, but he responded to the riot as a signal. The guard frowned and looked back.

"We will wait for the disturbance to be suppressed and return." He handed all Rebecca's purchases back to her and stood with a hand on his sword in a very guard like pose. Allin rolled his eyes. He doubted the guard was in on the plot, but he was also not in on the trap using Allin as bait.

"I refuse to stand around in the street." Rebecca swatted the young man's arm. "Either find us a place to sit and have tea or let us move on."

The servant's eyes lit up. "There is a place just a little farther along the road."

The trap ready to be sprung. Allin had to restrain a grin. He'd be glad to rid of the troublesome Alekar and his guild.

The guard picked up Rebecca's parcels and they continued along the street which grew more crowded as they went. Allin could smell the tension in the air. Their shadows became more visible as the mood of the people shifted.

"Wait here, I will have them set up a table for you." The servant bolted away into the crowd.

"Fool," the guard growled. "I will report him to Lady Wren."

Not the emperor? Something clicked in his mind, so it wasn't a complete shock when the guard tossed his burden at Allin, drew his sword, and tried to run him through. The sword scraped against the armour under Allin's clothes. Rebecca swung the fashionable bag she'd been carrying and hit the guard. He staggered under the blow. They'd put as much in the bag as they thought they could get away with before heading out.

Allin took the guard's sword and hit him again with the pommel, knocking him out completely. The riot had to be one of the most desultory attempts at a mob scene he had seen. The people shouted and wandered about, but they didn't break anything, probably because this was their home, and they didn't want to destroy it. No one attacked them until a movement on a roof caught Allin's eye. He stepped in front of Rebecca and let the arrow bounce off his armour.

"Watch the roofs to my back." Allin told Rebecca. Certain members of the crowd ran into alleys. Another figure stood up on a roof, but instead of firing at Allin or Rebecca the arrow flew over their heads to strike a figure behind them. Rebecca gasped, then a thud told him a body had landed on the street.

The arrival of the body sent the riot into high gear. The people were no longer interested in playing at trouble.

They wanted to escape, but the alleys were blocked by soldiers as was the street in both directions.

"Let them go." Allin shouted. "They just live here. None of them are a threat. Find a tea house and surround it."

A soldier stomped over to Allin. "Silence, who are you to give us orders?"

"The emperor's drinking buddy." Allin waved at the mess around him. "There are too many plots going on at once. If you start killing people because they're running away, you will create a real rebellion."

The soldier put a hand to his head, then shouted orders to let people go.

"Let's go find a place to drink some tea." Allin offered his arm to Rebecca.

The crowd split and went around him until there were more soldiers on the street than people. Those people pointed at Allin, but then glanced at the soldiers and tried to saunter away.

"Those people you can arrest." Allin told the soldier who still followed him. Again, he shouted orders. The street became a battle zone as the people who enforced the riot tried to fight their way out. Allin avoided the conflict until they arrived at a tea house that appeared to be a haven of calm.

"We're going in there to have tea." Allin informed the soldier. "Keep your men away until we've finished." The soldier shrugged and joined the fray on the street.

"Alekar, you might as well come out and have tea with us." Allin sat Rebecca against the wall and took the seat beside her, putting his sword on the table.

Alekar came out of the back followed by a half dozen men with crossbows. "My men will finish off your guards soon enough."

"Doesn't look like it unless you have another hundred men hidden in the basement of this place." Allin leaned against the wall. "You've lost the high ground and your cover. If you were smart, you'd have been gone by now."

"The emperor is dealing with his own problems, assuming he's still alive." Alekar sneered.

"You mean Lady Wren's attempt to take the throne. She's already failed. General Ordamy didn't get to be emperor without learning how to watch his back and know who he can trust. I'll give you even odds that he not only lets her live but continue to manage the keep." Allin took a flask from inside his tunic and offered Rebecca a drink. She swallowed and made a face, then passed it back to him. He drank the tepid water fortified with herbs Magpie had given him.

Alekar reddened and stepped forward.

"Not smart to get between your bowmen and their target." Allin capped his flask and put it away. "But you were never that smart. The thieves in my city know to stay out of my way. You walked out of the shadows and painted a target on your back, then were stupid enough to make a deal with the devil."

"You're still dead." Alekar shouted. "You and your friends in the keep."

"Wrong again." Allin smiled. "Henry has been the target of so many attempts on his power he can practically smell them. Lady Wren put us in that suite to isolate us and have us under her control, but as the emperor said, we're too valuable to kill. Henry has information she needs. He's also a better fighter than I am. I'd wager on him stark naked against any number of servants, even armed. You've seen his work."

"That still leaves you in my power."

"Do you think I'd really walk in here and sit down with no plan of action?"

"What? I don't see anyone rushing to your rescue."

"Don't need anyone." Allin sighed and shook his head. "You've over stretched your reach, betrayed the members of your guild, and now the emperor's legions are marching to destroy what's left. Can't you hear them marching? And you have forgotten the most basic rule of wearing a crown."

"And what is that?" Alekar sneered.

"There is always someone who wants to take it from you."

A crossbow snapped and the bolt travelled through Alekar's throat to bury itself in the wall above Allin.

"We leave now." One of the crossbowmen reset his bow. "The emperor can have the city. We'll leave him alone."

"I will pass on the message." Allin waved at the men. "Better hurry."

The six men ran out of the room.

The soldier Allin had been talking to walked in and nudged the body.

"Time to get you back to the keep." He picked up Rebecca's packages and handed them off to another soldier. They formed up around Allin and Rebecca to march them back up to the keep.

Emperor Ordamy met them at the gate.

"How was your day?"

"Pleasant enough. There will be a new king under the streets. They will have no interest in politics. How was yours?"

"A subordinate learned a valuable lesson." The emperor shrugged. "They too have lost interest in politics."

"I would like a bath." Allin took Rebecca's arms. "I feel the need to wash the dust of the city from me."

"I will have Lady Wren arrange it for you."

"My thanks."

***

"I hear one of Alekar's subordinates shot him in the back." Gurdin sipped on his wine. "How did you know that would happen?"

"It wasn't a certainty, but he had to have been upsetting people with his obsession with vengeance. When he started exposing the guild through his riots it would have become worse. Whether he won or lost the guild was dead. I pointed that out and someone smarter than him figured out the only solution was to disappear back into the shadows. The odds were pretty good that someone near him was smarter than he was." Allin swirled his wine and took in the scent. A fine wine, though not Fhayden. "I'm guessing you set a trap for Lady Wren?"

"Something like that." Gurdin stared into the flames. "She forgot I was still a soldier. The people who attacked me weren't ready to die for their cause, so they hesitated. That was all I needed. I will need to hire more servants. The ones who were serving you tried attacking Henry and Magpie in the baths. From what I've gathered it wasn't much of a fight. Magpie talked him out of killing them all.

"I've seen him fight. He's better than I am." Allin laughed. "I told Alekar I'd bet on Henry naked against servants. I didn't realize I was describing what happened."

"I thought they looked especially chastened." Allin sipped at his wine. "Now what?"

"I continue consolidating power. I'm in no rush. Rebecca's home is safe for a while yet. I never liked Ancanopolis. If I'm forced to act, I may put someone in place to run it for me."

"Don't look at me." Allin held up his hands. "My days of ruling are done. I knew that when I left to come north. Henry wouldn't thank you for trying to put him back on the throne either."

"I will find someone popular with the people. Neither of you work for that."

"Thank the fae." Allin took a long swallow of wine.

"Speaking of the fae. I received an interesting report from an old friend south of Stormhaven, near the forest. Apparently, he found that fae girl I was talking about. I've sent General Mihone to invite her to Dordnom. From what Willem said, she was heading in this direction anyway. She's young, but already canny about people, and she faced him with the sword without breaking and running or begging him to train her."

"Your friend must be very good with the sword." Allin rolled his shoulders. "I can't imagine a commander of a Thousand being a pushover."

"Willem claims he met a fae woman who made him the best swordsman in the world. He's down on the edge of my domain because my council couldn't trust someone who could beat all of them at once not to have ambitions to be general. They didn't know him well enough."

"Another person I'd like to meet, though not with a sword in my hand."

Gurdin laughed and drank his wine.

CHAPTER 9

Hob nodded at Marshal Hapten.

"Our scouts report no new activity at the Ancan encampment. There is some training happening, but mostly they are drinking." She frowned. "I've been taught not to complain about the folly of my enemy, but it bothers me to see such waste. They could have been helping with seeding or working on the road. A good road is important to maintain supply lines."

Frome stood, he'd returned from escorting the Fhayde army south. "The retreating Fhaydens have passed the point where our people know the land. Some of them appear to be familiar with the countryside there and have taken the lead. They were most grateful for our assistance and promised to let their king know."

"I've been in discussion with the people you sent me." Commander Betrice held up a scroll of paper. "We have an agreement I'd like you to hear and comment on." She unrolled the scroll and read. "Temporary agreement between the Free and the people of Caldera and Fhayde. The king will sign it, but it will be the people who keep the agreement. First. Caldera and Fhayde recognize the Free as a sovereign people and will make no attempt to enforce laws, customs, or beliefs on the Free in their own land. Only the laws obeyed by citizens of Caldera and Fhayde will be enforced on the Free living within their territories. Citizens of Caldera and Fhayde who travel in the territories of the Free will obey all laws of the Free.

"Second. The Free will be able to trade with Caldera and Fhayde without punitive taxes or fees. Merchants will be free to come and go in the course of their trade. Guidance across the pass to Caldera is mandatory but will not cost traders any money.

"Third. The King of Caldera and Fhayde recognizes the Free, but at this time will not be bound to come to their aid in present or future conflicts with the Ancan Empire or others.

"Fourth. The Free living withing the bounds of Caldera and Fhayde may return home at any time but will need the agreement of the local rulers of the land to once again live in Caldera or Fhayde. This isn't about people travelling to visit families and returning to their homes in Caldera, but those who pack up all they own to move back to lands held by the Free. Free who do travel only to visit shall not be held against their will.

"Fifth. The Free and Caldera and Fhayde will have ambassadors who will maintain a living relationship between the countries."

Betrice sighed and let the paper roll up again.

"Let me take this to our elders. We will respond within the week." Hob waved off the paper when Betrice would have handed it to him. "Few of us are literate. Arranging schooling for children is high on the list of things to accomplish. We have lost most of our original language, so we'll need to teach Ancan writing."

"Outside of the agreement of our nations, I have an interest in education. My family are teachers and we have worked for generations to increase literacy in Fhayde. We cannot teach your children, but perhaps we can help train teachers from your own people."

"We will speak more on this." Hob said. "If there is nothing else you Fhaydens need from us, there are things we must discuss alone."

Marshal Hapten and Commander Betrice stood, saluted and left.

"It is certain that the Ancans will attempt to take the city once more. We can't depend on the Fhaydens to defend it for us, though I'm sure they may do what they can. Their agreement states they will stand separate from our conflicts. If we accept it, we will be on our own."

"Kings dislike being bound." Duncan said. "If we are attacked, we can request aid, knowing it will come at a price. Our best hope at peace is a similar agreement with the Ancans."

"They have no emperor to sign and enforce it." Hob frowned. "I don't accept Haffmon as a true emperor. He will try treachery again."

"I expect so." Duncan sighed. "They hold many Fhaydens hostage. That may affect how the Fhaydens act during conflict. It might be wise to convince them to leave the city before the conflict starts."

"Perhaps after we have agreed on the terms of the truce, they will take the road home as well." Frome said.

"Would you leave people behind as captives of the Ancans?" Hob frowned. "I would be loathe to sign any agreement with people who did."

"Maybe if we helped free the captives." Duncan said. "It is sure they will come into play in any battle for the city. The Ancans haven't kept them alive all this time for no purpose. There are two ways I think they could be used. One would be to hold them close to the wall and demand the Fhaydens force us to open the gate. That is chancy as it would mean the Fhaydens would have to fight us in the city to gain control of the gate. The other possibility is they send a few of the captives who have 'escaped' to beg entry to the city. They could then open a small door as we did to let forces into the city."

"Either way, the goal will be to open a door or gate and let the enemy in." Hob tapped his chin. "Treachery is such a useful tool of war. What if we planned a trap based on their treachery?"

"It would make it even more important to have the Fhaydens out of the city before the conflict started so they couldn't reveal our preparations." A commander from the north said.

"Yet we don't want to create enemies by mistrusting friends." Hob stood. "We begin on our trap, and let the Fhaydens know, but from here we do the scouting of the Ancans. The Fhaydens don't leave the city unless they all leave and don't return."

"If we alert the Free as soon as the Ancans begin to move, we will need to hold the city for a week before the horde arrives. The Ancans will try their treachery sooner than a week. They are not a patient people." Frome said.

"True." Hob looked around the room at his gathered leaders. "I suggest we call the horde as soon as planting is done. They can wait two days away from the city. We'll have scouts sweeping the plain for enemies. Do you agree?"

"Agreed." Duncan stood.

"Agreed" The rest of his council stood as well.

***

Marshal Hapten accompanied Betrice to the room she used as an office.

"Come in sit down." Betrice waved at the only chair. "You look like you wanted to talk outside of Hob's command meeting."

"I expect they're talking about the same thing we are." Marshal Hapten settled into the chair. "We're his biggest problem. Sure, we're friendly, but he can't know what we'll do faced with hostages outside the wall. There's almost two hundred of us, all better trained than they are. It would be hard to stop us opening a gate if we decided to do so."

"We wouldn't betray the Free." Betrice leaned against the door.

"Maybe fifty of our people. Would you be able to stand and watch as they are murdered in front of us?"

"I..." Betrice looked down. "I don't know what I'd do. But I am sure whatever we do, the Ancans will kill the hostages anyway. They've proved to be that kind of people."

"Careful." Marshal Hapten held up a hand. "Two of the commanders were that kind of people. One wasn't, he's dead. I expect most of the Ancans are too busy obeying orders to think about them. But I agree for the purposes of this discussion, we need to treat all of them as bad enemies. Yet when they surrender, how will we treat them?"

"When they surrender?" Betrice laughed. "What would make them surrender?"

"They are camped on the trade route between Ancanopolis and Westburg. They control the supply lines, meaning the Free can't trade with the empire. But they are there waiting for reinforcements. As soon as Haffmon is secure enough another army will join them and march on Westburg. They'll be planning treachery of some sort, probably using the hostages to get past the gates. Then the city will become a deathtrap."

"I'm sure Hob will call in the horde again."

"It's planting season. There's plenty of work to be done. They can't afford to have everyone drop tools and show up here only to wait around. I expect it will take some time, and they need to hold the city for that time. Treachery will seek to open the gates before the horde arrives."

"Right, so we need to hold the city until help arrives." Betrice nodded. "We can help with that."

"No, it is asking too much trust from the Free. We will leave as soon as the scouts report movement from the camp. We can camp where we did before, and when the Ancans are organizing their attack, we strike and rescue the hostages." Marshal Hapten clenched her fist.

"That will be two hundred against thousands. We'd be better to attack the camp."

"We can't. Attacking the camp would turn into a running battle. They'd have nothing else to do but chase us. Once they're at the city, they couldn't afford to split their forces. We'll have a chance to run south."

"What about the people in the city?" Betrice slammed the door with a fist.

"I haven't got that far." Marshal Hapten hung her head. "We have no information from the city at all."

They stared at each other in silence, then started when someone knocked at the door.

Betrice opened it and glared at the woman standing in the hall. "Were you trying to listen in?"

"I heard some of your discussion from the hallway. You were not quiet. Come with me, Marshal, I think you and Hob need to discuss this together."

"You're that woman who came back with him. Willow, right?" Marshall Hapten stood. Her leg ached. She was tired and couldn't think.

"He asked me to be his sargent. Strange word. This is what I am doing."

"Okay, let's go." Marshal Hapten straightened. "I've learned to appreciate sargents."

Willow led them to the wall where Hob stared north.

"Our enemies are to the west." Marshal Hapten pointed.

"I believe our hope is to the north." Hob turned and nodded at Willow.

"You are both struggling with the same problem." Willow put her hands on her hips. "I believe it would be better to talk together. There is less chance of wrong assumptions."

"Very well." Hob leaned against the wall again. "Let's speak of trust between friends."

"You have plans to defend the city." Marshal Hapten leaned against the wall beside him. "But we're a problem. You know the enemy has hostages at best, at worst, they have some of our people who will fight against you. Even us sending scouts to watch the camp becomes a risk. How do you know we aren't plotting with them?"

"Are you?" Hob didn't look at her.

"No, that would be contrary to the orders Lady Robin gave me."

"Well then, that's taken care of." Hob sighed. "But not all my commanders are so trusting."

Willow cleared her throat.

"You're right, Willow. I haven't asked them. I have been influenced by Duncan's honour. I don't know how to explain that, but I haven't tried either."

"I thought about leaving the city at the first sign of movement from the enemy, but that creates as many problems as it solves."

"I can see that. It must be hard to have your people so scattered."

Marshal Hapten looked over at Hob, he glanced at her, then returned his gaze north.

"I thought of a way of using your hostages as a trap. We built another wall around the courtyard of the west gate, then we find an excuse to let them open the gate."

"You're talking about building a killing ground inside the city. It's risky. The wall won't be as tough at the city walls."

"True but it will delay them."

"How long do you need?"

"Probably a week if we don't want to interrupt the spring farm work. I thought about calling the horde sooner. The commanders agreed, but we need that harvest."

"We need information from the city." Marshal Hapten thumped the stonework. "That will give us a better idea of when they will attack. They have fields to plant too."

"Why don't you send Duncan with some scouts from the Marshal's troops?" Willow leaned on the wall on the other side of Hob.

"Why Duncan?" Hob asked.

"Both you and Marshal Hapten trust him, he speaks Ancan better than we do. He could be a trader."

"I'll have to ask Duncan." Hob turned around, "but it does get us the information we need."

"Did you really think I'd say no?" Duncan appeared from the shadows. "I came up to find you, then didn't want to disturb your conversation. You're my commander, I go where you send me."

"I don't deserve that kind of loyalty."

"Yes, you do." Duncan and Willow answered together, then laughed.

"Get ready then, Duncan. You leave in the morning."

***

Bodan sat at a corner table in the bar a mug of beer on the table in front of him. Sylve came over and plunked down on a chair across from him.

"What is it?" She wiped her brow with her rag. "This ain't a guard tavern."

"I needed to forget I'm a guard for a while." Bodan plucked at his shirt. "Thus the lack of a uniform."

"Fine for you, but half the place has made you for a guard and tips are down." Sylve complained. "You going to make up for that?"

"Come to my place, and I'll more than make up for tips." Bodan slipped a sliver of paper to her.

She glanced at it and sneered. "I ain't for sale. Should dump your beer over your head for suggestin' it." Crumpling the paper, she dumped it in his beer. "Drink up and git."

Bodan downed the beer and left, walking to the house where he and Tradkin had bunked until they took over the prison. Ironic that the section of the guard most loyal to Haffmon was full of Fhayden soldiers.

Sylve walked into the house hours later when the tavern had closed. "What's the problem, Bodan?"

"We haven't heard a peep from that army parked between us and Westburg. It's like as soon as we left, they gave up and made camp."

"So, they're waiting for orders, same as us."

"Probably, but it's getting onto war season. They aren't going to stay there forever." Bodan leaned back, making the chair creak.

"Fandin and Sherr said scouts are still coming from Westburg. What's left of the Thousand is holed up in there."

"We need to get in contact, make some proper plans."

"You want me to go to Westburg?" Sylve grinned. "Sounds like more fun than serving tables. How about I take Maci with me? She's even more bored than I am."

"Whatever you need. I want you to leave in the morning."

"Sure thing, Bodan."

***

Ham gritted his teeth to keep from wiping the slimy smile from Captain Hervithon's face.

"Some merchant is bringing supplies for the camp. You will provide a few women for entertainment purposes. In exchange your group will get better quality food for the next few days." The man appeared to think he was offering the deal of a lifetime.

"No." Ham cut the rest of what he wanted to say off, once he started, he might not be able to keep his hands from the smarmy ass's throat.

"Pardon?" The captain's smile slipped. "Let me rephrase. You will provide women, or we'll cut all your rations."

"No." Ham's hands twitched. "Let me explain in words that even you should be able to understand. We are prisoners of war, not slaves. Every person in my group is a soldier. None of them will be providing any form of entertainment. If you try to force us, we will fight back and die. Major Saligar has ordered the expense of keeping us captive and healthy. I'm sure he would be thrilled that you slaughtered all his hostages for the sake of slaking the lust of some visiting merchant."

The captain drew his sword. "I could kill you here and now and put someone else in charge."

"Sure you could." Ham spread his arms. "Try it and find out what would happen. I would rather die than continue this existence."

"You've already ordered them to rebel." Captain Hervithon lowered his sword.

"Nope." Ham met and held the captain's eyes. "I'm the only thing stopping them from giving up and tearing this camp to pieces. We aren't sheep, you stupid piece of horse dung. We're wolves, and we're just waiting for the right time to take you down. Don't forget it, don't turn your back on us. Sleep with one eye open, because the slightest mistake will bring hell down on your head."

"I'll cut your rations, double the guard. Even wolves can't fight when they're starving."

"And set off the very disaster you're trying to prevent." Ham moved until he was nose to nose with the Ancan officer. "I suggest you ask Major Saligar for orders before you do something even more stupid than you already have." He turned and walked away. "Give your merchant some of that red wine you're so proud of."

Ham hoped to feel the cold stab of steel in his back, but the captain was too cowardly to risk angering his superior officer. The guard at the prisoner's compound opened the gate, then closed it, dropping the heavy bar into place. Boredom had meant overbuilding the compound. The wall loomed double Ham's height with a narrow walkway for guards to patrol. Posts that had once sat on the ground were now sunk deep into the soil. The Ancans had built a fortress between them and the hostages. Nothing remained in the compound to make a weapon. They slept in tents on the dirt. All food and water came in through the single gate.

None of it lessened the fire burning in each of the prisoners. They had plans for every possibility. All of them with the single goal of causing as much death and destruction before the last of them died.

"Gather round children." Ham didn't raise his voice, even a whisper could be heard across the compound. Each time the Ancans worked on their fortress it grew smaller and his wolf pack grew harder to hold back.

They sat knee to knee, close enough to touch Ham.

"I had a gentle word with our loving Captain Hervithon." Ham scanned his group. The time of their incarceration had forged them into a deadly force. "I explained that we will not put up with threats or demands below our dignity. I believe once he's changed his small clothes, he will be contacting the major for orders."

"We should strike now." Merideth said. "We could break out and take half the camp with us."

"We could." Ham nodded. "But then what? We'll be dead, and they'll just bring in more soldiers to threaten our comrades. We are the key to get them into that city, deprive them of that and they'll find another. Our job is to take that key and at the right moment turn it into a weapon to drive into the heart of the Ancans so they will never even think of taking Fhaydens prisoner again, so the thought of fighting Fhayden soldiers will loosen their bowels."

The group growled and Ham smiled. They were ready.

***

Sylve muttered curses at the merchant. Why would he be bringing four wagon loads of lumber to the camp? It didn't make sense. The place was already more fort than camp. Yet even more intriguing than the lumber was the rope. The thickest rope she'd ever seen. The brief glimpses she'd had while they camped didn't sate her curiousity. The Ancans were up to something. The sounds of their merchant's camp came faintly through the screen of brush they sat behind.

"You aren't sneaking into camp." Maci handed Sylve a ration. "Bodan would have our butts in a sling, even if we didn't get caught. We check with Fandin and Sherr, then head onto Westburg. Like our *orders* said.

"I know, I know." Sylve bit into the ration. "I just hate to leave a mystery unexplored."

"We'll report it to Bodan. Commander Paychen may have an idea what they're building."

"We have a bit of light left. We need to leave a note at the drop so we can contact Fandin and Sherr tomorrow.

"Anything is better than watching you mope over those wagons." Maci jumped up and led the way deeper into the forest.

"I wasn't moping." Sylve followed her partner, putting the wagons and their cargo out of her mind.

To her surprise, there was a note at the drop already. They were to meet at location C. A sweep of her hand sent the twigs with the message into the brush. She crept back to Maci.

"C"

"Really?" Maci raised an eyebrow, but slipped through the forest to the location. It was the farthest meeting place from the Ancan camp. They hadn't used it because of its inconvenience, but it was probably the most secure.

At the location, Sylve and Maci slid through the grass of the meadow to peer at the people gathered in the hollow.

"I don't know most of the people, but that's Commander Betrice." Maci whispered.

"She's here on the way to the city." Sherr crawled up beside them. "Almost got us, but I knew you were coming. This is best overlook of the camp. We're clear."

The three of them stood and climbed down into the hollow.

"What brings you here?" Sylve asked after she'd saluted.

"Marshal Hapten wants to know what is going on in the city."

"That's a long tale." Maci settled comfortably and sighed. "I hope you have water. My skin has a leak."

Fandin handed her a skin and she drank thirstily until Sylve nudged her.

"Save some for me, I've been on half rations too." She finished the skin and handed it back to Fandin with a nod of thanks.

"You won't believe what Commander Paychen and Bodan have pulled off."

Betrice's face as they told the tale made Sylve giggle.

"So they all escaped the camp, but for a dozen or so people, then took over the job of running the prison?"

"Yup," Sylve responded. "We're part of Haffmon's most trusted division of guards. Haven't tried to get too close to Haffmon yet. If we get blown it would be a blood bath. We are training people for the arena. Haffmon wants to have regular games for people to bet on. He's bleeding gold with all the bribes he's paying. On the plus side, the people in the prison aren't fans of Haffmon, so the people who are still in cells in case of an inspection are recruiting an anti-Haffmon force. If he bleeds off enough of the guard to take Westburg, we may be able to start a rebellion."

"What about Sarge?" Commander Betrice asked.

"He's a personal prisoner of Haffmon's. They're holed up in an inn that's part of the more upscale districts of the city. No one gets in or out unless they are known personally to Haffmon. Sarge is alive, but weak, but we only know that from Haffmon's boasting. Sarge could be playing up his age."

"That changes things." Betrice poked a stick at their tiny fire. "Lady Robin gave us orders to collect what is left of the Thousand and retreat home. Circumstances in the empire have gone past anything we can do to change. We have an arrangement with the Free, that's what the people who farmed the eastern plain under the Ancan nobility call themselves now."

"Stories of massacres and horrors are rife in Acanopolis." Sylve shook her head.

"The Free did what they needed to get rid of the rule of the nobles. There wouldn't be any stories if they'd killed everyone." The man Commander Betrice introduced as Duncan leaned forward.

"True." Maci nodded. "I expected half of it is propaganda to excuse the cost of taking Westburg. That's along with the gory tales of the treachery of the Fhayden army who broke the truce of the white flag. Not a whisper that Haffmon ordered the breaking of the truce. I wanted to slip in some counter rumours, but Bodan said it isn't time yet. It would let Haffmon know there were people who knew the truth and were against him."

"Smart." Duncan sat back. "The Free don't care what the Ancans think. There will come a time for that when they've held Westburg and the Ancans are hungry enough to trade for food."

"What do we do now?" Sylve waved her hand at the gathering. "Do we continue on our separate missions, or join up?"

"I'm not sure I'd get more information going to Ancanopolis. I have strategies I'd like to discuss with the Marshal and Hob." Betrice drank from her waterskin. "Also, I'm not used to scouting anymore. I'm slowing down."

"I would like to continue to the city." Duncan said. "There are things I'd like to see for myself."

"Why don't I return with Commander Betrice to Westburg for now." Sylve suggested. "That way I can answer any questions that may come up."

"And find an excuse to try to sneak into the Ancan camp on the way home." Maci pointed her finger at Sylve. Sylve turned away and tried to look innocent. "I trust you would be able to get into the camp, but we don't have anything to share worth the risk. When it is time, you will be the one picked for the job."

"Pinky swear?" Sylve held out her hand.

Maci rolled her eyes and linked fingers with Sylve. "You go with the commander to Westburg on the condition you obey all her orders."

"Yes, sir." Sylve jumped up and saluted.

"I'll travel with you Duncan. From your pack, I'm guessing you are planning to be a peddler, maybe prevented from entering the plains by the awful Free, so you need to sell your wares in the big city. I'll work with you on roughing up your speech, you sound more like a noble than a poor peddler. Fandin, Sherr, keep a close eye on the Ancans.

They are up to something. As soon as you know something you let us know, even if you have to come and tell us yourselves."

"Sure thing." The two nodded.

***

Lyle staggered into a clearing. The witch's idea of training was excruciating, but it appeared to be working. He could win that strongman competition now. Trees much bigger than the block of wood used for the competition were nuisances to be tossed aside.

A bear charged into the clearing at him. Lyle swore and jumped aside. There were no sticks or rocks lying about, so he'd have to win without them.

The next time the bear rushed him, Lyle stood his ground and punched the bear in the face. It bowled him over and he tossed it aside, rolling to his feet just as it attacked again. This time it stood up and swatted at him with its paws. They gouged deep into Lyle's flesh. He shouted and pounded harder on the bear until it ran away.

The wounds from the claws healed as he watched, leaving scars behind. Another bear appeared, bigger than the first.

"Come on then." Lyle held up his fists. "Let's see what you've got."

CHAPTER 10

The first day of fights in the arena dawned with cloudy skies. Lencely, Rud, and Daggins dressed in civilian clothes for the arena. Though they'd be in the tunnels beneath the stands, Commander Themson didn't want any hint of official connection between the guards and the fighters.

Lencely figured Haffmon might make an appearance late in the day for the fights between Fhayden prisoners. Though they weren't to the death it still made his blood boil to see his people force to fight for the emperor's entertainment.

"Okay, Adam." Lencely patted the boy on the shoulder. He could have been older than Lencely, but he felt like a youngster. "Pay attention to your footwork and the distance between you and your opponent. Don't waste energy attacking if you're out of range. It will be just like the sparring in our arena."

"Darri will hit harder." Adam opened and closed his fingers. "I wish Becca was here."

"She'll be in the stands watching with the others. You'll join them after your match."

"You're sure I'm going to lose. What happens if I win?" Adam glanced at Lencely.

"If you win, you will be put on the list to fight later. You'll face a stronger opponent. It will be harder to get through the fight without getting hurt."

"I won't lose a fight to avoid getting hurt." Adam clenched his fists. "It wouldn't be right."

"Good for you. Go do your best. This is only your first contest, we'll keep training."

"Of course." Adam jogged out into the arena. Lencely had chosen another person from their group who was mostly on par with Adam. She was faster and meaner though. Either way one of his students won. He still found himself hoping Adam would win. The boy was so earnest. He worked hard and complained less than anyone else, if that was enough, he'd be a champion. Darri ran out past him into the arena.

Adam met the girl, Darri in the circle of rope that would be the boundaries of their fight. He reached out to shake Darri's hand, but she slapped it away. Some lessons in protocol and respect would be in order.

"Fight." The judge's hand dropped.

Darri jumped at Adam and landed a punch to his gut. He took a step back and settled into his stance while she threw punch after punch at him. He blocked the next one, and the next. When she drove in and tried to hit his face, he slid to the side, accidentally tripping her.

Instead of attacking his downed opponent, Adam backed up and waited for her. She jumped to her feet and charged in delivering a flurry of blows. Adam blocked most of them, but he backed up after each blow until he stood with his heels against the rope. He had to know he was in trouble. Darri wasn't going to let him escape to the side and he couldn't retreat any farther.

Darri knew it from the way she held her body. She waited until Adam made a move to the right then launched at him with a powerful kick. Adam shifted like he'd expected it and jumped left. Darri's momentum almost carried her over the rope but by some miracle she balanced just on the edge of the ring.

Adam delivered his only blow of the match. A punch, more of a shove to the stomach that sent her tumbling over the rope. She knelt on the sand and screamed in fury. Adam waited for her, then extended a hand to help her up. Lencely tensed as he waited for her to reject it, or worse attack him, but she took the hand. Adam pulled her up with an ease that surprised Lencely. They spoke a few words before she bowed to him and jogged out of the arena. Her face was a study in determination as she passed Lencely. The judge held up Adam's hand, then Adam jogged back to him.

"Darri is a good fighter." Adam said. "I'm glad I had a chance to fight her."

"What did you talk about at the end of the match?"

"Darri was mad. She was going to buy a treat for her family with the extra money for winning. I said I'd buy the treat and she and her family could join us for supper."

"You won't save any money that way." Lencely slapped him on the shoulder. "But it is a very kind thing to do."

"I'd rather have friends than money." Adam grinned. "She told me she'd kick my ass the next time., that trick would only work once."

"She's right." Lencely nodded. "But it worked well that once."

"I don't know what I'll do the next time. I don't want to hit people." Adam frowned.

"In the arena, honest blows are a form of respect." Lencely pushed him toward the stairs. "Go up and let Becca fuss over you."

The day passed, most of the pairs were evenly matched. Lencely noted a few who had held back in training to get an easier first match. They'd get their payback the next day. Like Adam's trick at the edge of the rope, it could only work once.

Adam came up late in the day to face, of all people Ulfred. The man had powered through three or four matches winning easy victories. People Lencely asked to face Ulfred started refusing. Adam heard and volunteered. Lencely wanted to say no, but the emperor had shown up and he didn't want to end the fights before Haffmon had seen at least one match.

"This isn't Darri." Lencely warned Adam. "Ulfred can beat anyone in our group, he'll take you apart."

"I want him to be able to show off in front of the emperor." Adam sighed. "I hope I can last long enough."

"Do your best and it will have to be enough." Lencely slapped him on the shoulder and sent him out onto the sand.

"I have to fight him?" Ulfred frowned.

"He only volunteered to give you a chance to fight in front of the emperor." Lencely replied.

"And so?"

"That's up to you." Lencely's hand stung after he'd slapped Ulfred's shoulder, but the man didn't twitch.

Once they were both in the circle, the judge made them face Haffmon's box and bow. The judge looked over at Lencely, then shrugged his shoulders.

"Fight." The shout echoed through the arena as it had all day.

Adam charged in and swung a fist at Ulfred. He had to reach up to hit the man's stomach. Ulfred swatted at him, but Adam danced away, somehow not tripping over his feet. He moved faster than he ever had without stumbling. Lencely watched Adam's mouth move, but was too far away to hear what he said. Whatever it was it sent a shock through Ulfred. The man stiffened, then dropped into a proper stance. He waved Adam in.

What followed was the most unequal match Lencely could have imagined. Adam attacked punching with all his strength. The smack of them landing carried all the way to where Lencely stood. Ulfred's return blow knocked Adam to his knees, but he jumped up to attack again. Then he lifted his arms soon enough to block Ulfred's punch. He still went down and had to roll to his feet, but he should have been out on the sand from any one of the blows he'd taken. It didn't look like Ulfred was pulling his punches. Lencely couldn't figure it out.

They circled each other and Adam visibly slowed in getting back on his feet while his opponent moved like he could go on all day. Finally, Adam fell and couldn't get up. Ulfred stood back while the judge called Adam out. When he'd finished, Ulfred ran to Adam's side and knelt. He picked up the boy to carry him off the field.

Even Lencely could hear the shout from the emperor's box.

"Not much of a fighter if he gave you that much trouble."

"Send one of your guards down. If he is still standing after taking one blow. I'll forfeit my prize money."

Arguing came from the box, but no guard showed up to challenge Ulfred. Ulfred bowed, still holding Adam, then turned and walked away.

"The emperor didn't sound impressed." Lencely took Adam from Ulfred.

"Wasn't the emperor who complained, but some hanger on." Ulfred brushed his hand across Adam's face, already swelling with bruises. "Give him my money from this match. He is braver than me." He walked away.

Lencely wished he had Lady Robin with her healing. He put Adam on a nearby table. The boy breathed evenly, then he opened his eyes as far as he could with them so puffy.

"Did I do okay?" It came out more a mumble.

"You did fine." Lencely said. "How did you last so long?"

"My brothers used to beat me. I learned how to take a blow. Ulfred hits harder than my brothers."

"You're crazy." Lencely growled. "Let me get an elixir into you and you can go to Becca."

"I can't afford an elixir." Adam tried to sit up. "I'll be all right in a few minutes."

"Ulfred gave you his prize money from the fight. You can afford an elixir."

"Why did he do that? He won't save anything that way." Adam put a hand to his head. "Ow!

Becca rushed in as Lencely made Adam drink the elixir, then gave him his prize money.

"He'll be okay. Just a little sore tonight."

"I don't know whether to smack you or hug you." Becca shouted at Adam but settled on hugging him.

"We have to buy some stuff on the way home. Darri and her family are coming." Adam looked over at Lencely. "Will you come too?"

"I shouldn't." Lencely said.

"Go." Rud walked in. "Enjoy yourself. Adam deserves some attention. Daggins and I will cover for you."

"Okay. I guess someone needs to watch Adam and all his winnings." Lencely followed Adam and Becca outside. The rest of the fighters had already left to spend their winnings or drown their sorrows.

Adam had Becca hold the money and do the bargaining. Adam sagged under a growing sack of provisions until Lencely took it from him. Adam chattered about the day, and the feast he was going to make as they walked.

"Well, well." A man stepped out in front of them. Lencely swore at himself. He wasn't wearing the uniform, so had no weapons. "You ain't so tough without your friends, are you? Just another guy slumming who ran into the wrong people. So sad."

There was a sound like two stones being knocked together behind Lencely. He'd really screwed up to let people in behind him.

"I heard people plotting against my friend." Ulfred stepped around Lencely. "I am not going to let you hurt him." He cracked his knuckles.

Lencely put the sack down and pulled out the large pot Becca had bought to hold the feast. A shadow rushed him from an alley. He swung the pot like a club connecting with the robed attacker's head. Lencely hoped the crunch wasn't the pot breaking. He struck another attacker's shoulder making the man drop his sword. Lencely handed the pot to Adam and picked up the sword.

Ulfred pounded the man who'd stopped them, batting aside the man's attacks with a knife. More shadows appeared on the road where two men lay motionless. Adam stood between Becca and another man, holding the pot like a shield. Becca reached into the sack and drew out a dried sausage. She slapped it against her hand. By her facial expression, the attackers were lucky it wasn't an axe or a club.

Lencely hefted the sword. It was shorter than he was used to. Good for fights in crowded streets or back alleys. Rud and Daggins were going to be angry they missed this.

"I'll give you one chance to flee." Lencely pointed the sword at one of the shadows. "Refuse and die."

The shadow jumped to the attack. Lencely remembered the fight with the assassins where Gord died. He met the attack, slicing at the hand holding a long dagger. Bones snapped and he drove the sword into the man's throat, stepping past to run the next man through.

Adam fended off his attacker with the pot, catching the knife inside it. Becca leaned over him and walloped the attacker with the sausage. The man's eyes rolled up in his head as he slumped to the ground. Not to be outdone. Adam hammered the downed man with the pot.

Lencely scanned the road, but none of the attackers remained standing.

"The roof, to your right." Becca shouted.

Lencely whipped the sword around as a crossbow snapped. He beat the bolt aside then ran for the building the shot came from. Ulfred met him there and boosted him to the roof. Lencely caught the crossbow man reloading. He slashed the string of the bow, then kicked the man's knee and put the sword to his throat.

"You're dead." The man growled. "The boss is weak, already he is surrounded by enemies. He can't help you."

"I don't need his help." Lencely pointed the sword between the man's eyes. "I will hunt every one of you down and put you in the ground crossways so your souls are food for the night hunters. For everyone you hurt, ten of you will die and rot for eternity." He kicked the man off the roof. The swearing from the alley where the man landed told him the man would live to send his message.

***

When Lencely arrived at the prison he ran to check on Rud and Daggins, but neither of them had been bothered. Their path home had been through a part of the city controlled by the Fhaydens dressed as guards. They wanted to rush out immediately to hunt down the people who'd sent the attackers.

"I sent them a message." Lencely breathed to still the anger still trembling in him. Ulfred had promised to guard Adam and Becca until the next training day. All Adam talked about was how the pot hadn't cracked with the abuse it had taken. Lencely's fear was for his squad.

"If they have truly declared war on the boss of the bully boys, they have nothing to lose." Daggins paced in the commander's office where Lencely had dragged them so they could talk without being disturbed. "No guard should go out alone. We don't know if this will spill over onto the streets."

"I don't care if it looks bad, we don't go out without our armour and batons." Lencely clenched his fists. "We can't trust Kraog until we know where he stands with this."

Commander Themson walked into the office and sat on the desk. "Report."

Lencely explained what had happened and their suggestions.

"We aren't going to wait." Commander Themson crossed his arms. "We need something to get closer to the emperor. We can suggest it was an attempt to rob and murder the first winner of his games. I doubt he'll be happy with that. If we play our cards right, we could get someone into his inner circle. Armour up. I'll rouse everyone else. Gather in the courtyard as soon as you're ready."

Lencely put on the guard's full armour for the first time. It wasn't as good as what he was used to, but it was much better than the contraband shirt he'd been wearing. He and Rud helped Daggins into his armour and chose swords.

"Listen up." Commander Themson's voice rang through the courtyard with almost two hundred guards. "Some of the bully boys attacked the winner of the first games and tried to rob him. Fortunately, one of our trainers was there and helped put down the attack. We are going to strike back hard and fast. I want the bully boys to get the message that they don't mess with the emperor's games. Each of your squad leaders has information about a bully boy business or safe house. We are going to hit them. If there is resistance, put it down, then confiscate anything of value you can carry. Report back here by dawn."

Lencely, Rug, and Daggins went with one of ten squads of twenty guards. The leader was Tradkin. As far as Lencely could see, all ten leaders were Fhayden.

"Right, boys and girls." Tradkin gathered the troop around him. "We're hitting what is rumoured to be the bully boy's counting house. Expect plenty of resistance, so try not to die. It means extra paperwork from me. Don't kill anyone who doesn't resist; it's bad form. We're guards, not hoodlums. On that note, I will pretend not to notice anyone who fills a pocket or two, but this money belongs to the emperor. He paid for protection, so now he's getting a refund."

They headed out into the night, most of them on the wagon Tradkin had found somewhere. From the exterior, the building didn't look any different from its neighbours, but muffled sounds of fighting came from inside.

"Ten of you, pair up and surround the place, cover windows, doors, anything someone could try to escape through. Give them one chance to surrender, then take them down. You all have plenty of strings to tied up prisoners. Remember your training, no sloppy knots. Lencely, Rud, Daggins, you're with me, along with you other six. We'll walk in the front. We aren't taking sides, arrest everyone."

A few of the guards frowned at Tradkin's orders.

"If you don't like the way I do things, you can walk back to the prison. Now." Tradkin didn't give anyone time to respond. "Move, now."

Lencely and Rud hoisted the ram from the wagon and staggered to the door, using the momentum to slam it into the handle. The latch gave way and the door opened into chaos. The room had to be ten paces square with tables laden with money, some of it now on the floor. Figures in shadowy robes fought with bully boys in heavy armour wielding clubs, a single door led to a back room. There were no windows Lencely could see. The other six city guards charged past them into the room.

"The ones in robes use poison." He told Tradkin.

"Thanks." Tradkin drew his sword. "Drop your weapons and get down on the floor. The emperor's guards are arresting all of you."

One of the bully boys glanced at Tradkin and paid for it with a knife to the throat.

"Clean them out boys." Tradkin set himself by the door. "I'll keep it sealed up tight."

Lencely drew his sword. "Take out the robed ones, and the others will surrender. Don't hesitate or you'll be dead. Keep on the outside of the fight."

They spread out, darting in to stab at their targets.

"The blighters are wearing armour." Daggins shouted.

"Try it this way." Lencely flipped his sword and holding the blade brought the crosspiece down on a robed fighter's head. The man stumbled, then went down under a guard's club. The bully boy jumped over the body to attack Lencely, who danced away from the club, flipped his sword back and stabbed the man in the armpit then face.

"The bully boy's armour is mostly show, it doesn't fit well. Look for the openings. We'll work as a team. I club them, you two make sure they stay down and keep the guards off my back."

The three-way fight was brutal, bloody and dangerous. Lencely couldn't take his eyes off anyone except Rud and Daggins. His squad mates kept him alive as more than one knife screeched against the steel of his armour. He didn't give anyone time to try for weak spots. He'd worry about prisoners when leaving someone moving didn't threaten his life. The other six city guards copied Lencely's squad's tactics after two of them went down to poison or the big clubs.

His arms ached by the time movement stopped in the room. They checked the bodies one by one, a few playing dead became truly dead when they attacked. A handful allowed themselves to be bound and searched for weapons. Tradkin gave the two downed guards elixirs, though the one with a knot on his head would still have to see the knacker.

Once the room was secure, Tradkin sent Lencely and Rud to check on the other guards. They'd gathered at the back where there was one door and two heavily shuttered windows. A pile of trussed prisoners lay against the wall of the building.

"Strange, none of them were carrying any gold." One guard winked at them.

"Don't care. Not my job." Lencely said. "Bring the prisoners around to the wagon, then you can help us load the gold.

"Who made you boss?" One of the Ancan guards sneered, but his companion swatted his head. "The boss sent them so you could pretend like you didn't take any gold. Get off your ass and get to work."

Lencely grabbed a pair of legs and Rud took the shoulders. They carried the prisoner around to the wagon and rolled them in.

"Hey, just the live ones." Rud said when the next one they picked up slumped bonelessly in their hands.

"He was alive when we clocked him," the complainer said.

"Must be the poison." Lencely shook his head. "Leave the dead for now. We'll send the slackers back to pick up the bodies later."

The complainer growled and stepped in close to Lencely, but the one who'd swatted him the first time dragged him back. "Don't want to mess with him, Hank. He knows how to use that sword he's wearing."

"And I don't?" Hank turned on the other.

"Not like he does." The second guard pushed Hank toward another body.

Once the bodies were loaded, Lencely led them around to the front where Tradkin was watching the four remaining city guards load gold and silver into bags and anything else that could hold them.

"I'm trusting you folks are already happy with your take, so get to work. Use cloaks, shirts, whatever you can find, we leave nothing but copper behind, and we take that if we can."

The sun peeked over the roofs of the surrounding buildings as they dropped the last load of silver into the wagon.

"Too bad we don't have time to load all the copper." Tradkin spoke much louder than he needed to be heard by the city guards. We'll have to send someone back for it when we have the time. It will be a few hours at least."

It took all of them pushing the wagon to get it moving and keep it moving back to the prison. People were already creeping into the building they'd raided even before the wagon turned the corner. He looked forward and pushed. The folk would remember the guard who'd left treasure for them to take.

***

Bodan accompanied the loaded wagon, now devoid of prisoners, as a fresh pair of horses pulled it to the inn where Haffmon had holed up.

A soldier stalked out and peered at the wagon.

"No one is allowed to stop here. Emperor's orders."

"This is for the emperor." Bodan smiled as if the other had greeted him with open arms. "The bully boys attacked the winner of the emperor's games and tried to rob him. It is common knowledge the emperor has been paying them to stay out of his way, so we took it on ourselves to raid a few places and teach the bully boys a lesson. Turns out one of the places was their counting house. Think of this as a refund of the money paid to them to stay out of the emperor's business." Bodan handed the soldier a pouch. "Take this to the emperor with our compliments."

The soldier poured out gold coins into his hand and glanced at the wagon. "Is it all..." he trailed off.

"Gold and silver." Bodan palmed a smaller pouch into the soldier's hand. "I'm sure the emperor will be pleased."

The solder ran into the inn, then shortly after he came out followed by squad of soldiers.

"Empty the wagon. Every coin in it belongs to the emperor."

A senior officer waved Bodan over.

"I'm Major Saligar, the emperor would like to meet the person who has brought him this gift."

Bodan followed the major into the inn. The emperor had set up court in the public room. He had a large, upholstered chair while officers sat at a table to his right. Sarge sat in a more comfortable chair to the left. He looked like he was sleeping. A young woman sat on a stool beside him.

"Welcome." Haffmon boomed. "I hear you brought some of my money back."

"As much as we could." Bodan knelt and looked at the floor. "I believe the bully boys will leave your games alone from now on."

"And if they decide to retaliate?" One of the officers asked.

"They might." Bodan paused to consider his words. "There may be some among the who believe they own Acanopolis, not the emperor. I don't think we should allow such a mistaken understanding among the rabble."

The silence stretched on as Sarge snored quietly in his chair. Bodan wondered if he'd laid it on too thick.

"He's right." Haffmon banged his fist on the padded arm of his chair. "To make the message clear we'll have more guards at the games and winners will be offered escorts." The others in the room nodded while Bodan hid his smile.

"You are dismissed with the emperor's thanks." One of the officers waved Bodan out of the room.

Bodan stood, bowed, and left to watch the soldiers finish emptying the wagon. He'd accomplished as much as he was going to for the day. As the person organizing the games, Bodan would choose the extra guards carefully.

***

Being old had its uses. Sarge could nod off at any moment and no one paid any attention to him. Most of the time he did sleep, but sometimes like today, he paid attention. Commander Themson was one of Robin's Thousand. Some of them roamed free. That was good. He'd make that part of his plan. There should be almost a hundred of them if everyone who'd escaped the camp remained in the city. He had to get word to his boys, and to Robin. If his plan was to work, it would need outside help.

Serena gently woke him, and they made their slow progress to his room. He sat in the more comfortable chair while Serena bustled about with blankets and pillows. She brought him tea along with a platter of cold meat and bread.

"I'm worried about Tom." She broke the food into bite size pieces and fed him. "If they were out last night fighting the bully boys, he might have been hurt. He acts tough, but he's new at being a guard. I don't know if he's even been in a real fight."

"Go out tonight and meet him." Sarge mumbled after swallowing a sip of the overly sweet tea. "Won't tell."

"What if you get sick, what if you..." she trailed off, her hand halfway between plate and his mouth. Sarge reached out and took the morsel from her and ate it.

"Everyone dies," he suppressed the sigh of exhaustion from feeding himself. "I will die sooner than most. No one can change that. Not you, not Robin, not the emperor himself."

"I don't like the emperor," Serena's voice dropped even lower. "He looks at me."

"Maybe we should arrange a distraction for him." Sarge put his hand on hers. "Tom may know of women from his work who could help."

"Tom isn't that kind of man." Serena pulled her hand from under his.

"He's a guard, maybe he's arrested someone."

Serena froze. Maybe he'd pushed her too hard.

"I'll write a note." Sarge wheezed. "That commander of his will understand the situation."

"Okay, I'll take Tom a note." Serena returned to rubbing Sarge's back.

She climbed out the window late at night. The downside to sleeping through the day was Sarge didn't sleep well at night, but he lay still and listened to her escape. He'd like to sleep, maybe he could dream of Robin. He didn't have much time left. Seeing her again was the only thing keeping him from giving up and leaving this world to deal with Haffmon on its own.

***

Lyle crawled out of the clearing and found a hole under a tree to sleep in. At least there was no bear in it. He'd had enough of bears. Turned out punching their skull didn't hurt them as much as it hurt him. Nothing much hurt them, but he'd got better at avoiding their claws. They'd got bored and wandered away. Probably the witch made sure they didn't eat him, but Lyle couldn't find the energy to care.

In the morning he climbed out of the hole and found a big stick before walking back into the clearing. The bears didn't show up, so he put the stick over his shoulder and walked in the direction the forest allowed him. He didn't get far before the path was blocked by a cliff.

"I guess I'm supposed to climb this. Forget that." He tried to make his way along the bottom of the cliff, but boulders rolled into his way and branches blocked him if he turned back to the forest.

"I wonder which one of us is more stubborn." Lyle muttered and sat on one of the boulders. He drank from the waterskin which never emptied and ate some of the bread and cheese he already tired of from his sack.

A bear came out of the brush and charged him. Lyle jumped up to stand on the boulder and used his stick to smack the bear about the head until it staggered away. Another came and he gave it the same treatment. The third bear was the biggest he'd ever seen. It ignored the stick and struck the boulder which cracked in half. Lyle jumped to another which the bear also broke.

"Oh come on." Lyle swung the stick which broke on the bear's head. He was sure the bear grinned at him before swiping at the boulder. This time Lyle had to jump for the cliff face. He clung to it with aching fingers.

"I guess you think you won." Lyle sidled along the cliff toward another boulder, but the bear moved faster. It picked up a chunk of rock and threw it to smash against the cliff just below Lyle's feet.

He looked down and spat at the bear before realizing his waterskin and sack of food lay on the ground by the first boulder. The bear ambled over them, then looked at Lyle.

"I don't suppose you'll let me pick them up before I climb this rock?" Lyle whined. The bear chomped down on the waterskin. Water exploded from the bear's mouth, then slowed until it dropped the mangled waterskin on the ground. It used its claws to tear open the sack, then snuffled at the bread and cheese before eating the pile of food. It circled like a dog before lying down on the remains.

Lyle cussed the whole way up the cliff. His hand bled from the rock and his boots were hardly more than rags. He looked for a rock to throw at the bear, but it had left. A few minutes along the path that opened up for him he met another cliff. Dangling from a branch at the top was a pack.

CHAPTER 11

Adam woke and stretched. Becca still slept on her side of the tent. He crawled outside and dipped water from the barrel to wash.

In the few days since the games, the clearing where he lived had turned into a miniature village. Tents filled the space in neat rows. He had a proper stone fireplace to cook on and pots to do the cooking. Some of it he'd bought with money from his first games, some he'd built with help of Becca and the others, and some somehow showed up.

Other families were stirring. Not all the children he'd met were orphans, some of the parents worked and couldn't get home every night. Other people had shown up with canvas and made themselves at home.

"We're getting short on grains for porridge." A man came over to Adam. "I'll pick some up on the way home tomorrow."

"Thanks, that would be great." Adam smiled and spotted a girl who didn't come up to his waist practicing sword with a stick. A boy only a bit older swept the area in front of his tent, carefully staying clear of the girl's stick.

Adam and the other trainees had a cheering section each afternoon. The morning they spent foraging for greens and tubers or improving the camp.

He put the large pot full of water over the fire and threw handfuls of grain in for porridge. They'd have enough for tomorrow. It helped that there were people who watched over their stores and made sure they didn't run out.

After breakfast, Adam and the other trainees headed for their arena. Becca had the camp under control. She spent some of each morning teaching who ever wanted to learn the little bit of writing and numbers she knew.

At the end of the day, Adam invited Lencely, Rud and Daggins to join them for supper.

"Everyone will enjoy seeing you, and having you eat with us will make them feel they matter."

"I have things I need to do." Lencely said, but Daggins elbowed him.

"We'll finish things up. I know the area you're living in. I'll drag Lencely and Rud there."

Adam went back to camp and built up the fire to start supper. They had a little bit of meat he should cook anyway before it went bad, so he'd make stew.

"Stop, that's not yours."

Adam looked up to see the little girl with the stick standing between three men and the road. The men had their arms full of whatever they'd been able to grab. A crowd gathered, but not too close. Adam and Becca were the only adults tonight. Adam strode over to stand beside the girl.

"Please return what you've taken." He crossed his arms.

The men laughed and one of them dropped what he held to swing at Adam. Adam stepped back and the man slipped and fell.

"Good one, Joh. You'll win in the arena for sure with that style."

Joh, climbed up and charged Adam, this time Adam stumbled on rock. Joh slammed into Adam taking him to the ground where he tried to throttle him. Adam stared up at Joh, but didn't do anything but hold the Joh's hands off. If he fought back, everyone in the camp would suffer.

Adam's arms were getting tired, then the other men started kicking him.

He heard the crack of a stick, and a heavy weight landed on him, but the kicking stopped. Becca was shouting something, but between the weight and his tiredness Joh had a grip on his throat and the world slowly faded away.

The weight vanished as Joh was hoisted off him. Adam took in a deep breath to see Joh fly out onto the road. Lencely reached down a hand to help Adam up.

"I think you probably could have fought back enough to save your life."

Daggins had one of the other men in a headlock. Joh had vanished down the street.

The third man lay still in the dirt.

Becca ran over and hugged Adam tight.

"You fool. We could get along without the money, but not without you."

"I know these three." Daggins dropped his opponent beside the one lying in the dirt. "I have an idea to send a message, but it will require relaxing one of our rules."

"Go on." Lencely crossed his arms.

"We put these three into the arena against Adam. One at a time." Daggins' grin became evil. "Then we let it be known that trainees are allowed to fight to defend their families. Adam's not the first to take a beating because of that rule."

"Works for me. Set it up." Lencely dragged one of the unconscious men into the street, while Rud took the other. Once they'd returned everyone's belongings, Adam served up supper.

"Good thing it is stew tonight. Anything else might have burned."

Becca sat close beside him and kept glancing at him. Lencely told stories which had the crowd alternating between laughter and moans. Rud stayed silent except to add something to the story once in a while. Then Daggins told a story that had the older boys in stitches while the younger ones looked puzzled. Adam's brothers had similar stories, he'd never seen the humour in them then, but listening to Daggins, he began to understand.

"Rud and I will take our leave." Lencely stood as the moon peeked over the broken roofs. Daggins will stay in case they try to come back."

Becca cuddled up to Adam when they'd crawled into their tent.

"I thought I'd killed that man." She whispered in his ear. "I'd do anything for you."

Adam put his arms around her and hugged her. "Thanks for the help. I'm sorry I put you in that situation."

She nodded and kissed his cheek before getting comfortable and going to sleep. Adam lay awake listening to her breathe. He knew from his gramma's stories what was happening. He was happy, because he cared deeply for

Becca, but the feelings his gramma talked about were missing from his heart.

He'd have to work harder and try to find them.

***

Adam worked hard in the training arena. Now they had wood swords and other weapons to work with. Lencely suggested they pick one to specialize in, and just gain a bit of experience in the others.

"You never know when your weapon will break, or be out of reach, so you need to be ready to use whatever is at hand."

A few new people joined the group and some left. Those in Adam's village, as they called it, mostly stayed, though a few took turns skipping training to guard the village. They wouldn't let Adam though, saying he was the best of them and should fight in the emperor's arena.

The day of the games arrived. Those who weren't fighting volunteered to stay home and keep the village safe. The rest joined Becca and the youngsters in the bleachers to cheer their friends on.

Adam's first match was against the man Becca had hit. The man charged with his club. Adam beat it aside with his sword. He used the sword because of the stories, but he liked the staff better. After letting his opponent wear himself out, Adam began his attack. He used each of the moves he'd been taught. Though the sword had been dulled, the man still grunted at each blow. When he'd been through all attacks he knew, he started again, only faster and combining them. The man threw down his club and ran from Adam.

The judge awarded Adam the victory. The one Daggins had choked into unconsciousness came next. He tried to run away, but Adam got between him the edge of the circle.

"Fight, you're getting paid for it."

The man spat at him and tried to run, so Adam herded him around the circle until he'd finished all the attacks he'd learned, then he kicked the man out of the circle.

When it was Joh's turn, the day had gone on long enough for the emperor to arrive, so they had to bow. Where the other two had fought in low boots, Joh's reached up to his calf.

"Look, you have a sword and I have this stick." Joh sneered in Adam's face. "But I'm still going to beat you black and blue."

"Do you know how to use the sword?" Adam asked.

"I used to be a soldier. Give me that sword and I'll kill you."

Adam handed his sword to the judge.

"I'll take the staff, give him the sword." The judge shrugged and traded the sword for Joh's staff.

Adam weighed the staff in his hands. Heavier than he was used to, and not as polished. It would do.

"Okay, soldier who steals from children. Show me what you know." Adam didn't quite shout the challenge, but he wanted the emperor to hear.

Joh didn't charge in right away, but circled Adam, getting used to the balance of the sword.

"I used to be the best in my division." Joh tried a thrust. Adam rapped him on the shoulder.

"Less talk, more fighting."

"I should have kept the staff, more reach."

"Was it drinking or stealing from children that got you kicked out?" Adam leaned on his staff. "Or maybe you're just a common coward."

Joh snarled and started a flurry of thrusts and slashes, trying to get inside Adam's reach.

"Right, coward it is. That should have been clear."

The staff creaked and groaned at it took the beating from Joh's sword. Joh's grin widened and he redoubled the attack. A few of the blows made it through Adam's defense. He'd have to get Becca to hug him gently for a while.

Joh jumped forward with a vicious overhead slash. The staff didn't break, but it bent in the middle and became useless. Adam tossed it outside the circle.

Joh began swinging the sword in figure eights, making it impossible for Adam to reach through. He backed away slowly.

"Maybe you shouldn't have thrown away your weapon." Joh jumped forward with a slash. Adam dodged to the side.

Lencely had said something about his trainer being able to see the rhythm of her opponent's attacks. Adam watched Joh. Figure eight, figure eight, slash. He always swung the sword a bit wider just before he slashed, and all his slashes had been from right to left. Adam dodged more slashes, but the pattern didn't change.

"If you were best in your division, it had to have been a pretty bad division." Adam timed his verbal jab just as Joh went wide for his cut. Instead of jumping back Adam lunged in and grabbed Joh's sword hand with his right and pulled down in the direction the sword was already moving. At the same time, he punched Joh just below the ribs.

The combination of the extra power on the slash and the Adam's punch made Joh lose his grip on the sword. Adam picked up the sword and walked to the centre of the circle where he stuck it in the sand.

"If you want your sword back. Come and take it."

Joh charged, but Adam met the charge head on with a blow to Joh's gut. Adam pushed the man back.

"Not good enough."

Joh tried more charges, tried running around Adam to reach the sword. Threw sand at him to blind him. Each time Adam stopped him and sent him staggering back with a hard blow.

Joh reached down to scratch his leg, then came at him with a lunge, knife in hand.

Adam batted the knife to the side, then took hold of Joh's knife arm at the forearm, put his other hand on Joh's shoulder and twisted to add momentum to Joh's lunge and threw him out of the circle.

Joh rolled twice, then pushed himself to his feet.

"I'm going to kill you."

"The match is over." The judge stepped closer to Joh. "You stepped out of the ring."

Joh turned to face the judge, putting the knife behind him to pass it to his left hand. Adam caught Joh's left arm and twisted it up behind until the blade touched his throat.

"Drop the blade." Adam whispered in Joh's ear. "You couldn't touch me with a staff, a sword, or a knife. You lost, you will always lose." He put more pressure on Joh's shoulder. "I could kill you right here, or—" Adam lifted and twisted the arm and the pop of Joh's shoulder echoed through the arena.

Joh screamed and dropped to the sand, leaving Adam holding the knife. He handed it to the judge, bowed to the emperor and walked out of the arena.

He made it through the door into the underground room before he doubled over and vomited what little was left in his stomach onto the floor.

"I didn't teach you that." Lencely handed Adam a damp rag.

"My brothers practiced on me." Adam spat the last of the bile from his mouth. "I always gave up, so I didn't know if it would work the way they said."

"And I thought my brothers were tough on me." Lencely pulled Adam to his feet.

"The emperor is calling for you." The judge stood in the door. "Your opponent has been carried away."

Adam sighed and breathed in deep.

"Let's go."

He walked with the judge past the sword still stuck in the sand to where he could have seen the emperor if he'd looked up. Adam knelt and studied the sand.

"You fought last week in the final match." The emperor's voice was rougher, deeper, than Adam expected. "Now this. I will keep my eye on you. You're interesting." A small purse landed in the sand beside Adam. "You had a grudge with that man."

"He attacked my family." Adam lifted his head enough to see the emperor's shadow on the sand. "I needed to make it clear what happens to those who threaten my family."

"Very well." The emperor's shadow vanished as he stepped back. "Continue keeping your family safe, buy them something nice."

"You may leave." The judge handed him the purse. "Thanks for your help."

***

Bodan glanced at the crumpled note in his hand, then at the young man, Tom, he'd said his name was.

"Why are you bringing this to me now?"

"My girlfriend brought it to me." From the redness flowing up Tom's face, she was more than a girlfriend now. "She's afraid of the emperor. Serena's just an innkeeper's daughter. The emperor might use her and throw her away, or worse have her disposed of."

"And what do you expect me to do?" Bodan raised an eyebrow. "There was this one brothel we visited." Tom's redness deepened. "A woman there suggested I could help her get out of the brothel."

"And she rewarded you in advance." Bodan sighed. *When did the new recruits start looking like babies?*

Tom hung his head.

"You have to be more cautious. You don't know who will call in any favours you offer. This is how the bully boys get people inside the guard." Keeping his tone fatherly challenged Bodan, but he needed this young man.

"I would never betray the guard." Tom's shining eyes contrasted with his rigid posture as he snapped to attention.

"Very good." Bodan stared at the young man until he started trembling. "You will go with Tradkin and arrest this woman. Put her in a cell, then inform me. I will take it from there."

***

Lencely laid on his bunk and sighed. Training the fighters was fun, but exhausting. He worked as hard as any of them to maintain his image of being unbeatable.

Daggins shook him.

"I need your help."

Lencely sat up. Daggins was white and shaking.

"What's the problem?"

"I need to check something out, but it is in the section of the cells we're not allowed to go."

"We'll go and talk with Commander Themson." Lencely stood and brushed off his tunic.

"We can't. He was the one who ordered the arrest." I heard Tradkin and Tom talking."

"You want to get into the restricted section of the cells, why?"

"I thought I recognized the voice of the prisoner." Daggins hung his head. "Please."

"We'll let Rud sleep." Lencely led the way out of the barracks.

The restricted cells were down on the basement level. They were barricaded by a heavy door. Tradkin sat in a chair, leaning it back against the wall.

"What do you want? Not supposed to be down here." He only moved to cross his arms.

"You'd be more threatening if you stood while you did that." Lencely shook his head. "Dealing with too many obedient soldiers has made you soft."

Tradkin laughed, then the chair slipped, dumping him on the floor.

"Ouch."

"You okay?" Lencely crouched beside him.

"Aren't you supposed to use my momentary weakness to overwhelm me and sneak into the cells?"

"What good would that do? Go tell Commander Themson I kicked the chair out from under you."

"As if." Tradkin stood up and groaned. "I have to stop doing that."

"That would mean learning from your experience." Lencely laughed.

Tradkin opened the door. "I wasn't specifically ordered not to let anyone in."

"Blame me." Daggins spoke for the first time since entering the basement. "The worst he'll do is put me back in a cell."

"If you think that's the worst the commander can do, you don't know him well." Tradkin waved them in

Lencely shivered when the door closed behind them. "This is where we are supposed to be." They walked down the corridor until Daggins stopped in front of cell.

"Mena?"

"What the hell are you doing here?" A woman came to the small window in the door.

"I thought I recognized your voice." Daggins tried to reach through the bars, but Mena slapped his hand away. "And you've always been partial to that scent."

"I let myself be sold to a brothel to save you from this." Mena slapped the door with her hand. "Did you waste your life, after all that?"

"Mum and Da died of that fever a couple years back. I've been taking care of myself since then."

"And here you are in a guard's uniform." She choked out the words like she was on the edge of tears.

"It is the only way I can work against that bastard." Daggins grabbed the bars. "I've been searching for you since they died. You're the only family I have."

Lencely turned and peered into the next cell. It was empty, but the despair in it clutched at his throat.

"You don't want me as family," Mena whispered. "I'm everything that Da hated."

"Not your fault." Daggins put his head against the door. "I wanted to hate Da for selling you, but Mum wouldn't let me. He got small afterwards, it was pathetic. Like he couldn't deal with his own failure."

"He never could." Mena reached through the bars and ruffled Daggins' hair. "I worried about you, boyo. You weren't ever the brightest. What gang did you run with?"

"Mostly Kraog's but I never took initiation." Daggins sniffed. "Even after everything I didn't want to disappoint Da."

"How did you meet that one?" Mena pointed at Lencely.

"In prison." Lencely answered for Daggins. "I was running with the wrong gang."

"You don't look like a gang boy to me." Mena sneered.

"Different kind of gang." Lencely shrugged. "Turns out we work well together."

"And now you're guards?"

"Yet another kind of gang." Lencely looked down the corridor as the door opened and Commander Themson strolled in.

"I hope you've noticed that the cells next to hers are empty." The commander frowned. "I expect you've already put a foot in my play. I need her to cooperate."

"I'll gladly go back in a cell to get her out." Daggins stood straight and met the commander's cold gaze.

"You too Lencely?"

"He's part of my squad." Lencely stepped up beside Daggins. "I share any punishment he gets."

"You boys are fools." Commander Themson stood nose to nose with Lencely. "I should put you on scrubbing the shit holes."

"Whatever you want." Mena banged on the door. "Ask, but don't threaten my brother."

"Brother?" Commander Themson's ominous presence relaxed. "I think we will be able to work together."

"Lencely, take Daggins upstairs. I sympathize with his being here, but I need to discuss things with his sister he is not allowed to hear." Commander Themson met Daggins' eyes. "She won't be any safer working for me, but it is her choice. Swear to me you won't try to find her or interfere. That could get her killed."

Daggins glanced over at Mena who nodded at him.

"I swear." He sighed. "I'll leave her in your care."

Lencely led him out of the corridor, nodded at Tradkin and headed upstairs.

***

Mena watched her brother until the bars blocked her vision.

"Okay, what do you need from me?"

"Would Haffmon recognize you?" the commander asked.

"Haffmon, if I get a chance, he's dead."

"That's not what I asked." The commander leaned against the wall opposite her cell.

"I was just a skinny kid when he ruined my family." Mena slapped at the tears on her face. *Why am I weak now?* "My father got into a debt he couldn't pay. Haffmon forced him to sell me to pay the debt. Da was always showing off how righteous he was, it tickled Haffmon to make him the father of a prostitute."

"So, he wouldn't look at you and know you." The clicking of the man's heels as he paced in the corridor sounded like the coins being laid out as the madame paid for her.

"What's this about? Haffmon is never going to bother with me again. He probably doesn't remember. We weren't the only family he ruined."

"I want to place you in the service of the innkeeper where Haffmon is holding court. I'm not interested in Haffmon, so you don't need to spy on him. However, the innkeeper's daughter is afraid of him, says he looks at her."

"He's the type. The one time I met him, he spent the entire time leering at me. Gave me the creeps." Mena shuddered. "I don't get the creeps anymore. I'd kill him given the chance."

"I'd rather you waited until we didn't need him." Commander Themson came over and peered through the bars at her. "He's a snake, but he's one of a nest of snakes. Kill him, and a worse one will step into his place before the end of the day. I plan to destroy the entire nest in one shot."

"I can wait my turn. There's no hope for me, but I want Daggins to have a good life." Mena turned and sat in the corner of her cell.

"Good. A woman will be down to help you wash up and dress the part we have in mind for you to play. You will be extra help, recommended by the daughter. She has her hands full with caring for an old man. You may be asked to help with that too. If he asks you to do something, I suggest you follow his order."

"Friend of yours?"

"Member of the same gang." The commander sighed. "You will be in grave danger. Even if Haffmon doesn't recognize you, the slightest indication of your hate for him could be lethal."

"I loathed most of my clients." Mena's skin crawled. "I'll be fine."

"One last thing." The commander's tone made her look up at him. "Never give up hope. Daggins wants you to live, and you need hope for that."

***

Lyle swatted another bug. They had to be biting dead bugs as much as him now, but they wouldn't stop. The waterskin only let him drink once a day, and the food in the sack was stale. The witch's punishment for his disobedience.

But she still needed him. There would be opportunities and he'd be ready to seize them. He slipped on a patch of mud and rolled down hill, bouncing off trees until he splashed into a swamp. The muck filled the air with such a foul smell that even the bugs left him. Lyle crawled out of the mud and sat on the bank studying the swamp. Though he had been doubting that any of his experiences were real, it wasn't time to put that to the test yet.

Tuffets of grass dotted the swamp and made an irregular path into the distance. When he put a foot on the closest one, it held his weight. He'd have to jump from one bit of grass to the next. Probably not all of them were safe. He tried another one and it sank as he put pressure on it.

Lyle studied the grass more. Some of the tuffs were yellower. They were the ones he could depend on. He adjusted his pack and took a long breath immediately regretting letting the swamp air into his lungs. His father would say he needed to chew the air.

Lyle hadn't thought of his father other than to hold him to blame for the mess since the witch sent him on this journey. He pushed thoughts of the old man out of his head and jumped for the first tuffet.

He made three jumps before he misjudged and ended up in the water. The tuffet held him as he climbed onto it. He'd have to do better. Just like life with his father. He always had to do better.

Chapter 12

Robin lay on her mat. Being in prison was boring. The captain had come and ordered Sam out of his cell, the big man hung his head and went back to work after the captain threatened his family. She had no one to talk to.

The forest sneered at her in her dreams, showing Lyle 'training' to become the forest's champion. Robin pitied the man. He was a bit of a jerk, but he didn't deserve the torture he endured. It only cemented her determination to avoid becoming anything like the fae.

This wasn't anything like the stories she'd read in Fhayde. The fae in those tales had been mysterious and sometime capricious, but they hadn't relished cruelty. She didn't know the stories from the north, maybe it was different here. That might explain the division between the land in Fhayde and the Ancan empire.

Her only remaining thread of hope was that Willem's friend, the emperor was a man who would listen. Though she had no idea of what to say to him that he didn't know. The empire had fragmented, with Haffmon ruling Ancanopolis, war felt inevitable.

"I want to go home." Robin told the uncaring stone walls. "I've probably missed Federick's wedding, and who knows what else?" She wiped the tears off her cheeks.

That evening the captain brought her supper himself.

"We've received orders to transfer you to the emperor's custody. You will be taken by coach tomorrow." He shoved the tray under the door. "Maybe the emperor's food will be better than ours."

He smirked at her and walked away.

The food was decent, probably leftovers from the guards' own meal, but cold and greasy. Robin ate it anyway. She needed the strength. Her constitution was tough enough not to reject the food, but she daydreamed about Seth's cooking.

In the morning, the first female guard Robin had seen showed up with a billowing pile of fabric over her arm.

"The captain wants you to wear this dress," the woman stammered. "The emperor would be insulted if you showed up as you are."

"I don't like dresses." Robin stood and took the dress from the guard. "Especially ones as overly fancy as this one."

"He said if you don't wear the dress, you will travel in prison clothes and shackles."

"That will be fine." Robin handed the dress back.

"Please," the woman had tears running down her cheeks. "If you don't put the dress on, he will put my whole family in the cells. We're behind on the rent." She looked down. "I know a great lady like you don't care about such simple things."

"I'm no great lady." Robin muttered. "Is there no depth this captain won't stoop to? You'll have to help. What's your name?"

"Kerie." The woman looked down. "I'm sorry, great lady, but I don't know what to do with such a dress."

"Then we will figure it out together." Robin took a deep breath and collected her wits. The two of them crammed Robin into a dress that probably should have had at least two maids to help. When they were done, Robin could hardly move, despite it being much too big for her. Probably what the captain wanted. She wondered where he'd put his hands on it, then decided she didn't want to know.

Robin picked up the skirts and concentrated on walking without tripping to the captain. "I will need my bag."

"Sam will hold onto your bag up front." The captain waved a hand. "You won't need it."

Sam helped her up into the coach, then it rocked as he climbed up onto the driver's bench. It started off down the road.

***

Robin couldn't find a way to stay on the seat with the combination of the ridiculous dress and the tossing of the coach on the rough road. She finally crammed herself in a corner between the bench and the wall. It remained gruesomely uncomfortable, but at least she wasn't falling off the bench every few minutes.

I'm not going to survive to get to the emperor at this rate. When they'd put the thing on Robin, neither Kerie nor Robin considered what would happen when she needed to answer the call of nature. Her stomach growled and she laughed. This situation was her own fault. She'd played up being the Lady Robin, and this was the payment. Stuffed into a dress making it impossible to move, then into a coach which would do well as a device of torture.

Shouting outside grabbed her attention. She tried to get up off the floor but tangled in the fabric. The door of the coach ripped open and a man in a mask leered at her before shooting her with a crossbow. The bolt slammed into her just above her heart and pinned her to the wall of the coach. A moment later two more men in masks dragged her out of the coach. Robin screamed as the bolt pulled through her and out her back. The men dragged her into the woods away from the road, but she caught a glimpse of Sam slumped over with a crossbow bolt in his neck.

"I happen to know there are bears in these woods." The man with the crossbow pulled up his mask and leered at her. "No one makes a fool of me and lives." The captain spat on her. "I will write a report about how I found the coach and my poor guard, obviously the result of a bandit attack, but you missing, clearly dragged away by animals. Everyone who sympathized with you is dead. You could have avoided all this by helping me out."

Robin stared up at the light shining through the trees. There were bears nearby, she could feel them. With the last of her strength, she called them. Better to be meat for bears than to listen to this mockery of a human being.

Her eyes closed before the bears arrived, but faint shouts of panic reached her. Her last thought was to hope the bears didn't get hurt.

***

"Rather a dramatic exit," the old woman chuckled. "You could have been a fae and lived for ages."

"Better to die than be like you." Robin snarled at the woman. "I saw what you're doing to Lyle."

"Making him strong. In time he'll be emperor and the world will return to the way things should be."

"And you dragged me here just to gloat?" Robin laughed. "You're more pathetic than that captain."

"All humans are like that." The woman brushed the air with her hand. "Now that you're too weak to resist, you're going to help me."

"No." Robin gritted her teeth and somehow sat up. "I will never be too weak to resist such as you."

The woman took a step toward Robin, but she faded away until Robin was alone in the cave.

"You're close enough to the border of our lands I could pull you into my domain." An old man leaned over her.

"Who are you?" Robin coughed and spat out blood.

"Another land." The old man held a kerchief to her face and dabbed away the blood. "I've felt you talking to other lands but couldn't reach you."

"And what do you want?" Robin couldn't keep the anger out of her voice.

"Peace would be nice." The old man sighed. "I'm going to let you sleep. If you wake up, we'll talk more."

Robin stood up and looked down at herself. She wore something hardly more than a long shift. Her legs goose-bumped with the chill. The cave had gone. A black plain stretched in all directions. Somehow even without light, she could see farther than she ever had. The faintest of tugs pulled at her. With nothing better to do, she walked in that direction.

***

General Mihone rode into the small village by the forest. He knocked on the door of the guardhouse, expecting Willem to answer. Instead, a mountain of a man looked down at him.

"How may I help you?" the mountain asked.

"I'm looking for Willem." General Mihone pushed aside his astonishment. "On the emperor's business."

"Come in." The mountain stepped aside and waved him in. "The commander is just finishing training. I've made tea for him. Would you like some while you wait?"

"Certainly." General Mihone sat at the table. "If it isn't too much trouble."

"None at all." The man disappeared into a back kitchen and came back almost immediately with a tray laden with teapot, cups, and a platter of food. "I should introduce myself, I'm Seth. One of Willem's guards and his cook."

"I'm General Mihone." The food looked good after the long ride. The general dug in without hesitation. Seth poured a cup of tea and set a pot of honey and another of cream beside it.

"I will let the commander know you are here." Seth went out another door, and a few minutes later returned with Willem.

"Ah, General Mihone." Willem saluted. "To what do we owe the pleasure of your company?" He sat opposite the general and helped himself.

"You wrote a report about a young woman. The emperor would like to meet her."

Willem frowned and his hand paused over the cream jug. "The emperor didn't hear? The captain of Stronghaven sent guards to arrest her for being a spy." He poured the cream into his tea. "I'm sure you would have had word from them by now."

"Nothing." General Mihone clenched a fist. "And you sent nothing?"

"Just a note to say that Stronghaven had taken custody of Lady Robin."

"You'd better give me the details." The general relaxed and sipped at his tea. "Call me Dyve as you used to, Willem."

"Very well, Dyve." Willem described the young woman's arrest. Dyve's approval of this Lady Robin went up as the tale was told.

"I need to get to Stronghaven as soon as possible." Dyve stood at the end of the tale. "There are unsavoury rumours about that captain. I would have thought you'd know."

"My interest has always been in outside forces." Willem frowned. "I heard nothing about this captain. If he is so chancy, perhaps Seth should ride with you. He has learned a lot and deserves a chance outside this village."

"I would appreciate the help, but I only have my horse and my spare."

"We can provide him with a horse, perhaps he can find a spare in Stronghaven."

"We'll set out as soon as he's ready."

"It won't take me long to pack." Seth ran out of the room. True to his word he was back before Dyve had finished his second cup of tea.

"We won't stop except to rest the horses." General Mihone said.

"Lady Robin is a friend of mine." Seth checked his horse over before mounting. "I will run if I have to."

***

They arrived in Stronghaven in mid-morning. General Mihone's appreciation of Seth had grown. The man didn't complain but had set up camp and somehow cooked a more than passable meal from what he had in his pack. They'd broken camp before dawn and when Seth's horse looked like it might go lame, he had indeed run to keep up with the general.

At the guard house, the gate was shut, and the guard wouldn't let them in until General Mihone produced the letter from the emperor ordering him to bring Lady Robin to Dordnom.

"My apologies, but we just put the Lady on a coach to travel to the emperor." The captain's expression rubbed General Mihone the wrong way, but there was nothing he could do.

"General Mihone." Seth interrupted them pointing at a bag on a shelf by the captain's desk. "That is Lady Robin's bag. She wouldn't travel without it."

"She gave it to me as thanks for the excellent treatment she received." The captain walked over and stroked the leather.

"What did you do with the contents?" Seth stalked over and picked up the bag. "She would have warned you that the contents were dangerous. Yet it feels full."

"General, I would ask that you control your man. He is insulting my honour."

"I'll worry about your honour later." General Mihone walked over to Seth and took the bag from him. Pulling it open, the general raised an eyebrow at the contents. "If she gave it to you as a gift, surely she explained the contents and how they are to be used."

"I have the bag as a keepsake."

"I'm taking the bag to the emperor." General Mihone closed it and handed it to Seth. "Keep it safe, Seth. It is indeed very dangerous."

"You can't do that. It's mine." The captain stomped up to General Mihone.

"I'm the general of the emperor's legions." General Mihone knocked the captain to the floor. "Seth, arrest this man on charges of insubordination."

Seth picked the man up like a toddler. "Who has keys to the cells?"

A woman guard stepped forward. "I do." She picked up keys from the wall and led Seth down a corridor.

"Is there anyone who is willing to lie for that poor excuse for a human, or will I hear the truth from you? Either way a division from my legion will be arriving to investigate the running of this guardhouse."

"We ain't saying anything. You don't have your legion here, do you?" A guard drew a sword and charged at General Mihone.

General Mihone waited until the last second, then separated the fool's head from his body. "Attacking a superior officer is a capital crime. I don't have time to sort out who of you are vile beasts and who is just foolish and fearful. March into the cells and I will lock you there until my legion arrives, or you can die now."

Two more men died on his blade before the rest dropped weapons and filed into cells. General Mihone stood over them while Seth searched them for weapons or keys. The men moped in their cells as Seth locked them in.

"There are guards out patrolling," the woman guard said, "they'll just let them out and it will go back to the way it was."

"There should be an alarm bell." General Mihone pointed outside. "Seth, go ring the bell until the guards show up."

"Yes, sir." Seth ran outside and the bell clanged.

"What is your name, guard?" General Mihone asked the woman.

"Kerie, sir." She gulped and dropped to her knees. "I'm not really a guard. The captain had me in to dress Lady Robin to send her to the emperor. He kept me around because I was—convenient."

What General Mihone could see of her face was bright red.

"I would hang him now if I had the time." He wanted to stay and repair this mess, but the emperor's orders had been explicit. Find Robin and bring her immediately.

The bell stopped ringing.

"Come." He strode outside, still holding his bloody sword.

The guards had gathered around Seth, swearing at him. A crowd outside the gate was shouting questions.

"Seth, open the gate and let the citizens in. They deserve to hear what is being said."

"Who are you?" One of the guards swaggered over to the general.

"General Mihone, commander of the emperor's legions." He pointed the sword at the guard and waited until the man saw the blood dripping from it. "I'm here to set things right until my investigation division arrives."

The man paled and scrambled back.

"Listen up." General Mihone switched to his parade ground voice. "I'm here on the authority of Emperor Ordamy. Unfortunately, I have orders which don't allow me to stay and investigate on my own. My people will arrive within a week and investigate everything that has been going on in this guardhouse. Until they arrive, my personal aide, Captain Seth will command, Kerie will be his second in command. They are to be obeyed absolutely. In addition, none of the people in the cells may be released. No guard may resign. If anyone leaves, they will be treated as deserters. If Captain Seth and Guard Kerie are not present and in good health when my squad arrives, they will have orders to hang all the guards present, then track down and hang any who fled."

The silence following General Mihone's declaration only lasted until the first shout from a guard. Seth clubbed the man to the ground before the man took a step.

"What about us?" A woman in the crowd shouted. "Who's going to keep us safe?"

"Safe from who?" Another woman shouted. "I'd rather thieves and brigands than these guards."

"Write your complaints down for the general's investigators." Seth bellowed. "If you can't write, come and I'll write it for you. You'll be making your oath about your complaint, so it had better be true when the investigators arrive." He swiveled to the guards. "You will patrol, but there is no need for swords. You'll be issued batons. Kerie, see to it."

"Yes, sir." She pointed at the door. "Swords in the cupboards. Take a baton. I'll be watching. With the Captain's permission I'll be locking the evidence room."

"You'd better sleep with one eye open." A guard shoved his way past Kerie into the guard house.

General Mihone followed the guard into the room, then cleaned his sword on the man's tunic. "Do you want to be locked up for your own safety? If you are already disobeying orders, maybe I should treat you like I did those." He pointed at the bodies on the floor. "I suggest you hand up your sword, then start cleaning up the front office. I'll watch while you strip them of their weapons and hang them up too."

The guard paled and dropped to his knees. "Don't kill me."

"Then I strongly suggest you follow your orders. Captain Seth speaks with my voice. Understood?"

Once all the weapons had been stowed and checked. General Mihone took Seth aside.

"Sorry to dump this on you. One consolation is you're a Captain in my legion now. Maybe that will keep you through the week watching this sorry lot."

"I'm honoured to serve you however I can." Seth saluted. "Bring my greeting to Lady Robin when you find her. I'll ask that you take her bag with you. She will be missing it."

"I hope so, Seth. I really hope so."

General Mihone checked his horses over.

"Sorry, but it's going to be another long ride." He mounted and took the reins of his spare then rode out of the guardhouse and through the town. The urgency he felt fought with the stone in the pit of his stomach saying he was too late.

He found the remains of the coach and what the scavengers had left of the driver late in the day. Dyve didn't feel like a powerful general as he dug the grave. He left the coach for his investigators. Anyone who'd already passed by hadn't stopped long enough to bury the murdered man, chances were there was nothing left to steal.

Since it was dark by the time the grave had been filled in, Dyve made camp nearby. In the morning light he tracked where the passenger had been dragged away. He'd seen the bloody crossbow bolt in the coach, all he expected to find was the need for another grave.

The trail didn't go far into the forest. A fancy gown lay crumpled on the ground, bear prints overlaid the boot prints in the dirt. He didn't find a body. Bears wouldn't undress a body before dragging it away and the dress looked like the wearer had vanished, not like it had been torn off. All the fastenings were intact. The only sign it belonged to someone from the coach was the bloody hole where the woman's heart would have been.

Dyve had fought in the legions for decades. He'd seen things most people would laugh off as impossible, but looking that dress, his skin crawled. Something he couldn't understand had happened as well as bloody murder.

Back on the road he stood and stared into the distance. Part of him wanted to go back to Stronghaven and hang the guards, but he couldn't be sure they were all involved in the murder. He also needed to bring the news of his failure to the emperor. The timing had been so close.

If he'd stopped in Stronghaven on his way, he'd have collected Lady Robin safely.

Dyve sighed and breathed the same prayer he did over every fallen soldier's grave and mounted his horse. Seth would have to deal with Stronghaven for now. Dyve's first duty was being General Mihone and that meant getting back to his emperor. If the smaller cities were in such bad shape, it would mean spreading the legions thinner to make sure the emperor's rule was felt in every corner of his empire.

***

Lyle stumbled through the ancient battlefield. Not even bones remained of any of the soldiers, but bits of armour and weapons were traps for his feet. He'd heard stories of battle from the guards, mostly repeating stories they'd heard during their training. Willem, the only one who'd seen real action in the north against the clans, didn't talk much about it. His usual comment was that there was nothing to be glorified in battle, only death was victorious.

Lyle began to understand the old man's reticence. If he'd seen this much suffering and death, he wouldn't want to talk about it either.

After walking all morning, Lyle came to a clear spot. In the centre old fashioned armour knelt holding a sword. A familiar force took over Lyle's body. He fought against it, but the battle was short lived. The witch's will made his hand reach out and take the hilt of the sword. He cut his left hand just enough to let a drop of blood fall on the sword.

The armour stood and faced Lyle, then waved at him to attack. Lyle trembled and fell to his knees to vomit. The armour stepped forward, grasped Lyle's throat and tossed him to the edge of the clearing. Even the bears hadn't been so strong. Lyle raised the sword then charged to the attack.

The armour stepped aside as he rushed past. He imagined eyes in the floating helmet narrowed in disappointment, like his father's so many times.

"I don't know how to use a sword." Lyle tried to drop the weapon, but his hand wouldn't let him.

Pieces of the armour floated over and attached themselves to him, finally the helmet settled over his head.

The desolate battlefield came to life. Men strove to kill each other. One charged at him, and his armour forced him to move. The sword slid between a gap in the other's armour and blood poured out. Lyle didn't have time to react as another soldier attacked.

The sun froze in the sky as Lyle fought for his life, but he learned what to do, how to move so more and more it was him, not the armour who brought death to those to challenge him. Exhaustion dragged at his feet, but he got no respite.

Finally he stood alone on the field again. His armour was bloody and battered, the sword notched, and the tip broken off. The armour fell from his body, crumbling into dust as it hit the earth. Lyle opened his hand and the sword fell and shattered. He shuddered and drank from his waterskin until it ran out. It might have been his imagination, but the bread and cheese from his sack didn't taste as stale.

Somewhat refreshed, Lyle walked across the battlefield. On the far edge he found a single sword stuck in the ground. He pulled it out and inspected it. It didn't look like it would break on the first blow, so he carried it along with him.

Chapter 13

Sarge liked the new girl. She was quiet and respectful, doing anything she could to help Serena. Apparently, they were old friends, though from where was a bit fuzzy. The result of Mena's appearance was that she became the one to sit with the dozing Sarge during the meetings with the emperor.

Sarge did notice she became tense while in the room with the emperor. He didn't think it was fear or concern about upsetting him. More like she was restraining herself.

"So how is the work on those war machines coming along." Haffmon pounded the table. "You know how much it is costing me to keep that camp there? The money from those guards is all but gone."

"Word is they are closed to finished." Major Saligar said. "They will be able to put the final touches on them while on the march to the city. We should be in a position to attack in no more than two weeks."

"I want that city back in my control in three weeks. Hang all those slaves, and we'll send the nobles back with quotas of food production." Haffmon banged the table. "Like Sarge said we need to move with deliberation."

"I'm not sure he suggested hanging a city's worth of slaves." Another officer whose name Sarge could never remember spoke up. "That's going to mean replacing the entire population."

"Hang the leaders then. Show them the empire isn't going to put up with them getting above themselves."

"Hostages." Sarge muttered.

"Right." Haffmon pointed at the forgettable officer. "Once you have the city, kill all the hostages too. We won't need them anymore."

Sarge coughed and cursed his inability to say more than a word or two at one time. Haffmon didn't have the patience to wait, and the others toadied up to him so much none of them were interested in anything except doing his bidding, then blaming each other for failures. Maybe the officer whose name he couldn't remember would listen.

"Him." Sarge pointed. "Tea."

Mena patted Sarge on the shoulder.

"What was that?" Haffmon glared in Sarge's direction.

"Sarge gets frustrated because he's so weak. Maybe Major Gregor could join us for tea. Sarge could explain what he means, and Major Gregor could then pass it on to you."

"Why not me?" Haffmon puffed up. "I'm the emperor."

"Exactly, your majesty. You are far too busy to sit down for tea with an old man for an afternoon. And Major Saligar has to run the city."

"Fine then." Haffmon jumped up from his throne. "Report when you're done." He stomped out of the room, probably headed for the bar where he'd do his best to get drunk. Major Saligar eyed Mena doubtfully.

Sarge figured Haffmon didn't have much longer as emperor. Saligar would take over, probably right after capturing Westburg. He already did most of the work. Sarge had to get rid of Saligar before he took over.

Mena lifted him and walked him back to their room. Major Gregor followed reluctantly. Sarge watched him argue against everything Sarge suggested. He wasn't a climber like Saligar, but he was competent, and that had its own risks.

The afternoon passed excruciatingly slowly, but Sarge did get across that the Ancan forces should hold the slave leaders as hostages to control the rest of the population, and that the Fhaydens should be shipped home to avoid upsetting the Calderan kingdom. They were better as failed examples than as martyrs. Sarge couldn't tell if the major agreed with any of it, but he did promise to explain at the next meeting.

Mena and Serena did a good job of taking care of the major without fawning over him. He wasn't a man to be impressed by compliments. The major took his leave politely, and the girls slumped in their chairs.

"At least he doesn't spend most of his time ogling you, Mena." Serena pushed herself up and started clearing the dishes.

"True. He appears to be the rarest of men, one who pays more attention to his duty than a pretty woman." Mena shuddered. "If Haffmon gets drunk enough, he'll be pawing at me again."

"I'm sorry I can't help you with him." Serena hugged herself. "I just can't deal with being close to him.

"It's all right, Serena. I've dealt with worse."

***

Duncan and Maci relaxed in the safe house.

"Bodan will be here soon." Maci poured herself more of the tea Duncan had brewed. "Now that he has a real job, meetings are a pain."

"I don't mind waiting. It gives me a chance to recover from all that walking. It's been a while. We did most of our travelling by wagon."

"Hard to hide a wagon." Maci nodded. "But they do make things more comfortable."

A complicated knock sounded at the door.

"That will be him." Maci jumped up and went to the door, peering through a crack before opening it. "You brought company tonight."

A man walked in with a young woman.

"I'm Commander Themson, from Lady Robin's Thousand. Mena here is one of my agents. Call me Bodan."

"Pleased to meet you, Bodan. Maci has told me a lot about you."

"Only half of it is true." Bodan rolled his eyes and pulled up a chair for Mena. "I'll grab more chairs from the other room.

When they'd all sat down around the small table. Duncan poured what was left of the tea. Mena declined. "I spend all day drinking tea with Sarge."

"It is good luck you being here." Bodan leaned on the table making it creak. "Mena has a report for you to take back to Westburg. She's been helping care for Sarge."

"Physically Sarge is very weak." Mena sighed. "But mentally he's all there. I think he's trying to set up Haffmon for a fall. It turns on Westburg. Haffmon has bet a wagon load of gold on taking the city and controlling trade through it. Major Saligar is ass kissing, but he's probably thinking of offing Haffmon and taking over, but he can't do that until Westburg falls. Major Gregor is the other one jostling for the General position, but Haffmon is keeping that as a carrot. Sarge wonders if Haffmon is able to appoint a General without the bureaucracy's cooperation, and they are still distancing themselves from him. The palace is occupied with rebuilding after the fire. A lot of this is Sarge's speculation. He's been talking to me while Serena is out with her boyfriend."

"Tom is a member of the guard under my command." Bodan grinned. "I've been subtly encouraging him to deepen his relationship with Serena. Mena has said that Sarge would like her out of the inn, so we may come up with a strategy to separate her from Haffmon completely."

"Anyway," Mena leaned forward. "Let me fill you in on the latest plans." She recapped what they'd talked about with Major Gregor. "The major is very skeptical about the siege engines. Says they are too vulnerable to fire. They've also slowed everything down while they're being built. He wants to insert some of the hostages in the camp into the city with instructions to open a gate or have all the other hostages killed. If that works, they don't need the engines."

"So Sarge's plan is to have the siege on the city fail, but will that be enough to destroy Haffmon?"

Duncan leaned back but stopped when the chair complained. "The siege could drag on for weeks, maybe months. We planned on holding the gap until winter closed the invading army's supply lines, but there's no similar time crunch here."

"There may not be a time crunch." Bodan grinned. "But his finances are in terrible shape. He's already spent most of the gold we recovered for him, but that was a one-time thing. There will be no second wagon load of money to bail him out. The palace is giving him nothing. As long as they keep their coffers closed, he's in trouble. He can't afford a long campaign."

"I still don't see them packing up and going home because he ran out of money."

"Was your father ever late paying his men?" Bodan asked.

"Hell no, he'd have had a mutiny on his hands." Duncan laughed. "Right, now I get you. No money, no army, or at least a very unhappy army. I need to get back to Westburg. All this information will make a big difference to how we hold the city."

"You say 'we' like you're one of the plains people." Bodan met his gaze. "Or are the last of the Thousand helping to secure the place?"

"I'm Hob's man." Duncan rubbed his chin. "It's hard to explain, but he is the reason there are people other than the Ancans holding Westburg. He was the spark that freed the plain. They call themselves the Free. I like that. But Marshal Hapten is also part of the equation. They are working together. If the city falls the Fhaydens are done for. If they can repel the Ancan force, then they can turn their eyes toward bringing the people in Ancanopolis home with them."

"Good to hear they haven't forgotten us." Bodan stood and paced around the room. "But disentangling us from Ancanopolis without bringing the whole place down around our ears may be a challenge. We need someone in charge who isn't interested in expansion."

"I will mention that to the Marshal." Duncan nodded.

"Maci, please escort Duncan back to Westburg, and try to keep Sylve out of trouble."

"Right. You know her." Maci laughed.

"Sarge keeps mentioning Lady Robin." Mena said. "Where is she in all this?"

"She headed north. Something about the land calling her. Marshal Hapten's last orders were to get everyone home. We haven't heard anything since Robin left."

"He won't be happy about that." Mena frowned.

"You can tell him Lencely and Rud are doing well, maybe that will help cheer him up." Bodan moved toward the door.

"I will tell him." Mena followed Bodan. "Nice to meet you."

The door closed behind them.

"Looks like we're back on the road in the morning." Maci sighed. "I'd just got used to sleeping in the same bed every night."

"I'll see you in the morning." Duncan shrugged. "I'll find somewhere to sleep. I have some thinking to do."

***

Lyle came out of the forest and found himself on a road. Roaring and screaming came from the south, so he turned that way and jogged along the gravel. It didn't take him long to arrive at a village in turmoil. A huge man wielded a beam like a club, smashing buildings and chasing villagers. Bodies already lay unmoving at the giant's feet.

He couldn't draw his sword dramatically as he'd been carrying it in his hand since he left the battlefield. He shouted and charged along the road into the village. People who were running in his direction swung wide around him, looking as scared of him as of the giant.

By the time he arrived in the square, most of the houses had been wrecked. The giant swung his beam at Lyle who had to roll under it, almost sticking himself with his own sword. Not a great start for a hero. The giant stomped at Lyle, who scrambled away behind the giant.

The oversized man was far too quick for his size. Lyle spent most of his time dodging the beam or the giant's feet. He needed time to think, to come up with a plan. *Who am I kidding? My plan would be to run away.* The witch wouldn't let him run. She made it clear he had to kill the giant or die trying. A test, she'd call it.

None of the things he'd been through prepared him to fight something more than twice his height and faster than him.

His back slammed into a wall as he got away from a kick. The giant swung his club overhead to crush him and the building behind him. Lyle waited until the giant started his downswing and dodged to the side. The beam hit the building, demolishing it and sending dust in all directions.

The giant grunted as he tried to lift the club. The building had collapsed in on it, trapping it for a few seconds. Lyle darted in. The giant tried a half-hearted kick, but Lyle swung his sword instead of dodging. The sword cut into the giant's ankle severing the tendon. Lyle almost died as he stared at the sword. It had been blunt as a club when he picked it up. At the last second, he moved so the giant's hand only brushed him instead of turning him into a pulp.

When Lyle stopped rolling, he jumped up to see the giant leaning on a building. The wounded leg bled profusely. Lyle ran in again, this time using the destroyed buildings as cover. He slashed at the other leg, toppling the giant. It was still a long bloody process to kill the giant, but finally Lyle stood on the giant's chest, sword buried up to the hilt.

"Sorry," he muttered to the corpse. "I guess the witch didn't give you any choice either."

He climbed down from the giant and looked for a way to wash the blood from him, but the entire square was fouled and not one house remained standing.

Lyle staggered out of the village and sat leaning against a tree. The villagers slowly came back and circled him.

"What do we do now?" they asked him.

"I don't know." Lyle leaned his head back. "I was just passing through. Maybe bury the giant?"

"How are we to do that?" A tall man stomped up to him. "It would take an army to bury that creature."

"Then maybe send a messenger and ask for help from the army." Lyle said. "Don't look at me. I'm too tired to do anything."

The man frowned and walked away, followed by the rest of the villagers.

"Not a word of thanks." Lyle muttered and closed his eyes.

Night was falling when he woke up hungry. The sack was empty, as was the water bottle. *Figures.* Lyle tied them to his belt anyway. Even empty they might be useful. He pushed himself up and walked back into the village. The blood dried on him cracked and peeled, making him itch.

The sword was still stuck in the giant. He climbed up and retrieved it. Then without anything else to do, he headed south.

When the road crossed over a creek, he took time to wash himself until no blood stuck to him or his clothes. Then he filled his water bottle upstream. At least he wasn't thirsty anymore.

He hiked until he came on the villagers, camped at the side of the road. They glared at him, so he kept going. The road forked with one going east the other continuing south. Lyle headed east as that road looked slightly better kept in the moonlight.

Lyle bedded down under a tree when the moon set and slept until the sunshine in his eyes woke him. Without anything better to do, he continued east, avoiding the villages with people who stared at him suspiciously.

The farms started looking bigger and richer. At one a dog came out to bark at him. Lyle hid under a bush until a man came and dragged the dog away. As he crawled out, his hand tangled in something. He pulled the something out and stared at the gold chain with a huge red gem hanging from it. Hiding it in the bottom of his sack, Lyle hiked east. That gem would sell for a small fortune. For the first time since the witch sent him on this horrible journey, things were looking up.

When he arrived at the city, the guards arrested him for carrying the sword. They found the gem. Even though he told them it was his, they took it away from him and tossed him in a cell in a small building.

"Those guys at the prison are getting all the good stuff." One guard tossed the gem in his hand as he spoke. "Let's sell this and split the take."

"I don't trust you." The other guard tried to snatch the gem from the first. They fought in the corridor until a third guard walked in and took the gem from them.

"Our division needs to get back in the emperor's good graces." The third one kicked at the two wrestling on the floor. "I'm taking this to the captain."

Lyle leaned against the wall of his cell. He imagined what would happen. This captain would take the gem to his superior until finally it got to the emperor. None of them would remember Lyle. He didn't even have his sword.

"Hey you." A guard with a blackening eye yelled at Lyle. "I'm not spending my coin feeding you. Get out."

"What about my sword?" Lyle asked.

"What sword?" the guard sneered at him.

Lyle left the guard station. No one would believe him about the gem, probably no one would believe him about the giant. He wandered through the city until it grew dark, and he came on a massive building. He wedged himself into a door and tried to sleep.

"You can't sleep here." A man held a lantern up. "You look strong, you want to fight in the games?"

"Does it pay?" Lyle shaded his eyes.

"Win or lose." The man looked around. "I'm trying to put together my own stable of fighters. You want to join me?

"May as well." Lyle followed the man into the night.

***

Lyle expected the fights to be easy after all he'd gone through. He won a few, but never made it to fight in front of the emperor. His trainer, Roph, was happy enough.

The man came in one day raving about how some stranger had killed a giant, then left it behind for the army to clean up. The emperor had been in a rage according to rumour because it meant spending money for soldiers to go to the village. The villagers wanted money to rebuild.

"That's heroes for you. Saving a village, then being blamed for the mess."

"You sound like you know something about it." Roph said.

"Some." Lyle sighed. "I used to dream about being a hero, but it just isn't what the stories make it sound like."

"Poor kid." Roph shook his head. "Apparently, they found the sword in a guard house in the west of the city. No one can move it. One of the villagers says it's the sword. He tried to pull it out of the giant but couldn't budge it."

"You want to go look at the sword?" Lyle couldn't help the spark of hope in his chest. Maybe if he claimed the sword.

"Why not? It's a few days before the next games."

They wound through the city until Lyle recognized the tiny guardhouse.

"This is it."

"You sure?" Roph peered at him.

"Yeah, spent some time here." Lyle led him into the building. A guard with a fancy uniform stood arguing with the two guards who had robbed Lyle.

"You don't remember anything about how this got here?"

"Nope." The guard's black eye had almost faded to nothing.

His buddy spotted Lyle and went pale, he strode up to Lyle. "You can't be here, official business only."

Lyle shoved him against the wall before picking up the sword.

"Blast. The thing's still dull as a butter knife." He sighed and thought about putting it back and walking out.

"The emperor wants to talk to you." The man in the fancy uniform said.

"Sorry, I'm out of here." Roph muttered to Lyle and bolted for the door. Lyle grabbed the guards and shook them. "Leave him alone. It's bad enough you stole from me. Don't be bothering my friend."

"They stole from you?" Fancy uniform frowned. "Maybe a red gem on a gold chain?"

"That would be it." Lyle spat on the floor. "That was going to set me up."

"Let's go." Fancy uniform pointed to the door. "The emperor will olwant to hear your story."

Lyle expected to be taken to the palace, but their coach pulled up in front of an inn.

"Let's go. Be polite, call him your Majesty if you want to stay on his good side. You'll have to put that sword down before we go in."

Lyle leaned the sword against the wall and followed fancy uniform into the inn. A man sat in a big chair. He looked ordinary, except for the glint of the ruby hanging around his neck.

Lyle bowed as best he could. "Your Majesty."

"Who are you?" the emperor pointed at him.

"Your pardon, majesty." Fancy uniform smirked at the emperor. "He's the one who killed the giant and found that gem."

"Oh." The emperor glared at Lyle. "Tell me about the gem. Did the giant have it?"

"Well." Lyle hesitated. *I can hardly tell him I found it under a bush hiding from a dog, can I?* "I took it from the giant. My sword is outside."

"Saligar, go get the sword."

Fancy uniform left the room, to come back a few minutes later. "The sword won't move from where he placed it."

"Really?" The emperor's expression became crafty. "Go invite one of those palace people to visit. Tell them I have the Emperor's Ruby."

"Very well." Saligar bowed and left.

"I hope you like beer, boy," the emperor said, "because I despise tea."

CHAPTER 14

Word got around about Adam's wins in the arena and the village grew in population. Becca organized work bees to make houses around the clearing safe to stay in. They had no more issue with people trying to rob them. Instead, they struggled to feed all the extra people. Not everyone wanted to work, she dragged more than one person out onto the street and dumped them in the dust.

"You don't work, you don't eat." She dusted off her dress and went back to work. The man she'd kicked out of the village rubbed the ear she'd used to haul him away, then slumped.

"Wait." He froze when she turned around to stare at him with her blue eye. He didn't want to work, but he didn't want to go hungry either. "I'll bring some food for you."

"No stealing." Becca crossed her arms. "The merchants aren't here just for your convenience."

He stared at his feet. "It's the only thing I know."

"Then you need to learn something else." Becca didn't budge. He wasn't the first thief to join them. Most didn't last long. Work was hard.

"Okay." He wandered away and she returned to what she'd been doing when she found him sleeping in the tent next to the firepit.

A man would be by to collect the ashes and the pisspots soon. He had a tendency to leer at her, so she didn't like to have him around for long. No one complained that she dealt with him herself.

The collection man came and went, then the thief she'd booted out returned with another man.

"What do you want?" She stomped over to meet them.

"Jorold is the leader of the gang who runs this turf." The thief hid behind Jorold when Becca put her hands on her hips.

"We don't pay protection."

Jorold put his hands up. "Let's not start on the wrong foot. I'm here to ask you to ally with us. We got members with families. Where we hole up isn't safe. We're too close to the Redhawks' turf. I'm hoping wc can move our families closer to you people. Gart here said you don't like thieves. Neither do we."

"Then what do you do?" Becca peered at him with both eyes. He didn't mean trouble, in fact he hoped she could make his life better.

"Mostly we escort merchants who have to come into the broken district. Usually, they're looking at land on the fringes, wanted to build warehouses cheap."

"Protection?" Becca frowned. People offering protection were worse than thieves.

"Not a racket." Jorold put his hands up. "Not since I took over a few months back. That's why the Redhawks are so angry at us, we've driven them off more than once."

"Right." Becca shook her head. "If those merchants decide they like the land, who do they buy it from?"

"Not us." Jorold laughed. "As far as I've seen, they just move in, shove anyone living there out and start building."

"Next merchant you escort, find out from the who owns the land they're buying."

"So you'll help us?" Jorold looked so hopeful, Becca couldn't help but laugh.

"It isn't my decision. I'll talk to Adam tonight. Stop by at supper time." She glanced over at Gart. "You too, I guess. I have a job in mind for you."

***

Becca served up bowls of stew while Adam greeted Jorold and Gart. A few of the people in their village already knew the men and assured Becca they were who they said.

"The streets around here are still dangerous." Adam sat and blew on his food. "Would your gang be interested in walking around the area and keeping it safe? The guards don't come except to train us."

"We wouldn't be able to do that and escort merchants." Jorold shook his head. "We aren't that big a gang. 'Tis why we're hoping we can ally with you. You'd be protecting us."

"Offer the Redhawks the job of escorting the merchants, you set it up and take a cut. They break the deal; they lose easy money and you cut them off." Gart shrugged.

"They're in no better shape than you. No one in this hell hole is."

"Could work." Jorold rubbed his chin. "But trusting them to a sit down is tough. There's bad blood there."

"Invite them here. We'll feed everyone. No weapons, anyone disturbs the peace, they have to deal with me."

"Sounds like a plan." Gart grinned. "I'll take them the message."

"Good." Adam spooned food into his mouth. "Games in two days, so make it for the day after the games. I'll have the day to prepare properly."

"Got it." Gart started on his bowl.

"That reminds me," Becca said. "I have a job I think will suit you, Gart."

He raised an eyebrow but didn't slow his consumption of the stew.

"We need to know what is going on in the neighbourhood. I think you will be good at keeping me informed about what is going on."

"I'm not going anywhere near the bully boys." Gart held up his hand, spoon still clutched in it. "But the rest, sure."

"The bully boys have a good idea of what will happen if they interfere with the games." Becca took a bowl for herself. "Adam's village is important to him. Messing with it will be messing with the games. He is after all, the only fighter to receive a purse from the emperor's own hand."

"I'm sure the bully boys are very aware of that." Gart paled.

Becca was sure Gart was still very connected with the bully boys, but he'd be useful to have around.

***

Adam did well at the games, no purse from the emperor, but he'd won all but the last match against Ulfred. This time he hadn't needed to be carried from the field. The emperor had a new person standing behind him in black armour. Two men in white robes flanked the emperor. They didn't look happy.

On the way back to the village, Adam bought some meat. Enough to make stew for a day or two. Some of the other members of the village also earned coin in the arena or at other jobs, so they had their own shopping lists.

Becca welcomed him with a warm hug and a kiss on the cheek. He was certain she wanted more than that from him, but he didn't know how to bring up the topic. His brothers had told stories, then bragged of their conquests, but Adam didn't get it. He was sure he loved Becca, but not the way the stories described it.

He put the question aside while he prepared and cooked the meat, then readied the stew for the evening meal. Full dark hadn't come when he declared it ready. The days were getting longer. Soon it would be too dry for a lot of the plants they foraged. Maybe they could plant a garden, but that would mean watering it, and so, much hauling water from the well.

Becca sat beside him, and without visitors, she snuggled up to him. He enjoyed the warmth both from her body, and from his heart. His life wasn't anything like gramma's stories, but he was more content in his little village than in a throne in a palace. At least he thought so, he'd never sat on a throne, but he imagined it would be lonely.

Becca dragged him to their tent before it got too late. He had a rest day on the morrow, but her work never stopped. She lay next to him, arms wrapped around him, tonight she stretched over and kissed him on the lips.

"Have you ever thought about having children?" She buried her face in his neck.

"Not really." Adam held her tighter. "Do you want some?"

"If you're willing." Heat from her face reached through his shirt.

He rolled on his side so he could see her face. She lowered her face, but he lifted her chin with a finger.

"I would do anything for you, Becca." Adam closed his eyes as he struggled with words. "I would die for you, so if you want children..." he trailed off then took a deep breath. "I just don't really know what to do. My brothers explained it in detail, but it never made sense to me."

"I don't know either." Becca barely spoke above a whisper. "Maybe we can learn together?" She kissed his lips. Adam opened his eyes and met her gaze. Her tears dampened his cheek, so he brushed them away, then tried kissing her. It was weird, but he could get used to it.

He woke in the morning tangled in Becca's arms and legs and smiled. He had some thinking to do, but the talk with Becca had helped. He didn't need to get up right away, so he did his thinking waiting for Becca to wake up.

When she opened her eyes, he grinned and kissed her nose.

"Before we get up and start work for the day, I have a question." She tilted her head, he'd got used to her looking through each of her eyes.

"Okay, ask." She made no attempt to separate from him.

"In all the stories gramma told me, the hero married the princess." Adam took a deep breath. "I know I'm far from being a hero, but would you marry me? Then we can work on children together."

Of all the reactions he was expecting, it wasn't laughter. It started with a bitter edge to it, but mellowed quickly and she pulled him tighter. Adam waited for the laughter to finish. Becca would explain if she wanted to.

"Ever since I was little," Becca whispered into his ear, "I've been told that is one question I would never hear. My father said I was too ugly, and no one would take me. You looked at me the first time and saw me. You called me a princess. As ridiculous as it was, that changed my life. You are my hero, and I love you. I will marry you, Adam. We can ask Gart tonight if there is a priest or magistrate to wed us."

"I love you too." Adam moved her head so he could kiss her. "I promise someday to build you a castle to live in."

"I don't need a castle if I have you."

Reluctantly Adam rolled on his back. "I have work to do if we are going to entertain guests."

"Me too." Becca took his hand and squeezed it. "I'm happier than I ever have been."

"I'm glad." Adam sat up and caressed her cheek.

The day went quickly, but Becca found excuses to be near him and bump into him. Then he saw her over talking to one of the women taking care of the younger children. She looked over at him and he waved at her. She turned red and waved back.

Gart led three men and one woman into the village in the late afternoon. Jorold followed soon after with a woman he held hands with and an older man. He walked straight over to Gart. Adam went over and joined them.

"Greetings, I'm happy you have come to speak with me in peace." Jorold said.

"I still limp from that bruise you gave me with your club." One man scanned Jorold, then glanced at the woman, still holding his hand. "I'm glad you trust us enough to bring your woman to the talk."

"I want to introduce her to Adam."

"I'm curious about Adam. From what I've heard he should be a huge man."

"I'm Adam. Glad you came." Adam laughed at the expressions on the people.

"I'm Zeke, leader of the Redhawks."

"Welcome, Zeke, and your companions. We will have proper introductions at the fire."

Adam led them to where they'd set up seat in a semicircle around the fire with their biggest pot set warming on the side. "Please sit, we haven't much more than water to drink, but there is plenty to eat."

Jorold pulled out a flask, but the woman stopped him.

"Not until after we talk."

"Whatever you say, Liza." Jorold smiled and put it away. Zeke had also taken out a flask but followed Jorold's example.

"What are you looking for?" Zeke leaned forward. "Free food is always good, but there has to be a catch."

"You are our guests." Adam frowned. "We will feed you whatever you decide unless you start fighting. Then Becca will toss you out on your ear."

"Believe him." Gart laughed.

Becca served up bowls of stew and handed them out. A young man followed her with a basket of bread. The visitors ate heartily, dipping chunks of bread in the strew. Jorold and Zeke chatted like they weren't enemies. The women also talked with Becca about things Adam couldn't follow. There was a lot of laughter, so they were enjoying themselves.

Adam watched as the village came by to get their food. They were almost to the point they needed another fire and stew pot. Some of the women who helped him cook offered to cook at the second fire. In some of the stories his gramma told him there were armies who had mess tents. Maybe that would work.

"So you want to start your own guard force." Zeke interrupted Adam's thoughts.

"I guess so." Adam nodded. "I hadn't thought about it that way. With the village getting bigger, we need to keep the dangerous elements away."

"It's a good idea." Zeke nodded. "I think we may do something similar on our turf. We want it safe, but not so safe that the merchants won't hire us."

"Speaking of merchants." Adam sopped up broth with his bread. Becca took his bowl and refilled it. "Do you know how they know who to buy land from?"

"Far as I know, the palace owns any land without people living on it. Clear the people out and you can buy the land from the palace."

"Not the emperor?" Jorold held his bowl out for a refill.

"He's the emperor, and not the emperor." Zeke leaned forward and lowered his voice. "He owns the guards and he's popular enough with the people, but the palace won't give him anything. Something about not having the emperor gem. I think they just don't like him. He was involved with that cursed sword before he tried to take Westburg. The priests have a lot of pull with the palace."

"How do you find a priest to get married?" Adam asked. Becca turned pink.

"You don't need a priest unless you're a noble." The old man who came with Jorold waved his hand. "They cost a lot of money. You want to get married; this is what you do. Get a broom. Hold hands and ask each other if you want to be married. If you agree, just jump over the broom holding hands. Done. That's what Jorold and Liza did."

Becca disappeared while the people around laughed. Adam didn't mind. These were possibly new friends. By the time Becca came back with a broom made from a stick with twigs tied to it, the entire village had gathered around. He hadn't seen them all in a group for a while and there were more than he expected.

"It's good luck to have lots of people watching." Liza took Jorold's hand, and he smiled at her.

"We only had a few witnesses." Jorold stood up and pulled her to her feet. "Let's show them how it's done.

Becca put the broom on the ground and Liza and Jorold looked in each other's eyes.

"Do you wish to wed?" They spoke together, then laughed and jumped over the broom. The crowd cheered.

Adam stood and walked over to Becca. Part of him listened to the calls and advice from the crowd, but most of him was looking at Becca. He took her hand and looked into her blue eye.

"Do you wish to wed?"

"I do." Becca squeezed his hand. "Do you wish to wed me?"

"I do." Adam gave her a quick kiss.

They jumped over the broom, and the cheering just about deafened him. Becca wrapped her arms around him and held him tight. They held onto each other for a long few breaths. Then the people came and slapped their backs and offered hugs. Some of the women had tears in their eyes.

Jorold offered Adam his flask. "A drink to celebrate."

The liquid burned on the way down and warmed him to his toes.

"Thanks." Adam squeaked out.

The night became a celebration of the new couple. Zeke and Jorold apparently had settled everything they needed to, since they joined in the festivities with no hesitation.

Late in the night, the guests, now friends, left to go home. They walked together, not just for safety but to continue to plan.

When Adam and Becca finally crawled into their tent, Adam was tired beyond anything he could remember. Maybe it had something to do with the sips from Jorold's flask.

Instead of lying down on their mat, Becca undressed. He couldn't see much but shadows, but he'd helped her wash at the buckets, so he had some idea of what she looked like.

"Your turn." Becca sat beside him.

Adam stripped and put his clothes at the side of the tent with Becca's dress.

"I asked one of the mothers what we need to do to have a child. I'll explain it to you."

None of it made much sense to Adam, but all of it made Becca happy, so when they were done, he was content.

***

When Adam went to train in the morning, his friends told Lencely and the other trainers about the night before.

"Congratulations." Lencely slapped Adam's back. Rud and Daggins shook his hand. That was it before they started training. If anything, they worked Adam harder than usual. He sparred against Ulfred, who kept up a running stream of advice on fighting.

At the end of the day instead of dismissing everyone as he usually did. Lencely waved over Becca and the children and women who'd come to watch the training.

"You are like their lord." Lencely pointed to the crowd. "Take care of them, and that means taking care of yourself too. You can't rule from weakness. My father taught me that. It took a while for what he meant to sink it. Be strong so you can love the people you watch over." He handed Adam a handful of copper coins. "Buy your lovely wife a treat. Whatever she asks for."

Adam put the coins in his purse and grinned at Becca. "Let's go shopping."

Of course, the entire crowd of women and children had to tag along.

Adam wandered through the tiny market near the edge of what they called the broken district as Becca looked at each booth. He expected her to get fabric for a dress, or maybe jewellery. She stopped at the jeweller's booth and examined the contents all of it old and worn. She picked out a men's ring and handed it to him.

"A lord needs a ring." She slipped it on his finger. It fit like it had been made for him. "I'll hold it while you are training and fighting, but I want you to wear it the rest of the time."

"If I have to wear something as a lord, then you need to wear something as my princess." He scanned the table and saw a necklace with a red stone. "Here." He put it around her neck. "The emperor's own gem couldn't look any better on you."

The owner of the booth cleared his throat and put his hand out. "That will be three silvers for each."

Adam looked in his purse and started counting out the coppers, then at the bottom a bit of gold glinted at him. Surely Lencely hadn't given him gold along the copper? Adam shook his head, but the merchant still stood with his hand out.

"Here." Adam handed him the gold coin. The merchant's eyes bulged. "A friend gave it to me to celebrate my marriage."

"I don't have change for this." The merchant's hand closed around the coin as he scanned the crowd.

"You can owe it to me." Adam smiled at him. "Until you've paid it off, you're under my protection."

People murmured, and he realized there was a much bigger crowd than his own people.

"You're the one who runs the village," someone said.

"I am." Adam straightened his shoulders and looked around the crowd. "I take care of my friends."

"We want to be part of your village." Two women came up to him, then others, most of them looked like they worked in brothels.

"Ye can't be stealing my women." A man in mismatched finery stomped over to Adam. "You take my women, I'll be shutting down your new friend."

Adam punched the man in the gut.

"It isn't wise to threaten my friends."

Other men stepped out of the crowd. The merchant handed Adam a club, then frantically packed up his wares.

"Only four of you?" Adam found himself speaking words he hadn't planned. "How brave of you. Becca, if you and our friends could stand back, I don't want to get blood on you."

"How sweet." The first man pulled a knife from his boot and slashed at Adam. Adam stepped out of range of the knife, then lunged in, bringing the club down on the man's head with a crunch. He swivelled to face the next one, kicking out to catch the man's knee. The man went down screaming. The last two charged at the same time, one holding a club, the other a rusty sword.

A rock hit the man with the sword, and he staggered back. Adam brushed aside the club from the other man, then drove the end of his weapon into the man's throat. The man fell back gurgling. More rocks hit the swordsman and he dropped his weapon and fled.

"Who runs this turf?" Adam asked one of the women.

"Paolo." The woman kicked the overdressed man lying on the ground. "Looks like there is an opening at the top."

"I will need to talk to Jorold and Zeke." Adam said as Becca enveloped him in a hug. "But I can see it isn't safe for you here. I will need to arrange for people to patrol the market and keep it safe. In the meantime, stay together. You're stronger as a group."

The woman who had approached him first dropped a rock. "We will do as you say, Adam."

Adam scanned the market and most of the merchants had packed up and left. "I'll return the club next time I see the jeweller."

***

Adam stayed up to keep watch at his village that night with a few of the other trainees. When six men swaggered down the road smacking their hands with their clubs, they were met by grim faced trainees.

"Adam, you stay back. Let someone else have a turn." Darri stepped between him and the men. The others followed, making a wall between the village and the invaders.

"Kids, what can they do?" The man who had fled with the sword sneered, but he waved the others ahead of him.

The other men edged around him and stalked toward the line egging each other on.

A shrill whistle cut through the air, freezing the men on the spot.

"Sorry to be late to the party." Jorold's voice floated through the night. "But I had to let the Redhawks know what was happening. You idiots are hardly subtle."

"We've got you cut off. There's no escape." Zeke walked out of the shadows to stand beside Adam. "You know, you should have sent us a message. We would have made sure they didn't get this far."

"Sorry, I didn't think of it." Adam shrugged. "Let's get them to talk." He strolled through the line of defenders. "Stay with me and keep alert."

The men bunched together. "You aren't taking us down without a fight."

Adam stopped. "Not interested in fighting. I have a message for your boss. I'd like to talk with them. We'll meet in the training arena. Tomorrow, after training is done. They can bring a few people, if they start a fight, they won't make it out of my turf alive. I'd like to negotiate a peace between here and the emperor's arena. I shop at that market a lot on my way home."

"And if we decide just to wipe you out?" the man with the sword sneered.

"You're welcome to try." Adam said. "I will be inviting the Kraog to the meeting. They might not be as ready as you are to start a war."

"We'll just go home and teach a few people that we're the boss." Swordsman hefted his sword. "Blood on the cobbles is a great instructor."

"I haven't said you're going home." Adam walked toward the man. "I don't like people threatening my friends. Drop the sword and I might let you live until the meeting tomorrow."

The man shouted and charged at Adam. Darri jumped forward, rolling under his sword and tripping him. She picked up the weapon and sat on him. "Terrible sword. The ones at the arena are sharper, and they're supposed to be dull." The man squirmed under her, and she thumped him with the hilt of the sword until he stopped moving.

"Who's next?" Adam crossed his arms. "You're keeping me from my new wife."

The other men dropped their weapons and fell on their knees.

"We don't want to go back,' one said. "The boss will kill us for failing."

The others started saying the same thing.

"I need someone to carry the message."

"I'll get Gart to carry it in the morning." Zeke said. "I'll pass the word to the Kraog."

"While he's there, ask him to see if anyone's been hurt." Adam put his hands on his hips. "Jorold can you take care of these for me? I don't want them in my village, but maybe you can make something out of them."

"If you say so." Jorold strolled onto the street and stared at the men quivering on the street. "Okay, you heard Adam. On your feet, you're coming with me. Better pick up the sleeping one." He offered Darri a hand. "Good work, girl. I'll bet on you next time you fight."

"You want the sword?" Darri held it up.

"Nah, you won it fair and square."

Darri waved the sword at Adam. "Do you think Lencely will let me keep it?"

"If you promise to run through the drills with it." Adam smiled at her. "Now that things are quiet again, I'm going to bed."

"I'll keep watch." Darri wiggled the sword in her hand. "It really is awful." She grinned at him.

Adam crawled into his tent and undressed. Becca snuggled up against him and he fell asleep.

Chapter 15

Adam walked to the training arena with Darri hugging her new sword. Somehow, he'd made everything between the village and the training arena safe. If he made this deal, he'd control a large portion of the broken city.

Kraog controlled a swath to the south of his village. A lot of that turf was outside the broken city where he was building his village. If they agreed to leave him alone, maybe he could pay them to watch the borders. There were still people who thought that lives in the broken city were worthless and came to murder for sport. He'd lost a couple of people to that, even with Jorold and Zeke's groups patrolling.

Adam made it through training, but Darri thumped him a few times for being distracted during sparing.

"You're the boss, but here, you're just my opponent." She stuck her tongue out at him. Darri was a lot younger than Becca, but almost as protective. "You doze off in the games, you'll be done."

"You're right." Adam shook himself. "Let's go another round and see if you can land something on me when I'm awake.

"There are a lot of people around." Lencely said to Adam after they'd finished training.

"I called a meeting here." Adam shrugged. "It felt like a safe neutral space."

"You need any back up?" Lencely frowned.

"Don't think so." Adam looked around. "Come by the village tomorrow and I'll tell you about it. Bring Rud and Daggins too, they haven't seen the place in a while."

"Sounds good." Lencely grinned and walked away.

Adam sat in the sand with Darri and a few other trainees who refused to leave. Becca waved and led the women and children away with her.

A man walked out onto the dirt with a pair of big men flanking him.

"You Adam?" He peered down like Adam was a bug.

Adam stood. "That's me."

"What's stopping me from killing you right now?"

"There are people watching." Adam waved them in. "You may be tough, but I have twenty people hoping you make a move. You aren't very popular."

The man laughed. "My guys are worth ten of..."

Ulfred walked back into the arena. "I saw all the muscle around and had to stick around in case there was a fight."

"You work for me," the man said.

"Not anymore. The fights pay me better. My family lives in the village now, they're out of your reach."

"Nowhere is out of my reach."

"The men you sent last night send their regrets." Jorold joined Adam. "They quit. That little girl beat the crap out of the first one, the rest folded and begged for their lives."

"I'm no little girl." Darri glared at Jorold.

"Sorry." Jorold winked at her. She huffed and laid the sword on her shoulder.

"Hi Koan." Kraog walked over. "Sorry to be late. Zeke has the Redhawks working the perimeter. If you value your men, you'll order them to step onto the dirt. My boys are trying to restrain him, but you know how much he hates you."

"What is this?" Koan sputtered. "I run everything between here and emperor's arena."

"That's what I wanted to talk about." Adam crossed his arms. "We shop at the market on the edge of the broken city. It seems a lot of the people there don't feel safe."

"So what?" Koan sneered, he moved to step into Adam's space, but his bodyguards held him back.

"I have space for them to live around here. It might be rough to run a turf if no one lives there."

"You can't get through my turf without passing me. Accidents happen." Koan growled.

"About that." Gart joined them. "Good to see you, boss."

"Thanks for carrying my message." Adam nodded at the man.

"Sorry, what was I saying? Oh right. The bully boys attacked one of the emperor's fighters. His guards trashed all their hidey holes, including where they kept all their money. The guard gave it to the emperor as a gift. Said it was a refund for the bully boys not staying properly bribed. I heard it took two horses and twenty men pushing to keep the wagon moving it held so much gold. They didn't even bother with the copper. You may have enough muscle to take on Adam, but the guards will make you very, very dead. They aren't as forgiving as Adam here."

"It is my territory; the bully boys will back me up."

"No, they won't." Gart brushed some dirt from his shirt. "That's what I just said. They will do nothing against the emperor. Nothing. Attacking Adam is out. You're on your own."

"I'm done here." Koan turned and stomped away. "Stay out of my territory if you want to stay alive, if you bother me, then some of your friends will start dying."

"I can't allow that." Adam shook his head. "I was hoping I could negotiate something with you but that is impossible." He waved his hand.

"You going to attack me here? You think you can get away with that? I have friends in the guards." Koan ignored his guards and got into Adam's face.

"I'm not a murderer." Adam met Koan's gaze. Koan's knife ground against the armour under Adam's shirt. "Though it does appear that you are. I borrowed the armour from the men I didn't kill last night. It appears they told Zeke a lot about you."

Darri's sword crashed on Koan's shoulder and he collapsed, dropping the knife in the dirt.

"Get them." Koan hissed.

"Are you kidding?" The bodyguards stepped back hands up. "You don't pay us enough to commit suicide for you." One grabbed Koan's head and snapped his neck. "I never did like you."

"We will follow your orders." The other guard said. "I'm getting tired of being the one to beat people up. I'm getting old, maybe it's time to retire."

"Runners are headed to the market, they will tell anyone who wants to settle near here, is welcome, as long as they obey the rules."

"The brothel girls too?" the other guard asked.

"Anyone." Adam said. "I can have people help clear space and make houses safe to live in."

"Madame Carsti will probably take over the territory. Someone has to run it."

"That's fine." Adam sighed. "I don't want to run the city, just build a place where my friends will be safe."

***

Adam walked to the market with Becca.

"We really need another stew pot." Becca said. "With the way we've been growing we'll need to be able to cook more food all at once."

The market had grown. While many people had moved closer to Adam's village, others had come in to replace them.

"Hey, Adam." One of the brothel women came over to him. "When are you going to come a visit us?"

"Never." Becca bared her teeth at the woman.

"Sorry, I didn't mean like that." The woman laughed. "You two are a legendary couple. No one would dare get between you. But you can stop in for tea and meet Madame."

"Do we have time?" Adam looked over at Becca.

"Might as well let the new cooks do their work." Becca shrugged and waved over a young man. "I have some things I need delivered to the village. I'll pay two coppers."

They bought a pot and filled it with food. The young man needed to get help from a friend, but they carried the pot away.

"Aren't you worried that it won't make it there?" the brothel woman asked.

"I know their mother." Becca smiled. "It will get there with nothing but a bit of bread missing."

"Very good. Follow me." The woman started along the street, looking back over her shoulder. "You can call me Rose."

The brothel didn't look any different from the buildings around it. The big man at the door saluted Adam.

"Welcome, Adam, and Lady Becca. This is much better work for me."

Becca blushed as they passed the man and entered the house. The women clustered around them.

"Adam, we're so happy to see you."

"Lady Becca, what a pleasure to have you visit." One of the younger women led them through a curtained door and set them at a table. "Please sit. Madame will be with you soon."

A boy brought a tray with a teapot and cups. He carefully put his burden on the table, then ran off.

"Ah, you've met my grandson." A woman walked in to sit across from them. "A pleasure to meet the people who have made my life so much easier." She poured tea for them and slid honey and cream over.

"This isn't what I expected." Becca looked at Madame tilting her head to see through both eyes.

"And tell me, what do you see through those eyes of yours?"

"You are genuinely pleased to have us here." Becca picked up her tea. "And the women are happy here. You are still a dangerous woman."

"I am, and so are you, my dear." Madame also picked up a cup and sipped at it. "One of the emperor's kitchen staff used to visit regularly before the fire and everything fell apart. This is the last of the tea he gave me."

"He's the father of your grandson?" Becca also sipped her tea.

"You are perceptive. Sadly, I don't know if he's alive or dead. My daughter married another man, but he didn't want her son."

"I wouldn't leave my son for any man." Becca frowned.

"Everyone has a sad story." Madame sighed. "You are making the city safer again, so we are getting more customers. I feel I owe you something."

"Spend it on your women." Adam glanced at Becca. "They deserve a treat once in a while for no reason."

"I can see why Becca is so taken with you." Madame smiled. "You both are always welcome here. There may come a day when we can help you as you've helped us."

"I'm happy to be friends."

Madame and Becca talked more, mostly about children. Adam sat back and enjoyed listening. Madame reminded him in some ways of his gramma.

On their way home, Becca held his hand and hummed to herself.

***

Adam made it to the last fight before the emperor. Ulfred had been defeated by the man in the black armour. The judges announced him as the emperor's champion.

He faced the champion. The face inside the helmet looked ordinary enough, except for something in the man's eyes.

"Adam." The emperor spoke. Adam recovered quickly from his shock to kneel properly. The man in the black stood motionless. "I hear you are organizing the broken city."

"I am trying to keep my friends safe." Adam's palm sweated. He didn't like this talking to the emperor.

"You might be a good soldier in my army." The emperor drawled.

"I wouldn't be a very good soldier." Adam replied. "Let me keep the city safe so you can use your soldiers for other things."

"You are saying you can keep my city safe while the guards are away?"

"Not the entire city, but the part that the guards don't like." Adam lowered his head farther.

"Maybe that is enough." The emperor sounded doubtful.

"I will do my best for my emperor." Adam said.

"Fight my champion. If you win, I will give you any one thing you want. Lose and you will owe me your life."

Adam stood and looked up at the emperor. The man had his hand around a huge ruby. Adam's eyes widened, but he couldn't say anything but "As you command."

As he faced his opponent, the invisible control on Adam didn't fade. He could dodge and parry, but each time he tried to strike, his arms froze. Adam gave up on attack and tried to lure the champion out of the ring, but the invisible hand forced him back to the centre.

The champion's face stayed eerily calm, as if he didn't care how the match went, or he already knew the outcome.

"Are you being controlled too?" Adam asked the champion, but the man made no reply. Maybe he couldn't.

The most frustrating thing was that the champion's attacks were nothing special. He moved slowly, his footwork was a mess, half a dozen times if Adam had been able to attack, he could have landed a solid blow. The whole time the emperor held that gem. The ruby that should have been around Becca's neck.

"Why do you mock me?" the champion finally spoke.

"I can't fight properly with the emperor's hand on that ruby." Adam threw his sword down and shouted in rage he couldn't remember ever feeling before.

"What makes you think that?" The champion frowned and aimed a wicked cut at Adam. Adam stepped away. "You're lying."

"Why would I lie?" Adam growled. "Your emperor is a thief and a cheat." He turned his back on the champion, and waited for the blow to land.

"Your Majesty." The champion said. "He refuses to fight. The match is over."

"Strike him down." The emperor shouted.

The crowd erupted in boos. They stomped their feet. Guards who tried to stop them were knocked down and stripped of armour and weapons.

"We must get you to safety." Guards gathered around the emperor.

"My people." Adam held his arms up. "Peace. Wait for the blow to fall before you rage."

The arena went deadly quiet.

"I will keep my friends safe." Adam turned to face the emperor. "They will not revolt, but I will not fight again. I won't risk their lives for coin. Go fight your war. The city will be here when you're done." Adam walked out of the arena, all the time his shoulder itched waiting for the arrow or bolt to strike him.

"Let's get you out of here." Lencely rushed Adam to the door. "I thought there was going to be a riot."

"We can't win as long as he has that ruby." Adam punched the wall. "That champion of his must have found it and given it to him."

"I'll let the commander know." Lencely said. "You get yourself back where you're safe."

Adam marched out into the street and was immediately mobbed. He wasn't afraid. These were his people, his friends. They swept him along the streets until they reached the broken city.

"We'll rise up when the emperor goes with his army." Darri tugged at Adam's shirt.

"He won't go with his army. He'll send people off to die for him. The only thing we can do is protect ourselves." Adam took Becca's hand. "I said I would keep his city safe, but not for him. That ruby is the key."

***

Lencely stood at rigid attention while Commander Themson raged.

"That damn stone. It changes everything. We aren't up against a few underfunded guards, but the entire Ancan army. They'll be calling up the reserves to throw at Westburg."

"Didn't a lot of the army give their parole not to fight against us again?" Rud asked.

"Against us. It doesn't do any good when they're fighting against the Free and what's left of our people. And your friend Adam showed Haffmon the extent of his influence. Haffmon isn't going to allow that to go unanswered. With money from the palace, he'll be able to subdue the city and bring it all under his control."

"Will he do that before he sends out the army?" Lencely asked. "It would be like fighting a war on two fronts. He needs to deal with Westburg, then with the city."

"You're right, but the slightest sign of trouble and he'll order a blood bath. The people with Adam aren't the tax paying ordinary citizens, they are the marginal, best forgotten ones. The citizens may sympathize with Adam, but they won't risk their lives for him."

"Haffmon will move to the palace as soon as it is in good enough repair." Commander Themson stopped. "The palace will need more labour. What if Adam's people took work at the palace? They could learn the layout of the new place. It would be helpful if it came to a straight up fight in the streets."

"I'll talk to him." Lencely relaxed slightly.

"No good, Haffmon will be angry with us as the people who trained Adam. I'm sure we'll be watched at best, but probably we'll be split up into other divisions so the brass can keep a better eye on us."

"Maybe it's time to stop being guards." Daggins leaned against the wall. "That being at attention thing is tiring. Don't know how you do it."

"If we leave, we're deserters." Rud relaxed as well. "They'll hunt us down."

"Only we don't properly exist." Daggins said. "We're guards because we wear the uniform and say we're guards and act like guards. If we take off the uniform and stop acting like guards, how are they going to find us?"

"Daggins is right." Commander Themson rubbed his temples, "But I'm reluctant to hang out the guards who do have families and histories."

"Order them transferred to other divisions." Lencely sighed and leaned against the desk. "The brass will probably order it anyway. Send them off tonight, then we put on civvies and vanish into the broken city. I'm sure Adam would appreciate any help we gave him.

"We don't have time to write up orders for everyone." Commander Themson shook his head. "Send them home. Tell them our division is in deep trouble with the emperor. They are to report tomorrow with the expectation of being transferred to a new command. I will talk to our people and send some out to catch the folks on patrol. We need to empty the prison of our people too. Get on it, boys. We don't know when Saligar is going to show up with his guards to transfer us by force."

Lencely ran to the barracks.

"Bad news," he shouted. "The commander is sure the emperor is going to be angry at us for the near riot at the arena. Everyone is to go home. Turn up tomorrow ready to be transferred to a new division. You don't want to be here when he shows up angry."

The barracks emptied quickly of Ancans. The Fhayden guards dragged their feet until they were alone.

"Ditch the uniforms" Lencely ordered them. "Keep your weapons and anything else you think might be useful. We're pulling a vanishing act."

With the ones who sat in cells for show, there were about a hundred Fhaydens, twenty of them out on patrol. Commander Themson ordered a few people to make contact with the patrolling guards and give them orders.

Within an hour of the decision, Lencely led twenty-five guards, now dressed in nondescript clothes into the broken city. They'd raided the armoury, so each guard carried a bag with weapons and armour. Rud and Daggins led two other groups on different paths. Commander Themson had gone with the people sent out to make contact with their people on patrol. He was confident he could lead them into the broken city after hearing all the reports from Lencely's squad.

***

Once Bodan had found all the people out in the city, he returned to the prison. Saligar's men already crawled through it like ants. Their shouting gave him a picture of the chaos in the prison. Bodan watched until morning when the Ancan guards returned. Saligar tore a strip off them, demoted them and set them to the worst areas of the city to patrol. Bodan heaved a sigh of relief when Tom wasn't singled out. The kid was a bit of an ass, but he didn't deserve death.

Bodan headed into the broken city, following the route Lencely described. He found the training arena easily enough. The other Fhayden had already set up a rough camp.

"Any trouble?" Lencely appeared beside Bodan.

"No, the brass were furious that guards had let us pull the wool over their eyes, but no one was singled out. Maybe when Saligar cools down he may wonder, but a hundred people and their families is going to take a lot of resources to watch. Likely they will find themselves on the front lines of the battle for the city."

"We need to get Tom out of the way." Lencely said. "He can put Serena and Mena in danger, and if they figure out we've been using him, they'll guess we know their plans."

"What are you thinking?" Bodan asked.

"We grab him. Make it public, like someone has a beef against him."

"Make it happen, but no plans to rescue Sarge, they'll be looking for that." Bodan sighed at Lencely's mutinous frown. "He's safe enough for the moment, even in the palace. We wait until the time is right."

"And when will that be?" Lencely groaned.

"When making a move won't get us all killed." Bodan waved his hand in dismissal before he gave in and did something stupid.

CHAPTER 16

Robin had no idea how long she walked through the darkness. She didn't get tired, thirsty, or hungry. The only proof she had of her existence was the tug that pulled her. It gradually strengthened until she could see light ahead of her.

What was she doing? Sarge would be mad at her. She'd forgotten his teaching and got herself killed. He'd always told her to think ahead, plan for the worst.

After more endless walking, she arrived at a tree. Though to call it a tree did it an injustice. It loomed over her like a mountain. The faint glow of its leaves vanished above her. The trunk took her more than a count of a hundred to walk around. She had to scramble over roots taller than her on her way. The thick ridges in the bark made it easy to climb.

When she arrived back at where she'd started, Robin looked around. There was no other light breaking the darkness. She craned her neck and wondered how tall it was. She'd climbed enough trees as a child. Her mom used to say she was like a squirrel. Robin dug fingers and toes into the rough bark and started up. It distracted her from her failure.

Like with the walking she didn't get tired. Climbing was at least different than walking. The branches when she reached them were immense. She stopped on the first one to look out over the darkness, but she could still see nothing. The branch swept away farther than she could see. Robin kept climbing.

The branches came more often. Some of them almost as big as the trunk, others tiny in comparison. Robin came on one that had broken off. She'd seen no sign of its wreckage on the ground.

The longer she climbed the more she expected the trunk to thin, but still looked like a flat wall and her an insect on it. The light grew brighter as she passed more branches, on some of them she could make out other branches splitting off them.

One branch had leaves she could see, so she walked along the branch weaving around the smaller limbs extending from it until she reached one where the leaves looked close enough to touch. The bark on this limb wasn't as gnarled and rough, but she still had no problems climbing it. She reached something of a cup made by branches that reached out in different directions. Robin walked around trailing her hand against each branch until a thrum ran through her. She climbed that branch until the leaves surrounded her. Putting her hand on the leaf sent a thrill up her arm and she heard a thought from someone gathering firewood. They were looking forward to the warmth of the fire and the company of the one they loved. Robin moved on touching leaves here and there. She found a leaf that crackled under her touch. The thoughts were of being tired, but content. Life had been good. Robin rubbed a tear from her cheek and kept climbing.

Now she paid more attention to the leaves. Some were soft as velvet, others rough, and even thorny. She wondered what her leaf would be like.

In the distance a leaf glowed a bit stronger than its neighbours. Robin climbed over to it and put her hand on it.

Robin She almost fell from the shock. Robin gripped the branch tighter and put her hand on the leaf again.

Robin, must live to see Robin. In all this huge tree, had she found Sarge's leaf?

I'm here Sarge. She thought to the leaf.

You're alive?" Relief washed through her.

"I think so." Robin spoke out loud. "I'm in a strange place."

I wanted to see you again, but I don't know if I have the strength.

Sorrow ran through her.

The new emperor here is greedy and vile. I've been trying to stop him, but I failed. It's up to you now.

History ran through her mind. Emperors of countries she'd never heard of, why some lived and some failed. Bloody wars fought over a throne that echoes through centuries of darkness. Robin wept at the enormity of the possibilities. Even her friends in Caldera weren't safe. As she thought of them leaves far away glowed brighter. Maybe... Robin concentrated on the tug that had brought her north. The man who had been emperor. She spotted a leaf in the opposite direction to the ones in Caldera.

It took a while for her to reach it. She had to climb down to the cup and climb a different branch. Now she was impatient to arrive, so the journey had length, but she reached the leaf and put a hand on it. The man was only thinking of how much he loved the woman with him. Robin yanked her hand away. Maybe if she climbed higher a place would appear that would let her back into the world. She had work to do. She wouldn't become fae like the forest wanted her, but power was a weapon too, and she would need everything she could find to follow Sarge's commands.

Robin moved with purpose now. Not impatient, but determined. She reached the end of the branch where a leaf dangled. The branch had become thin enough to move beneath her weight. She shimmied up the branch to where she could almost touch the leaf. The movements of the branch warned her not to go any farther, but the leaf tormented her with its closeness. She stretched out her hand and as she fell her hand brushed it.

***

Robin screamed before she realized she lay on the floor of a cave. The old man huddled over a cauldron.

"So you made it." He ladled some of the contents of the cauldron into a bowl and handed it to her. She took a sip, and it burned all the way through her. Lines of red, green and gold coiled over her skin each one telling her a story.

"There are clothes in the corner." The old man pointed with the ladle.

Robin drank more of the soup, if that is what it was. She'd been naked for however long in his cave. A few more minutes wouldn't matter. Her heart measured time. She breathed in smoke from the fire and herbs cast into it. Her stomach rumbled with hunger, and she laughed.

Once she'd had a few bowls and didn't feel so empty, Robin took a proper look at herself. She was still herself, small, pale, black hair. Scars ran along her skin. One pockmarked the skin over her heart. A matching scar would be on her back.

The clothes in the corner turned out to be a sample of every kind of clothing that could be worn. Robin picked through them, settling on a green dress that felt like the softest of the leaves she'd touched. It fit her like it had been made for her.

"I see." The old man sat cross legged on the floor. "Tell me why you chose that dress."

"Swords and shields have their place." Robin ran her fingers along the fabric. "But to heal this land will take more than that."

"Only this land?"

"You know about the tree." Robin looked up at him. "Isn't that why you sent me there?"

"I have seen the tree in dreams from far away."

"Everything is connected to the tree. If it becomes disconnected, it ceases to exist." She recalled the missing branch and shuddered. "The forest thinks it has edges, boundaries, and seeks to stretch them, not knowing what she is pulling asunder is connected to her."

"It has been a very long time since someone came back from the tree." The old man smiled at her. "Don't think life will be easier for it. You can still be hurt; you'll hunger and thirst. Like anything that lives, you will die."

"I have work to do before then."

"Even if it ends with your death?"

"Even then." Robin stood. "Now that time has started again for me, I have places to be."

"Farewell then, Robin Fastheart. I don't think we will meet again in this world."

"Farewell." Robin bowed and left the cave. She turned until she had the direction she needed, then started running.

***

Allin sat in the throne room listening to Emperor Ordamy run his country. The guy impressed Allin. Ordamy meddled as little as possible. The response to the problem of guard corruption in the smaller, more distant cities was to set up a better system to communicate in both directions. He expected regular reports from the captains, he asked questions and sent instructions, or rather his chief of staff in charge of domestic affairs did.

General Mihone hadn't recovered from his perceived failure in Stronghaven, but Ordamy had already moved on, sending a cadre of experienced legionnaires to take over the work of keeping the city safe. Seth and Kerie were on their way to the capital. Ordamy didn't waste a single talented person.

The doors to the room opened and a guard ushered in Seth and Kerie. They must have made extraordinarily good time. Ordamy hadn't expected them for another few days.

"Greeting Emperor Ordamy." A young woman Allin hadn't noticed followed them in. "These good people told me they were on their way to see you and I attached myself to them."

"And who might you be?" Emperor Ordamy glared at her.

"Pardon my rudeness." The young woman bowed. "I am Robin."

"Lady Robin Fastheart?" General Mihone sat up straight. "I thought you had been murdered."

"They tried very hard but failed." Robin smiled at him. "Seth told me many good things about you. Kerie too." She waved at the pair, who tried to look like they hadn't been holding hands.

"General Mihone." Seth saluted. "Captain Seth reporting for duty."

"I resigned my position as guard." Kerie lifted her chin. "But I wanted to accompany Seth."

"If I recall, your appointment was somewhat irregular." Emperor Ordamy tapped his fingers on the arm of his chair. "I will grant you permission to resign. Captain Seth, I will leave you in General Mihone's care."

"Thank you, your Majesty." Seth saluted. General Mihone waved him over and they left the room. Captain Seth probably faced a grilling on how he met up with a supposedly dead woman, then arrived several days early.

Allin grinned, he'd like to be a fly on the wall for that conversation, but the one in front of him looked to be equally intriguing.

"Lady Robin." Emperor Ordamy inclined his head. "I have heard some of your doings. What I don't know is why you are here, alone, in my domain."

"The land called me here." Robin stood relaxed, like she could hold that pose forever. "I was seeking the past emperor. I believe he is here." She blushed slightly.

"Henry has renounced being emperor. He is my guest."

"Very good. I would be delighted to meet him."

"You won't meet him if you're intent on making him emperor again." Emperor Ordamy frowned.

"You said he renounced that position. It isn't up to me to convince him otherwise."

"Then why are you here?" The emperor shifted in his chair.

"Your domain is threatened on three fronts. I may be of some assistance."

"Three fronts?" The emperor's frown would have made most people quake in their boots. "I am aware of the clan threat in the north. The plains peoples claim to freedom may become an issue in the future. What is the third?"

"The forest to your south has corrupted some of your people, though a few of them were all too ready to be corrupted. She has turned her attention to the emperor in Ancanopolis."

"The forest corrupted?" Emperor Ordamy's frown deepened to the point where guards shifted to make ready to seize the intruder.

"You are aware of the warning I gave on the border that whoever crossed the border to shed blood would be cursed to destruction. That was a warning the land gave me. Sadly, it wasn't properly received by the Ancan forces. Anca fractured and it will be generations, if ever, before it becomes the Ancan empire again."

"The land gave you this warning?" The emperor sat back in the throne as if suddenly certain he dealt with a lunatic.

"Part of the reason you sent for me, before I was murdered was because of the stories I was fae." Robin lifted her hand and her sleeve fell to reveal symbols in green running along her arm. "I am a shieldmaiden. I serve the land."

"Surely the land in Fhayde has little interest in what happens in Anca?"

"All the lands are connected." Robin lowered her arm. "What happens in the empire affects Caldera and Fhayde. For centuries, since before there was an empire or Fhayde, the lands have disagreed. Don't ask me what lands can disagree about. That led to the fighting on the border as each land tried to use their people to overtake the other. The curse came from deeper than either as an attempt to end the division."

"So now what?" The emperor slouched in the seat and put his elbow on the arm to support his head.

"Imagine the Ancan empire as a hand." She held up her arm again hand clenched in a fist. This time the marks were gold. Allin shook his head, that didn't make sense, maybe it was the light.

"Now that what binds the hand into a fist is gone, the fingers are left to do as they please. The plain will become a farming society with a fierce dedication to freedom and responsibility." She held up one finger. "The nobles on the border are already making trade deals with Fhayde." She held up another. "You have declared yourself emperor of the north to maintain the safety of the land you love." She held up another finger. "Farther to the north, the clans are moving to gain land where they can grow more food and live a less brutal existence." Another finger lifted. "In Acanopolis the Emperor's Ruby has reappeared. It is a relic of the fae, connected to the land. The emperor there plans to recreate the empire. He will fail, but his failure will bring more destruction and heartache to the lands that once made up the empire. I have learned that I sought the emperor so he could announce the dissolution of the empire and give the lands the ability to develop as they choose. That is no longer possible."

The emperor had shot upright in his seat when Robin mentioned the Ruby.

"Are you sure of this?"

"You will receive confirmation of this soon. But yes, I am sure."

"And you expect me to invade against the Ruby?"

"I'm not suggesting you invade exactly." Robin sighed. "Your forces would be destroyed. I don't want that. You are doing important work here."

"What do you mean, not exactly?" Emperor Ordamy leaned forward.

"You will hear this from your own people, but I don't expect you to believe me now." Robin looked around the room, maybe to gauge the response of the others present. She spotted Allin, and though they had never met, she smiled and nodded at him. "Duke Allin can tell you stories from our ancient history. Giants threatened the fae in the land before there were humans there. Giants have come out of the forest to block the road south to Ancanopolis. One has been killed by a young man the forest set up to be a hero, and maybe the next emperor in Anca. The others are ravaging the road, heading north. You will need to deal with them one way or another."

"Giants." The emperor stood. "I have heard as much as I can take from you at this time. Duke Allin, since she recognizes you, perhaps you will let her join you in your suite."

"I appreciate your ear, your Majesty." Robin bowed deeply. "I thank you for your hospitality." She turned and walked out of the room. Allin jogged to catch up to her.

"That wasn't the best way to get the emperor to believe you."

"He doesn't need to believe me today. He will tomorrow or the next day." Robin put a hand to her head. "I'm tired from my journey. I would appreciate a chance to lie down and rest."

"Of course, Lady Robin." Allin couldn't stop the edge in his voice. "How did you know me?"

"Your portrait hangs in your palace." Robin smiled. "It doesn't really do you justice."

"I always hated that thing." Allin shook his head. "Giants, really?"

"Tomorrow, Duke Allin, or the next day."

They walked in silence to the suite. The guard waved them in. Robin headed straight for the couch, curled up on it like a cat and slept immediately.

Rebecca came out of their room and raised an eyebrow at him. He put a finger to his lips and guided her back into the room.

***

Robin spent the next three days chatting with Duke Allin and Rebecca. Henry slowly came around to believing she wasn't asking him to return to being emperor. As he relaxed, Magpie opened up.

"You're fae? Like my mistress' nanny used to talk about?"

"Yes and no." Robin shook her head. "I'm not completely sure myself. I'm a shieldmaiden, which the fae had before there were humans. Some human women became shieldmaidens too, until they could become knights. Most of the fae were farmers and foresters and the like. Just like most humans have jobs other than knight. Shieldmaidens were the protectors of the land. But now." She shook her head. "It goes deeper than that."

"But you look like the fae."

"I always have." Robin rolled her eyes. "My parents look nothing like me. The fae intermarried with the humans. Sarge says the genetics lined up in my case. I have no idea what that means. Maybe the land saw the need for someone like me back when I was born."

"Can you talk to the land in the north?" Rebecca asked.

Robin closed her eyes and listened, following the branch of the land they sat on to where it split off to become the land of the north. She shivered with the cold. Snow still covered the land in many places, especially in the north where the mountains curved around to meet the ocean.

"The land to the north where the clans live is tired, it wants to sleep for a while. The clans are hungry and desperate. Moving south means fighting with your people, but staying is a slow death. They will invade when the weather breaks in the mountains."

Who are you? A voice echoed in her head.

"One who listens to the land." Robin replied.

Our land is dying.

"Not dying, but tired. It wants to sleep."

We starve, the animals are gone.

"Send ten hunters with your chief to the southlands to talk."

Our chief is dead, I am dying. It is too late.

"What is going on Robin?" Rebecca knelt in front of her. "Who are you talking to?"

"A shaman from the clans. They are starving."

"Tell them to move south. I will find a way to help them. Rebecca Ormdottir says this."

We will come. It is better than starving here.

The voice vanished and Robin fell over exhausted. The fire had been lit and candles guttered on the table.

"You sat for most of the day." Allin tucked a blanket closer around her, then dabbed a kerchief to dry her cheeks. "You may be extraordinary, but you are still human."

"Sarge told me that a lot." Robin closed her eyes and slept.

***

Rebecca knocked on the door and asked the guard to see if the emperor would meet them.

"It's urgent." She scrubbed the tears from her eyes.

"I will go." The guard shook his head. "But don't expect anything." He locked them in their room, leaving Rebecca pacing. She could feel the pain of her people dying, even if they were clans-people. Their fate tugged at her heart.

A knock at the door made her spin and run to the door. It opened to reveal Emperor Ordamy frowning at her.

"I am not used to being summoned." He walked into the room and sat. "But I just received a report of giants moving north, threatening the villages on the road. I am curious what new disaster Lady Robin has to report."

"Robin is sleeping." Allin bowed to the emperor.

"Enough of that, I am Gurdin here. No emperor would answer the summons from prisoners in his palace."

"Gurdin." Henry looked up from the sofa where he sat with his arm around Magpie. "A good strong name, I believe it means plow blade in the old tongue. 'That which opens the earth.'"

"Fascinating." Gurdin nodded at Henry. "Now what is so urgent?"

"The clans-people are dying." Rebecca knelt in front of the emperor. "Robin talked to a shaman. "The land can't support them. I want to help them."

"They are our enemies." Gurdin frowned.

"Neighbours more than enemies." Rebecca pushed back the fear in her heart. "If I can make peace with them, it will secure our northern border."

"Our northern border?" Gurdin's frown deepened.

"Yes. We have traded and fought with the clans for centuries before Anca claimed us."

"So I should call my legions home?"

"Let me go north and make peace." Rebecca put her hands out to plead. "I will give you whatever you demand, if you let me do this one thing."

"You have nothing I need." Gurdin moved to stand.

"You need peace in the north." Robin pushed herself into a sitting position. "The east is troubled, but its ire is directed to the south of you."

"You were right about the giants." Gurdin spoke reluctantly. "And peace in the north will give me space to make a treaty with the plainspeople." He took Rebecca's hands. To her surprise his hand shook. "Even an emperor may feel fear."

"How may I aid you?" Rebecca squeezed his hands.

"Go north. I withdraw any claim I have to the land or responsibility for it. When you have your peace, we will talk about trade and how we may strengthen each other." Gurdin stood. "I will have a letter for you to take to my commander there. Make ready to travel tomorrow. You will ride. It is faster than a coach."

"I will travel with her." Allin moved to stand behind her. "My daughter will need me."

"We too will accompany her." Henry looked at Magpie and smiled. "We have become family, and I have never seen snow."

"As much as I would like to help." Robin rubbed her eyes. "I am called elsewhere. Perhaps I may find time to find you in the future."

"Is dealing with giants where you are called?" Gurdin asked.

"Your legions will have little trouble with them. They are strong, but not wise. It is sad they have been brought back into this world only to die."

"And where will you be going then?" Gurdin knelt to look into Robin's eyes.

"The fate of two lands hangs in the balance." Robin sighed. "I must do what I can to tip the balance toward peace."

"You can't save the world by yourself," Allin said.

"True, but I have friends there to help." Robin smiled and stood. "It has been a pleasure meeting you Gurdin, may you reign long and peacefully." She bounded out the window.

Rebecca ran to the window.

"I expect she knew it was a third story window." Allin came to stand beside her but saw no sign of Robin. "She'll be fine."

CHAPTER 17

Lencely sauntered along the street in front of the inn. New guards stood outside in palace armour. They glared at him suspiciously. He couldn't see any other activity.

"You, boy." A man stepped up beside him and took his arm. Another poked him in the back with a blade. "You're that trainer from the arena. The major has a few questions for you." They forced him into the house where Major Saligar sat in a large wooden chair.

"Just me." The major smirked. "When all those guards vanished, I got to thinking about who they were. The empty prison gave me the answer. You were those Fhaydens from the camp. That meant you'd eventually want to rescue your precious old man."

"Sarge is more than just an old man." Lencely wanted to spit at the man, but the room was full of guards. "He's the reason you lost at the border."

"And the reason Haffmon is sitting in the palace on the throne." The major stood and walked over to Lencely, then slammed his fist into Lencely's gut. "That throne should be mine."

"Maybe if you can claim Westburg, you'll have a chance." Lencely grinned and met Saligar's gaze. "Victorious generals have become emperors before."

"You sound like your Sarge." The major hit him again, this time sending Lencely staggering back. "Haffmon gave command of the army to a general from the palace."

"And you're going to take out your frustration on a kid instead of doing something bold like a future emperor." Lencely laughed. "Even Haffmon could spot you as a fake."

"I could kill you here." Saligar drew his sword.

"Are you sure no one here will run to Haffmon to say you killed the only source of information about his enemy. That could get them promoted to your job after you hang."

"My men are loyal." Saligar put the point of the sword to Lencely's throat.

"I'm not your man." One of the palace guards stood in the door. "Draw blood and I might kill you myself." He dragged Lencely out of the room. "You keep your mouth shut about this."

"Sure." Lencely shrugged. "Whatever you say."

The palace guard threw Lencely into a coach, then climbed in with him. They rattled through the streets to the section of the palace that had been obviously made ready in a hurry. The guard dragged him out of the coach and down a hall. Two other guards opened double doors, then closed them with a boom.

"My emperor." The guard went to his knee, forcing Lencely face down on the floor. "I've captured one of the Fhaydens. I believe he is one of the boys who served the old man."

Lencely peered up as Haffmon shifted on the throne. Lencely grinned, the man didn't look comfortable.

"What is funny, boy?" Haffmon put a hand on the ruby hanging on his chest.

"No need to compel me." Lencely let the magic flow over him without fighting it. "I was just thinking how uncomfortable the emperor's throne is."

The guard slammed Lencely's face against the floor. Black dots swarmed in Lencely's head. He dove into them. *Let them question an unconscious man.*

***

A cold cloth woke Lencely.

"He's awake." A woman's voice spoke.

Lencely tried to sit up. The world spun and he vomited on the floor.

"Easy Lencely, you took quite a blow to the head." The woman mopped his face again.

"Lencely," Sarge said. "Idiot."

"I missed you too, Sarge." Lencely rolled so he could see Sarge. The old man had tears in his eyes.

"Rud?"

"He should be reporting to Commander Themson that I've been captured."

Sarge nodded.

"Looks like they've been doing a decent job of taking care of you." Lencely tried sitting again. This time he made it upright. "Thank you." He tried to grin at the young woman, but his split lip twinged and made it more of a leer.

"I'm Serena." She wrung the cloth. "Sarge has talked about you."

Lencely almost asked about Mena but bit his cheek. People would be listening. He debated bringing up Saligar's comments, but chances were too great it would get back to Saligar or that guard, who probably planned to blackmail Saligar. Instead, he looked around the room. Nothing fancy, a bed where Sarge lay, a cot for Serena. He guessed he would be sleeping on the floor once he could move safely.

"I haven't seen Robin in a while, but Commander Themson says she headed north." Lencely touched his swollen lip. It made talking a challenge, but he didn't want to sit in silence. There were so many things he wanted to tell Sarge but couldn't because of listeners. "Haffmon has this gem that can compel people to obey him. That's what he used against Adam." Lencely realized Sarge didn't know about Adam, so he talked about the training and how Adam had his own way of seeing the world. He stayed away from how Adam was building a network of alliances in the broken city and was popular enough with the crowd that he scared Haffmon into leaving him alone. Lencely talked until Sarge nodded off. He crawled onto the floor and insisted Serena take the cot.

"You're the one who will have to get up if he needs something. I'm useless right now." Lencely took the blanket Serena gave him and slept in the corner.

***

Bodan took a deep breath and turned back to face Rud. The boy quivered on the edge of panic. "There's nothing we can do right now. With any luck, they'll put Lencely with Sarge and hope he talks too much." Their campfire was one of a dozen on the training arena.

"What if they torture him?" Rud groaned.

"Word is the emperor has this gem that makes people do what he wants." Daggins twiddled a stick in his fingers. "I don't think he has complete control, or Adam wouldn't be alive. Haffmon will try to use that on Lencely. We'll need to have watchers out and be ready to duck and cover. The broken city is bigger than most people think, we'll have plenty of places to hide."

"I've got scouts in place already, but more would be good. We'll hope that they just seal us off and hope to starve us before they get back from Westburg."

"If they take Westburg, we'll be in trouble." Rud tossed a stick onto the fire. "They'll march in and destroy us."

"If it was that easy, they'd have done it years ago. The broken city is here because there's no one who can fix it. Adam might, if they give him a chance." Daggins snapped the stick and tossed the pieces back on the wood pile.

"Our priority needs to be finding supplies and growing food." Bodan stretched. "You might have trouble believing me, but I used to be a farmer. Most of us have skills that have nothing to do with war. Let's get together with Adam and make some plans. We need to know where the water is, and where we can plant gardens."

"Don't you need seeds for gardens?" Rud looked up.

"We have seeds, they're just inside the food we eat. It's bit late to plant, but better late than never."

Bodan surprised himself by enjoying the process of collecting seeds and planting them in prepared ground. It was nice to do something that wouldn't end up with people dying. He'd been a regular for so long he'd almost forgotten his roots.

Adam held regular meetings. He helped resolve issues of territory and assured people that no one was going to seize control of wells. Without the training for the arena, the fighters grew bored, so he assigned them to Bodan's people to help with the gardens and either tearing down unsafe buildings or fixing them up. Moving families into houses freed up ground to plant food.

Not quite a week after Lencely's capture a scout reported that the Ancan army had formed up and marched toward Westburg. Bodan's first thought was to run after them and scout their progress, then he shook it off. He had no one to report to, once they were well on their way, he'd send out a few people to watch for their return.

***

Ham sat in the middle of the tight circle of his people in the largest tent.

"The army marched in today." He told them what they already knew. The camp had been chaos as the new forces showed up and the new command structure tried to shape the camp the way they wanted. "From all the bellyaching, the new people are palace forces. I have an idea of what Hervithon planned, but I can't say if the new brass will buy it. With all the shouting it doesn't sound like either group is happy. That could be a chance for us, or disaster. All I can say is, be ready."

They'd already eaten the small rations the Ancan gave them, so they split up to their tents for sleep. Ham sat in the yard in the dark, listening trying to pull crumbs of hope from what he heard. They'd all grown used to the reality they were going to die, but Ham didn't want them to die in vain as prisoners. If it came to it, they'd revolt and take as many of the Ancans with them as they could.

The sound of feet on the sand brought him to full alert. He didn't recognize the sound, after the weeks of captivity, he could identify everyone by their breathing.

"Hey." A woman's voice spoke in Fhayden. "Ham, dang, but it's good to see you alive."

"You're one of Bodan's," Ham whispered. "What the hell are you doing here?"

"Nothing like a bit of friendly chaos to allow entry into a camp." The woman pointed at the tent. "I would be more comfortable if we weren't visible."

Ham led her to his tent.

"I doubt Bodan ordered this insanity."

"Nah, he'd have my ass for sure, but he's in Ancanopolis pretending to be a city guard. I'm Sylve."

"So Sylve, what is so important that you risk your life and ours by coming here?"

"I'm glad you asked." He could imagine the grin on her face from her voice. "There's about two hundred of us in Westburg, a hundred or so in Ancanopolis."

"There are fifty-seven of us." Ham's heart sank. So many lost.

"Marshal Hapten sent about five hundred home after the battle. Lady Robin left her with orders to rescue all the remaining member of the Thousand and get them back to Fhayde."

"And Lady Robin?"

"She went north. We don't know why or where, but the land told her to."

"The land." Strangely, that helped Ham relax. He didn't understand Robin's connection to the land, but it was familiar. "What happened at the battle?"

"Major Saligar murdered his own general and tried to kill Lady Robin and the Free. She helped them to escape. Marshal Hapten said she was frantic trying to find you on the battlefield."

The words flipped a switch in his head. He remembered fighting back-to-back with Temanjin, being struck on the head and falling.

"What can we do to aid Lady Robin's cause?"

"I'm not sure." Sylve hesitated. "The marshal has discussed plans with Hob, the leader of the free, but I don't know what they are."

"Let Marshal Hapten know we are ready to act, but we don't want more dying trying to rescue us. If the chance comes, we will welcome it, but..." Ham paused to sort out his words. "We have already come to terms with our death, but don't make us watch our friends fall in a hopeless battle."

"I understand." Sylve stood. "I'd better vanish before things get too quiet." She vanished as quickly as she came.

"It doesn't change anything." Merideth slipped into the tent.

"No, it does." Ham stared out at the night. "We haven't been forgotten. If all we have is a plan to die, then we will die. We need to make a plan to live."

"We will still probably die." Merideth said.

"True, but we act with a purpose, and we choose to live if we can."

"That will make us weaker."

"It will make us stronger." Ham lay down. "You'll see."

***

Two days after the armies joined, Ham and the other prisoners were roped together and set to march in the centre of a square of fully armed and armoured guards. Captain Hervithon walked beside Ham for a short distance.

"You are fortunate, the new brass didn't see any use for you, but the major argued that since you were here, it didn't cost anything to use you." He patted Ham's shoulder. "You're going to give us the city."

"The major facing some political problems?" Ham said. "Tell him he has my sympathy."

The captain laughed and left.

They rested, slept and ate in their ropes. Ham had to tell more than one person not to loosen them.

"Let them think us cowed, but one person slips their bonds and the rest of us will be hog tied and put on a wagon."

The march stopped when they could see the city walls in the distance.

"We have scouts out a day's march past the city." Captain Hervithon smirked. "No sign of a horde. They should have had them here to throw us back."

"Probably busy in the fields." Ham said. "At least they'll get to eat this winter." He looked around. "I wonder how many fields were left untended to make this army. I hope you have lots of savings to spend on food."

"We'll own the plains by then." The captain laughed. "Slaves don't know how to fight."

"They beat you once already." Ham shook his head. "Doesn't bode well for this time being easy."

"They have to be here to fight." Hervithon stood. "And they aren't here."

When morning arrived with no horde surrounding the city. Ham had to fight the loss of his hope. Hervithon was right, it would be easier to fight the Ancans while they were getting set up.

Ham and his friends were marched to the south of the city and put in a group, then their ropes staked to the ground. Soldiers with crossbows patrolled just within shooting range.

"See how they pay us compliments." Ham rolled his shoulders. The ropes were annoying, but it was too soon to make a move. He needed to see what Saligar planned, and how the city responded.

"What the hell are those?" Befal nudged Ham with his foot.

"Don't know." Ham stared at the machines. "I think maybe they're supposed to throw things."

They watched as Ancan soldiers maneuvered the things into position aimed at the city. Each had a wagon parked beside it.

"They're made of wood," Merideth said. "You want to go over and see if they burn?"

"Quiet you." One of the crossbowmen shouted. "No talking."

"Just because you're bored, doesn't mean you have to be mean to us." Merideth whined like a child.

The man raised his bow.

"I would check with Saligar before you start killing his hostages." Ham shouted. "He doesn't seem like the forgiving type."

The crossbowman hesitated while Ham prepared to snap the ropes and charge him.

"Stand down, soldier." Hervithon sauntered over. "There are latrines to be dug. Go beg for a shovel." He took the weapon and shoved the man away. "You were ordered to watch for trouble, not create it, next man to threaten the hostages won't be digging latrines, I'll have you buried neck deep in one." He unloaded the crossbow and put it on the ground. "You won't escape that easily." He pointed at Ham, Befal and Merideth. "Bring those three with me." He ordered the men who stood back snickering at the guard's misfortune.

Ham followed Hervithon to where Major Saligar sat beside a man in gold plated armour, a helmet rested on the ground beside his chair.

"You will be allowed to escape tonight," Saligar said. "You will run to the small door in the wall on the east wall, bang on the door, plead, beg, whatever, but gain entry to the city. If you fail, the rest of you will be executed. When you get in the city, you will have two days to open that small door, or I will start executing hostages."

"What if I want to open the gate?" Ham asked.

"Do what you're ordered, or your people die." Saligar stood and put a knife to Merideth's neck. "It would be easy to kill her now and pick another for your little adventure."

"Put your toy away." The man in the gold armour growled. "You begged me to allow this. Now you're playing foolish games with people who don't care if they die."

Saligar put his knife away and dropped in his chair.

"They need to know I'm serious."

"Then act seriously." The man in gold stood and stared into Ham's eyes. "I don't think this nonsense will work. Prove me wrong and I might allow you to live."

Ham glanced at Befal and Merideth, they nodded.

"Fine," Ham shrugged. "I will set a watch on the wall, if one of my people dies before I open the door, the deal's off."

"Two days from tonight, then they die." The man sat down and waved for Hervithon to take Ham and the others away.

Hervithon took them to where the Ancans were setting up camp by the east wall. "Can't have you giving any last orders to your people. It would be unfortunate if they did something foolish before you had your big chance." He tossed them each a shovel. "You might as well be useful while you wait for night."

Ham didn't mind digging. It helped to focus his rage. They demanded that he betray his own people. Either the ones inside or outside the wall. He would have two days to save them all. Somehow.

Hervithon showed up as dusk turned to full night.

"The soldiers have been ordered away, but you'll want to be quiet. No one else is in on the plan, make too much noise and they may shoot at you."

"Right." Ham smashed his fist into Hervithon's face. The man went down instantly. "Merideth, you and Befal get into the city. Warn them what is going on. I'll circle around to our people and get ready to free them."

"What about him?" Befal nudged Hervithon with a foot.

"Let him sleep." Ham pointed toward the city.

"They'll see only two of us and know something is up." Befal crouched and started stripping the armour and uniform from Hervithon. "He's about my size. I'll go to our people. You take him into the city with you. Don't worry about us. They aren't going to let us live if you open the gates. In two days, we will show them why it isn't smart to try to tame wolves."

"You won't be able to play Hervithon for two days." Merideth hissed.

"Go," Befal said, "before they wonder where we are."

"Come, Befal is right." Ham hoisted Hervithon. "We will try to get to you before the two days is up."

He ran through the night, Merideth like a ghost beside him. They banged on the door, and to Ham's shock it opened immediately.

"In." Marshal Hapten ordered them.

Ham and Merideth slipped through the door. The marshal closed it and dropped heavy bars in place.

"This way," she ordered and led them into the city. They wound through streets until reaching a courtyard. High walls blocked them. Ropes dropped from the wall then put their feet in loops in the ropes and were hoisted to the top.

"What is going on?" Ham asked. "How did you know we were coming?"

"We've been watching you since you arrived. It was obvious what they were about when they took you around to the east side."

"I guess that's why you're the marshal." Merideth drawled. Ham laughed and almost dropped his burden when Hervithon moaned.

"Who's that?" Marshal Hapten led them along the wall to a rooftop, down some stairs to the street then along the street.

"I couldn't resist hitting him," Ham admitted. "He's been such a pain in my side. Then things got complicated, and I brought him because we needed three people to enter the city."

"We'll lock him a cell for now." The marshal passed through broken gates into a building that once must have been a luxurious residence. She had Ham pass the captain to two other Fhaydens.

"I was hoping to be there when he woke up."

"No time for petty revenge, soldier." They entered a room and Ham stopped to stare.

"Lady Robin?"

"In the flesh." She walked over and caressed his cheek. "You have no idea how good it is to see you alive."

"I do." Ham swept her up in a hug. "I know exactly how good it is." Robin wrapped her arms around him and held him tight. He finally sighed and put her down. "When did you start wearing a dress? It looks good on you."

"That's a long story that will wait for another time." Robin grinned. "We have things to discuss. First, I must introduce you to Hob. He leads the Free."

"We were looking for the horde. Where is everyone?" Ham asked.

"All in good time." Hob smiled. "It is an honour to meet you. Lady Robin puts great value on you."

Ham's face heated and Merideth laughed. "Never thought I'd see Ham blush.

"He hides his soft side well." Robin sat and waved at them to take a seat.

"I've been discussing things with Hob since I arrived last night. The Free don't need the city. It is convenient, but a walled city is just an invitation to people to try to take it. Hence the army outside. The problem is that they can't afford to just let Anca have it. It would be too easy to turn it into a base to run attacks into the plains."

"Why not just drive them off like last time?" Merideth asked.

"How much blood would you shed over something you didn't need?" Hob asked. "We could drive the Ancan army back, but it would cost us in blood, and they would return. I want peace, not a long drawn out war."

"Right." Merideth leaned back. "I hadn't thought of it that way."

"We came to help bring peace." Robin frowned. "That is still our task."

"There won't be peace as long as people like Saligar are around." Ham thumped the table, then looked at his feet. "My apologies, Lady Robin. I spoke out of turn."

"No, you spoke the truth, and call me Robin now. It is simpler." She smiled. "There are things in motion that neither Saligar nor Haffmon are aware of."

"Robin." Ham said, and the world didn't stop turning around him. "How may I help?"

"Tell me about the hostages." Robin's eyes grew hard. "I am leaving no one behind."

"Belaf is with them. In two days, they'll revolt because either we'll have opened the door and they will be of no more use, or we won't, and they will be executed as punishment for our failure. There are fifty-four of them. Each of them ready to die, but I want them to live."

"Two days will be enough time." Robin nodded. "You've done well. I'd like you to stand by my side, like before."

Ham looked at Robin, then at Merideth. He wanted to stand with Robin, but he owed the hostages.

"It's okay, Ham. This is what you trained me for." Merideth saluted him.

"She'll also have me and the other two hundred of our people to help." The marshal said.

"How will you get to them? You won't be able to fight through the Ancan army. I don't want more of my comrades to die for our freedom."

"We have a tunnel." Hob shrugged. "Our people have always had tunnels out of places the masters wanted us locked in. We didn't know about them when we took the city, but there are several excellent tunnels leading out into the plain. One of them ends very close to where your friends are being held. Duncan will lead you there."

"Tunnels." Ham stared at the ceiling. "That does help. We'll need a distraction."

"That's where you and I come in." Robin said.

"And I," Hob added.

"Your people need you. If something goes wrong..."

"If my people can't rule themselves without me, they are in trouble."

"You promised to meet up with Willow."

"I did." Hob nodded. "You'll just have to keep me safe. It won't be the first time."

"Very well." Robin sighed. "Ham get some rest. Merideth will brief Marshal Hapten on the setup around the hostages. Don't visit your friend. You'll see him tomorrow."

Chapter 18

Robin woke before the dawn and climbed the stairs to the wall. Members of her Thousand patrolled where they were visible, then one by one, they were replaced with straw figures. Hob had already prepared them, it seemed a pity not to use them. The soldiers descended the steps to where Duncan, Marshal Hapten, and Merideth waited for them. Sargent Temanjin had insisted on standing with her. He had the right, so it would be him, Ham, Hob and her, plus their very unhappy prisoner.

Hob walked up beside her. "You used to look north all the time."

"I accomplished what I could in the north. Now the south pulls me."

"You've been away from home for a long time." He leaned on the wall. "I will miss this view."

"It is a very good view." Robin nodded. "You will find new ones."

"When this is done, I would like to travel north and speak with this Emperor Ordamy."

"He is as honourable as Haffmon is treacherous. Tell him I recommended you speak to him."

"I will do that. I wonder what is farther north. The plains continue past the most northern villages."

"There are people there too. They could be friends. They are more hunters than farmers, but you could teach them."

"That sounds better than war." Hob sighed.

"You could still go to Willow."

"It was her who insisted that one of the Free needed to stand in the gap. She just wishes it wasn't me."

"I will do everything I can to see you back to her."

"I know."

The sun crested the horizon, and the plain glowed with golden light. They turned and descended the stairs then walked to the west gate. Sargent Temanjin and Ham waited for them. Hervithon, as Ham introduced the prisoner was bound and gagged.

Robin helped pull the gates open enough for the four of them to walk through. Ham laughed. "I asked Saligar what would happen if I opened a gate for them. He got mad at me. I expect he's at the east side waiting for the door to open."

"I'm sure he'll get word soon enough." Robin smiled and lifted the white banner. "Let's see if this new general will honour the white."

A soldier approached holding his own white banner.

"Are you surrendering?" He shouted.

"In a manner of speaking." Robin replied. "I would like to speak to your general."

"He will not come to parley. You have committed treachery before."

"Is that the story Major Saligar tells? No matter, shouting distance is fine for what I have to say."

The soldier ran off, leaving several to watch them, unsure of what to make of the sight of four people standing in the open gate. Robin crossed her arms and ordered herself to stay calm. No noise from the south was good news.

A man in gold armour rode up as a troop formed up around him.

"I'm General Kashon," the man boomed. Saligar probably heard the man on the east side of the city.

"I am Robin." She put a hand on Sargent Temanjin and Ham. "These are my men who were by my side when we treated with Major Saligar. Hob, leader of the Free was also there, only one of his companions made it out alive."

"And where is he?" The general asked.

"You may meet him yet." Hob said. "He is doing a job for me."

"Ask yourself, General Kashon, how six of us slayed twenty warriors, a general and a major while Saligar escaped without a scratch? If you are half the commander you appear to be, your skin must crawl in his presence." Robin made her voice as loud as the general's. The soldiers shifted slightly.

"Speak what you desire. I care not about past events."

"What I desire?" Robin scoffed. "I desire peace. I came under a white banner offering aid to any who asked it. That banner was betrayed, many of my people died, others suffered in captivity while the treacherous plotted."

"It is too late for peace." General Kashon dismounted and moved to the front of his men. "I don't want to shed the blood of good men, but the emperor orders it."

"I have met your emperor. He arranged for a cursed weapon to be used against one of my men."

"The court didn't find him guilty."

"What does your gut tell you when you stand in his presence? The stench of his deeds must waft from him."

"He is the emperor. I follow his orders."

Saligar galloped up on a horse.

"What are you waiting for. Attack, kill them all."

"And so he said when he murdered General Thadonix," Robin shouted.

"Hold fast." General Kashon bellowed and the soldiers froze. "Do not interrupt me, Major. Your actions lead me to believe Robin's words."

"I will have all the prisoners killed." Saligar shouted before General Kashon knocked him to the ground.

"You have no prisoners." Duncan walked out through the open gate. "They got tired of waiting and left. They have better things to do with their lives than die at your command."

"And who are you?" General Kashon ignored Saligar as he jumped back on his horse and galloped south.

"Duncan, I am Hob's aide."

"Another survivor of treachery."

"Only because of Lady Robin's bravery."

"Is anyone else coming through those gates?"

"The city is empty." Hob stepped forward. "While it is useful, it is not worth my people shedding their blood. You may have it. On one condition. A treaty signed with the Emperor's Ruby with a penalty of death to any who break the treaty."

"Why sign a treaty when we can walk in and take the city?" General Kashon raised his fist. "My emperor will not be held to such a treaty."

"Meaning you want to be left the option of treachery and broken treaties." Hob shrugged. "Without that treaty, you will not have the city."

"And you four are going to stop my army?" Kashon pointed forward with his arm.

Robin sighed. She'd learned a lot on the walls of the city listening to the Land. It tolerated the city but would be happy to be free of it. The land shuddered and the gates of the city collapsed. Walls tilted and fell inward. Dust flew up from the destruction. The Ancan soldiers fell to the ground as the land quaked. Even the general staggered while his horse fled. The engines of war tilted and sank into the ground. In a few minutes the city of Westburg ceased to exist. Not even a pile of rocks marred the plain.

When the land stopped shaking. Hob stepped forward. "Look around General. What you see is the horde of the plains."

Robin knew they were there, but it was impressive anyway. Thousands of flags fluttered at the head of as many armies.

"You refused the treaty." Hob shouted. "Now hear our demand. No Ancan army may step foot on the plains without facing death. We could destroy you here and now. We could have destroyed you and kept our city, but we wanted to give you a chance. You failed. All your people must be off the plain by sundown. Any who remain will die. If you return, you will die. This ban will stay in place until the emperor himself comes and kneels before us to sign a peace treaty sealed with the stone."

"Tell your emperor, the only reason you live, and the only reason this army doesn't march on your city is because the Free don't want it." Robin's voice carried to the farthest soldier in the Ancan army.

"We retreat." General Kashon's voice was almost as loud as Robin's.

"One last thing, General." Ham stepped forward. "Take this piece of human garbage with you." He bent and cut the cords binding Hervithon, put the man on his feet and gave him a shove. We freed our people your army held.

We will free the people who are trapped in your city too. Tell your emperor not to try our patience."

"I will give him the message." General Kashon ordered a soldier to pick up Hervithon who stumbled toward him.

***

Once the Ancan army had marched west toward their capital, Robin joined her troops. They greeted her boisterously.

"You will always be welcome on the plains." Hob told her as he stood with Willow.

Robin hugged him tightly and whispered to him. "You are allowed to love again. Let it be a sign of your peace."

Hob nodded and when she let him go, he reached for Willow's hand. She smiled as if she'd expected it, then they walked away into the horde.

"Duncan. I will let your father know how proud he should be." Robin saluted him. "Go with your friend."

"What are your orders, Lady Robin?" Marshal Hapten asked.

"We will follow the Ancan army. Not close enough to be a threat, but close enough to keep them nervous. As soon as we reach the city, we look for our people. Duncan said they are in a part of Ancanopolis called the broken city.

"I can guide you there." A woman stepped up and saluted. "My name is Maci, I'm one of Commander Themson's squad."

"Where's Sylve?" Ham asked.

"Commander Betrice is giving her special training." Marshal Hapten laughed. "It was the best compromise we could come up with between a court martial and a medal."

"She deserves it." Maci said. "I'll take you to her when we make camp for the night."

Marshal Hapten had the Fhaydens lined up and ready to march within the hour. "No need to rush, we're going to be bumping into the Ancans soon enough regardless."

On the march, Robin made a point of greeting each individual soldier and thanking them for being there. Sylve struggled under a weighted pack.

"Commander Betrice said you marched with one." She gasped. "How did you do it?"

"I wore weights since I was twelve." Robin winked at her. "I got used to it. It will make you stronger, eventually."

Sylve straightened and took a few steps before she was gulping for breath again. Commander Betrice took pity on her after an hour and let her march without the pack.

"I see you're not wearing a sword. Does that mean you've given it up?"

"The sword isn't what I am wielding right now. I haven't forgotten it."

"Oh, then you won't mind another match?" Betrice grinned.

"We'll hold it where the Ancan scouts can watch." Robin laughed. "Show them what they missed."

"Or what they're in for." Betrice's grin widened.

***

Major Saligar fumed at the injustice of General Kashon's actions. Not only had the man refused to attack the city, he'd struck the major. Then to add insult to injury, the general seriously considered whether the major had been telling the truth about the treachery during the parley in front of the city gates before the first battle.

The major led his strike team away from the main camp. Nothing had been said about the ragtag batch of Fhayden soldiers following them. The general acted like they didn't exist. Major Saligar would deliver punishment to them for daring to ruin his plans.

They crept up to where they could see into the Fhayden camp. Saligar motioned for his troops to get ready to attack. The Fhaydens were gathered in a circle around two women. One wore armour and carried a sword and shield, the other in a dress wielded only a sword. They fought in a display of talent Saligar had trouble understanding. The men beside him shifted nervously.

"Get ready to attack." Saligar whispered.

"Nope, not happening." Captain Hervithon whispered back. "You see those women? They're playing, having fun. Imagine if they got serious. The two of them could destroy us themselves while the others watched.

Besides, those prisoners haven't had a chance to get back at us yet. I told you this was a bad idea."

"They've made you a coward, Hervithon." The major loosened his sword in its sheath. Once the bulk of his soldiers charged, he'd head in and...

An arrow appeared in the dirt in front of him.

"You idiots are as stealthy as toddlers." A woman's voice from the darkness spoke. "I didn't want to spoil the fun, but if any of you move so much as a finger's breadth forward. We will empty our quivers into your sorry hides, then let the crew below chew you up. Go back to your camp and give thanks to whatever gods you have that we're in a good mood tonight."

Captain Hervithon stood and walked away followed by the rest of the force. Major Saligar took a last look as laughter floated up from the fight below. The women were doing cartwheels and spins while they fought, faces filled with joy.

"Go home, Major. You'll face them soon enough."

The thought of facing either of those warriors loosened Saligar's guts. He fled the scene before he humiliated himself in front of that faceless voice.

A summons awaited him in camp. Saligar was forced to march between two of Kashon's guards to the general's tent.

"You have fun?" The general sat with a glass of wine. He wore a rich robe. "The scouts told me their camp is more secure than ours. The only reason you're alive is because someone a lot smarter than you gave orders not to kill."

"There's only two hundred of them." Saligar hissed. "We could slaughter them."

"Leaving aside that one of them brought an entire walled city down and made it vanish. The two hundred and sixty-one of them would tear our heart out. Sure we would win, but we'd lose at least four soldiers for each of them, probably more. That's if they stood and fought. They're much more likely to retreat into the forest and fight a running battle all the way back to Ancanopolis. That could double our losses to night attacks and exhaust our forces." The general took a long sip of his wine and eyed Saligar. "I will not sacrifice hundreds, if not thousands of good soldiers to ease your wounded pride. If you leave the camp again, don't come back, because I will hang you and deal with the emperor later."

The bulk of the guards flanking him kept Saligar from charging the general. The man sat as if he didn't think Saligar could touch him, even while he sat in a fancy robe.

The major spun and stomped out of the tent, the general's laugh following him and flailing his pride.

He rode in silence on the march and sulked in his tent while they camped. He couldn't get the vision of the Fhayden women playing at fighting out of his head. He needed to destroy them so he could live in peace again.

They camped a day's march from the city. Less than a day if they pushed hard. But General Kashon dallied on the road. Maybe reluctant to tell the emperor of his failure. Saligar hadn't seen any messengers riding ahead. Perhaps Kashon aimed to minimize the situation. The major grinned, he'd go and inform the emperor himself and warn of the Fhaydens coming to the city and the danger they posed.

He had his staff saddle his horse, and filled his waterskin with wine then rode out of camp. No one stopped him. The major rode most of the night then stopped at an inn on the border of the city. In the morning he had them prepare his horse and he headed for the palace.

The new section looked raw against the blackened stone of the old palace. Swarms of workers were tearing down old buildings while another swarm worked to build the new part. He threw his reins to one of the guards and swept into the palace. The hall took him straight to the throne room. No more warren needing slaves to act as guides.

Haffmon slumped in the throne while bureaucrats buzzed around him. Behind him stood that kid who claimed to have killed a giant. His black armour had dulled, and he looked sullen and more bored than the emperor.

"Your Majesty." Saligar went to his knee. "I come to report."

"You failed." Haffmon played with the ruby on his chest. "You went up against slaves and lost."

"General Kashon wouldn't even fight them." Saligar lifted his head and winced at the rage on Haffmon's face.

"That witch was allowed to destroy my city." Weight landed on Saligar's shoulders and pushed him into the stone floor. "Now she's coming here." Boots clanked on the stone floor, then something struck his back. Blood ran out, his blood. Then the sword in his back was wrenched out and Saligar's vision went black.

***

Lyle clanked back to his place behind the emperor as palace servants frantically cleaned up the mess.

"Your Majesty," one lay face on the ground in front of Haffmon. "Your champion has damaged the floor again. And this mess. It isn't seemly."

"I don't care." Haffmon kicked the servant away. "Take your babbling away. General Kashon will be here soon. Let him see the blood on the floor."

"But –"

Haffmon kicked the servant again and they scurried away. He never had Lyle kill any of them.

All week the emperor had been bringing in people he thought had wronged him, he tormented them until he got bored, then had Lyle kill them. It wasn't at all what Lyle had expected from his position as champion.

A champion should fight worthy battles, slaying fearsome enemies, not slaughter merchants. That red gem on Haffmon's chest was the reason Lyle was stuck as executioner. He didn't even try to refuse orders anymore. The ruby left him with no more will than a puppet. Lyle loathed the emperor, but with no way to challenge the compulsion, the loathing turned inward.

He had started by imagining hundreds of ways to kill the emperor, all of them ending with him holding the Emperor's Ruby and sitting on the throne. Now he imagined ways to die to free himself of the eternal dullness of meaningless killing.

He stood behind Haffmon waiting for the next corpse to arrive.

CHAPTER 19

Robin marched with Ham and Temanjin at her side. They'd taken a side road and marched long into the night to get ahead of the Ancan army. After a short night, they marched again. Sylve led them through the city toward the broken city and her comrades.

She looked forward to seeing more of her people, but something in the city nagged at her. Not like the call that had guided her through her journey, but a wrongness, as if the land itself was sick. Tonight, she'd listen and see what needed to be done.

The city around them grew poorer and more wretched until most buildings were derelict. But there were signs of rejuvenation. Gardens grew in blank spaces, and in others piles of material were evidence of new work happening. People waved at the marching army as if they knew who they were. Probably the word had gone out. The scouts would have arrived already and informed Commander Themson of their route.

More and more new construction lined the road while tents filled in spaces. Then they arrived at a large clearing, filled with tents. Fhayden soldiers stood in a square. None of them wore uniforms, but their discipline shone.

"Welcome, Lady Robin." Commander Paychen stepped forward and saluted. "I must admit that I've mostly had an advisory role here. Commander Themson has been the driving force behind our survival and the building of the relationships with the delightful people of the city." He waved Commander Themson forward.

"I think I finally understand the nature of our mission," Commander Themson grinned. "We are working our hardest to fulfill it."

"I see that." Robin smiled back. "At ease, friends." The tight square dissolved and the troops behind her and the ones in front of her meshed in a celebration. They would honour the dead again tonight, but for now, joy reigned supreme.

"Lady Robin." A new voice spoke to her.

"Right, this is our inspiration for all the work." Commander Themson came to stand beside her. Robin turned to face the newcomer.

"Adam." She laughed with delight. "So, this is what you got up to. Wonderful."

Adam knelt before her, with a young woman, not much older than him beside him. "Lady Robin, welcome. May I introduce my wife, Becca."

Robin lifted Adam and Becca to their feet.

"You don't need to kneel for me." Robin looked around. "You do me too much honour. Tell me what you're doing. I saw the work on the way in. Is that all your doing?"

"I have friends across the city, we are working together. The emperor and his palace have ignored the broken city for years. So we are doing what we can ourselves."

Something caught Robin's eye. "Is that a fox? What is it doing in the city?"

Adam turned to look as a wave of dread washed over Robin. Whatever was wrong had grown worse and threatened to consume the city.

"I must go." Robin put her hand to her head. "Follow as you can." She bolted away through the gathered people, heading toward the writhing hatred radiating from the palace.

***

Lyle watched as General Kashon moaned under the weight of Haffmon's anger. It would be a while before he was sent to end the man.

"You didn't even attack. You let my city be destroyed. You let *her* live."

"You have her mentor and the boy." Kashon somehow spoke through the agony. His armour started to buckle, yet he didn't sound panicked or afraid.

"Lyle, fetch them." Haffmon sneered. "We'll see if they have any use."

Lyle walked through the halls to the room where they kept the old man.

"Come." He waited while the boy picked up the man and followed. The girl clutched a cloth in her hand and stared after them.

"Wait here." The boy ordered the girl. She nodded as the door closed.

The boy carried the old man as if he was weightless. Something about the boy's face made Lyle uncertain. Boy though he might be, he knew exactly who he was. Lyle almost wished he could ask him about it.

They arrived at the throne room and Lyle pointed to where Haffmon would be able to see them without turning away from the general on the floor. The boy put the old man gently on his feet.

The emperor's slave, Mena had brought wine for Haffmon. He sipped at it as Kashon squirmed.

"Haffmon." A woman appeared in the throne room, then froze like a statue. She looked vaguely familiar, but not enough to matter. Lyle waited for the order he expected was coming. The old man had awakened and stood beside the boy, his eyes fixed on the woman.

"Lyle, kill the boy for me." Haffmon chuckled and waved his wine glass in the air. "Just to start the discussion."

Lyle drew his sword and stabbed at the boy.

The old man stepped between him and the boy, so the sword buried itself in his shoulder.

"You idiot." Haffmon dropped the glass. He was going to say something else, but Mena swept up a shard of the glass and plunged it into Haffmon's neck. The emperor let go of the ruby to try to stem the bleeding, so Lyle charged the throne, swinging his sword to cut through the back of the throne and Haffmon's neck. He pushed the corpse to the floor, then picked up the chain to hang the ruby over his own chest.

"I remember you now." Lyle pointed at the woman. "You're the reason I'm in this mess."

He charged her, but she evaded his sword, again and again his blows brushed by her. Kashon tossed her his blade. She caught it while spinning out of his reach, then went on the attack. It was all he could do to stay alive, even with his armour absorbing her blows.

Then a memory of Haffmon holding the ruby floated into his mind. He switched to a one-handed grip on his sword and put his left hand on the ruby.

"Stand still."

The woman's eyes widened as her feet stuck to the floor and Lyle began his attack again, but still she beat his blade aside. Finally, he swung at her head, shifting at the last second to cut her sword. The blade shattered and pieces flew across the room. Lyle kicked her stomach and sent her crashing to the floor.

"Do not move." Lyle stalked over to her. "You will die now, for what you've done to me." He raised his sword to strike. Even now she showed no fear.

***

Adam stood in shock as Robin vanished in front of him. Then Fox arrived and nipped at his leg.'

"You must go after her. Bring the knife and the waterskin she gave you." Adam didn't stop to question why Fox was here. He checked for his knife and waterskin on his belt, then ran in the direction of the palace.

"This way. Lady Robin needs us." By the time he'd reached the market, the army had caught up with him.

"The palace is this way." Daggins took the lead. "The guard isn't going to be happy. They'll think this is a riot or something.

"We'll deal with the guard," Rud came up on Adam's other side. "You go help Robin."

Adam ran, not wondering why he didn't tire, the palace appeared in the distance with soldiers milling about.

"We don't want a full-fledged battle." Commander Themson shouted, but he was drowned out by a roar as a crowd of people flowed past them and plunged into the soldiers.

"No killing." Adam shouted. Officers of the guards were shouting similar orders. He ran through the space the crowd opened and into the palace. The double doors at the end of the hall stood open, the guards that should have been there missing.

The man in the black armour loomed over Robin, his sword raised high and face contorted in hate. He moved the hand clutching the ruby to his sword as he swung down.

Adam drew the blade Lady Robin gave him and lunged forward to catch the sword with his knife. He was going to die, but Becca would understand.

"No," he shouted. Becca shouldn't need to understand. Adam twisted his knife as the sword made contact and pushed it aside. His momentum carried him forward, so he stabbed the man through the gap in his helmet, then snatched the ruby from his chest.

The man in black armour fell and shattered against the floor like he'd been stone, not flesh and blood. The ruby in Adam's hand flared to life showing the forest that filled the room.

***

Lencely held Sarge as the room changed. As soon as Lyle put on the ruby, trees burst through the floor. Lyle fought with Robin and she moved like quicksilver passing through trees like they weren't there. He pulled Sarge away from the fight, Mena appeared at his side and helped him find a safe corner.

Lencely jumped up to help Robin, but he had no weapon. Hers had just shattered, and Lyle knocked her to the floor. He couldn't save her.

Then Adam charged in, pushed the blade aside and killed Lyle. When he touched the ruby, the light in the room changed. The trees glowed softly.

Sarge stirred and Lencely dropped to kneel at his side.

"Time, Lencely." Sarge rasped.

"I know." Lencely grasped Sarge's hand as Rud skidded into the room. Mena waved him over.

"Rud." Sarge closed his eyes. "Live."

The hand went limp in Lencely's hand. He wanted to howl with the pain in his heart, but all he could do was lean over Sarge and weep. Rud shook with sobs too. Lencely knew he should get up, check on Robin, talk to Adam, but the pain paralyzed him.

***

Robin stood in the cup of the tree. The forest faced her filled with rage seeping out like black swamp water.

"I'm not done. My forest will grow." The forest aged as she spoke.

"You've put too much of yourself into a revenge against time." Robin sighed. "Sleep now, dream, and grow in wisdom."

"No," the forest stomped her foot like a child, then wailed like an infant.

Robin picked her up and cuddled her, like she'd seen mothers do.

"Sleep." The baby's eyes closed, and it curled into a ball. Robin put her down in the cup, pulled a blanket out of the air and wrapped the forest in it.

"You'll make a good mother someday." Sarge put a hand on her shoulder.

"Someday." Robin spun and clutched Sarge into hug. "I have so much I want to tell you, to ask you."

"I know." Sarge held her in strong arms. "I know, but it is time."

Robin stepped back. Sarge stood strong and tall. "I will miss you."

"Good, we're supposed to miss people." He cupped her cheek in his palm. "I'm proud of you. I have been since we met. Always stretching to do what was right. If I hadn't wasted my life fighting wars, my daughter might have been like you."

"It isn't fair." Robin clasped his hand.

"No, it isn't." Sarge smiled at her. "Never stop trying to fix that. Grow old, tell your grandkids about me."

"I love you, Sarge." Robin collapsed to her knees.

"I will always love you." Sarge kissed her hand then vanished. The living cup became the cold stone of the palace floor.

Lencely took her hand and pulled her to her feet. He led her over to where Sarge lay. Rud sat despondently with tears running down his face. A girl also knelt beside Sarge.

"I need to tell Serena."

"I'll take you to her, Mena." Lencely helped her and led her away.

"He's gone, Robin. What will I do now?" Rud looked at her with reddened eyes.

"Take what he taught you and teach it to others." Robin knelt beside him. "It's right and proper to grieve." She put her hand on Sarge's chest. "But you can't grieve if you don't live."

"Lady Robin." Adam put a hand on her shoulder. "Sorry to interrupt, but someone wants to talk to you."

She stood and took a deep breath, then turned to face the next challenge.

"I was in the neighbourhood after chasing the giants back into the forest." Emperor Ordamy crossed his arms. "They were a lot harder to kill than you said."

"I didn't think you were going to go yourself." Robin looked around at the chaos in the throne room. "You aren't worried about walking into this disaster?"

"The young man with the ruby has everything under control. I think he will make an excellent ruler."

"You're right." Robin brushed tears from her eyes.

Emperor Ordamy handed her a kerchief. "Take some time for yourself. I'm familiar with grief. We will honor him best by living."

"You know who he is?" Robin glanced over at Rud, now standing at attention over Sarge's body, Lencely beside him. Mena and another woman, probably Serena knelt beside Sarge.

"Your Sarge is as famous as you are." Emperor Ordamy bowed his head. "I would have liked to talk to him, but I have the honour of knowing his pupil."

"Sorry to keep bothering you, Lady Robin." Adam had the ruby tied to his belt, alongside the waterskin and knife. "Your people are asking for you." As Robin walked out of the palace, Becca passed her carrying a fox like a cat.

"I know it's undignified, but you need to put up with it. There are too many people around for you to be running wild." The fox yipped, then whined.

Robin shrugged and headed outside. General Kashon leaned against the wall, his armour off.

"General." Robin inclined her head.

"I sent most of the army home. They have better work to do than standing around here."

"Thank you for the sword. I'm sorry I broke it."

"No matter." General Kashon held up the hilt with a finger's breadth of blade attached. "I like it better this way. I will hang it on my wall and tell the story of its breaking until I die."

"Anca needs a general who doesn't mind peace." Robin leaned against the wall beside him.

"I think I will stick around for a while. The pay's good, and I can train up some of the next generation."

"I'm sure Adam will be pleased."

"The young man with the ruby? I'm waiting my turn to speak to him. He was dealing with the palace staff before Gurdin strolled in."

"He's Emperor Ordamy now."

"Really?" Kashon pushed away from the wall. "I'll have to get him to buy me a drink and tell me about it."

Robin walked until she found the Fhaydens. They cheered when they saw her, then mobbed her, patting her on the back, hugging her. More like family than an army. When she burst into tears, she had to explain about Sarge. Marshal Hapten immediately took Commander Paychen and Commander Themson into the palace.

"We'll look after him."

Robin's grief took on a new shade with people who'd known him. They told stories and laughed and cried with her until Lencely and Rud appeared, carrying Sarge on a stretcher. Marshal Hapten and the Commanders formed an honour guard behind them. Mena and Serena followed after them.

"Serena!" A shout went out from the crowd and a young man ran over to Serena. "I've been so worried about you. Your father said the emperor took you and that old man."

"That emperor is dead, good riddance." Serena threw herself into Tom's arms. "But so is Sarge, that poor old man."

People, both soldiers and civilians stood at attention, hands on their hearts as the procession passed. Robin teared up again, but she straightened and saluted.

"Where should we take him?" Lencely asked.

"To our camp for now." Robin said. "We can talk to Adam later about where we can lay him to rest."

***

The next day Robin and her army followed Adam to a hill in the broken city.

"I just learned about this place myself." He leaned down to pat the fox. "Fox passed it and told me about it. It is the most peaceful spot I can think of."

Lencely and Rud set to with shovels and dug the grave. Squads of soldiers took turns standing as honour guard. Not just Fhaydens, but General Kashon and his staff, and Emperor Ordamy with his guard.

Becca stood beside Robin the entire time.

"In a way, you brought Adam into my life." Becca kept her eyes on him as he checked with one group then another to keep things running smoothly. "I can never thank you enough for that."

"Adam is lucky to have someone like you." Robin smiled. "He was very earnest when we met. He still is, but it suits him."

"Emperor Ordamy wants Adam to be emperor in Anca. Adam doesn't want to be emperor."

"Call it anything you want, but he's exactly what Anca needs. What do the heroes get called in the old stories?"

"King Adam does sound nice." Becca smiled. "The palace people are upset because he wants to live in the broken city."

"They'll sort it out." Robin patted Becca on the shoulder. "They don't have a choice."

Robin watched them lay Sarge to rest beneath the flowers.

Lencely and Rud stood back as the army filed past putting shovel after shovel of dirt on the grave. Robin, at the end of the line put her hand on the soil. Power flowed out her until a tiny shoot sprung up. She stood and dusted off her hands.

"Didn't know you could do that." Lencely said.

"Neither did I." Robin smiled. "There are lots of things I've yet to learn about myself."

"I've decided to stay here with Adam. I want to see what he does with this place." Lencely straightened his shoulders.

"I'm going home." Rud shook his head. "Don't know what I'll do when I get there."

"You're from Vilscape, right?" Robin asked.

"Yes, it will be a long journey home through Fhayde."

"I'm planning to visit my home in Caldera; we could travel through the plains together. I've never seen the pass myself."

"I heard about the battle there." General Kashon walked up to them. "Adam is talking about sending a peace envoy to the Free. I'd like to be able to visit and apologize."

"That's one busy kid." Emperor Ordamy joined them. "He asked me to send a trade proposal for him to look at, and suggested we cooperate setting up a patrol on the road to discourage any more giants from bothering the villages. He didn't even ask what villages were mine and what were his."

"I still want that drink." General Kashon poked the emperor. "I need to know what to avoid so I don't get roped into running a country." The two of them walked away like old friends.

"Are you upset I'm staying here?" Lencely looked at her.

"No," Robin hugged him. "I'm glad you found a place." She looked around. "Anyone have a sword I can borrow?"

After picking one from the many offered to her Robin made Lencely kneel.

"Put your hand on the blade." He looked at her strangely, but did as she said.

"Lencely, do you swear to protect the weak, uphold the peace, and live with respect for all living things?"

"I do, sure, but what?"

Robin laid the sword on his shoulder. "I knight thee Sir Lencely of Caldera. Guardian of the peace." She handed him the sword hilt first. "Rise and take your sword. Wield it well."

Lencely stood staring at her with open mouth.

Cheers broke out around her as people gathered to congratulate him.

"You deserve it." Robin put her hand on his shoulder. "We are now equals."

Rud slapped Lencely on the shoulder. "Sir Lencely, it has a nice ring to it."

"It does." Adam grinned and shook Lencely's hand. "I'm glad you're staying. General Kashon is looking for some new officers to train not to fight. If you'd like, I'll suggest you."

"Please do." Lencely saluted Adam. He looked at Rud. Are you okay, I mean not being knighted here?"

"I want my father to be there." Rud grinned. "He always said I'd never amount to anything. I'm going to make him eat his words." The two hugged, then followed the crowd who were meandering away back to Adam's village.

Robin sat beside Sarge's grave.

"I'm going to do what you suggested. Live a long life and teach people everything you taught me."

"Sounds fine to me." The fox sat beside her and curled his tale around himself. "You do realize that your work is just starting?"

"It might be nice to just live a normal boring life." Robin ran her fingers through the fox's fur.

"I tried normal. It didn't suit." The fox looked up at her.

"I think you're right. I didn't go through all of this just to stop now. There are a lot of branches on the tree."

"Sure." The fox stood up and shook himself. "Are you staying here, or coming to join the party?"

"You know." Robin got up and dusted herself off. "A party sounds good right about now. Farewell Sarge, I'll bring my children to meet you."

OTHER BOOKS BY ALEX

Series:

Calliope Books
Calliope and the Sea Serpent
Calliope and the Royal Engineers
The Third Prince and the Enemy's Daughter
Calliope and the Kershan Empire

Spruce Bay Books
Wendigo Whispers
Cry of the White Moose
Disputed Rock

The Belandria Tarot
The Devil Reversed
The Regent's Reign
The Empire Unbalanced
The World Widens
The Fury Unleashed

Blue in Kamloops
Tranquille Dark
Columbia Smoke
Victoria Run
Rivers Trail Hunt

The Fae
Call of a Hero
Shieldmaiden's Quest
Return of the Fae

Stand-alone books:

Bigfoot Country (anthology
St. Peter's Fish and Other stories (anthology)
Mythical Girls (anthology
Leedles and the Golden Tree
Generation Gap
The Gods Above
Tales of Light and Dark
Like Mushrooms (poetry and photography)
The Heronmaster
Blood and Sparkles, and other stories
Princess of Boring
By the Book
Sarcasm is My Superpower
Playing on Yggdrasil
The Unenchanted Princess

Read short stories and excerpts from his novels at alexmcgilvery.com

www.ingramcontent.com/pod-product-compliance
Lightning Source LLC
Chambersburg PA
CBHW060311310726

48976CB00007B/2294